Other Books by Jane Kirkpatrick

NOVELS

*The Daughter's Walk**

Portraits of the Heart Historical Series
*A Flickering Light**
*An Absence So Great**

Change and Cherish Historical Series
*A Clearing in the Wild**
*A Tendering in the Storm**
A Mending at the Edge

*A Land of Sheltered Promise**

Tender Ties Historical Series
*A Name of Her Own**
Every Fixed Star
Hold Tight the Thread

Kinship and Courage Historical Series
*All Together in One Place**
No Eye Can See
What Once We Loved

NONFICTION

A Simple Gift of Comfort
Homestead: A Memoir of Modern Pioneers
Pursuing the Edge of Possibility
*Aurora: An American Experience in
Quilt, Community, and Craft**

*finalist and award-winning work

Where Lilacs Still Bloom

"When reading any of Ms. Kirkpatrick's books, I become engaged, almost instantly, on many levels at once. *Where Lilacs Still Bloom* is simultaneously a strong and gentle read of beautiful, spare language. It wooed and won me to Hulda's story even as it coaxed me to look at my own life as well. Who am I staking up? Do I tend to my husband and my children as well as to my calling? The sweet message that lingers long after the book is closed is the promised truth of sowing and reaping, in gardens, and in life."

—SANDRA BYRD, author of *To Die For: A Novel of Anne Boleyn*

"Jane Kirkpatrick reimagines the true story of a nature-loving wife and mother who studied Luther Burbank and devoted herself to breeding new and improved varieties of lilacs. Families suffer, thrive, and evolve as new flowers emerge in a gentle tale as sweet as its fragrant garden."

—JANE S. SMITH, author of *In Praise of Chickens* and *The Garden of Invention*

"*Where Lilacs Still Bloom* is a charming, delightful story of Hulda Klager's courage and perseverance on many levels, her gentle defiance of convention, her triumph over natural and personal disasters, and her desire to be sure her work is truly God's will. Neither the author's nor Hulda's use of botanical research ever overpowers Hulda's story but makes plain for readers her patience and ruthless care in her quest for the blooms she envisions."

—CAROL BUCHANAN, author of *Wordsworth's Gardens* and winner of the 2009 Spur for *God's Thunderbolt: The Vigilantes of Montana*

"Having worked with the history of the Thiel and Klager families for over six years now as a board member, I was excited to read how Jane gave the family members such character. I particularly enjoyed the relationship between Hulda and Frank and the way Jane portrayed the youngest daughter, Martha. I loved reading *Where Lilacs Still Bloom* and visualizing what it must have been like to live in that old house when Hulda and her family lived and gathered there."

—JUDY CARD, genealogist and Woodland, Washington, historian

"Extraordinary book. Jane skillfully drops the reader into Hulda Klager's loving, hardworking pioneer life. She chronicles Hulda's family and botanical triumphs and struggles. Thank you for this magical story."

—REBECCA W. ROBERTS, secretary of Hulda Klager Lilac Gardens

JANE KIRKPATRICK

Author of *The Daughter's Walk*

A NOVEL

Where LILACS STILL BLOOM

WATERBROOK
PRESS

WHERE LILACS STILL BLOOM
PUBLISHED BY WATERBROOK PRESS
12265 Oracle Boulevard, Suite 200
Colorado Springs, Colorado 80921

Scripture quotations are taken or paraphrased from the King James Version and the New American Standard Bible®. © Copyright The Lockman Foundation 1960, 1962, 1963, 1968, 1971, 1972, 1973, 1975, 1977, 1995. Used by permission. (www.Lockman.org).

This book is a work of historical fiction based closely on real people and real events. Details that cannot be historically verified are purely products of the author's imagination.

Grateful acknowledgment is made to the Hulda Klager Lilac Gardens of Woodland, Washington, for the use of the photograph on page xi. Used by permission.

ISBN 978-1-4000-7430-3
ISBN 978-0-307-72942-2 (electronic)

Copyright © 2012 by Jane Kirkpatrick

Published in the United States by WaterBrook Multnomah, an imprint of the Crown Publishing Group, a division of Random House Inc., New York.

WATERBROOK and its deer colophon are registered trademarks of Random House Inc.

Library of Congress Cataloging-in-Publication Data
Kirkpatrick, Jane, 1946–
    Where lilacs still bloom : a novel / Jane Kirkpatrick. — First edition.
        p. cm
    ISBN 978-1-4000-7430-3 (pbk.) — ISBN 978-0-307-72942-2 (electronic)
    1. Klager, Hulda, 1863–1960—Fiction. 2. Housewives—Fiction.
3. Immigrant families—Fiction. 4. Plant hybridization—Fiction. 5. Lilacs—
Fiction. 6. Woodland (Wash.)—Fiction. I. Title.
    PS3561.I712W53 2012b
    813'54—dc23

                                                                2012002016

Printed in the United States of America
2012—First Edition

10 9 8 7 6 5 4 3 2 1

To Jerry, who at eighty began a new garden with me.

Cast of Characters

Hulda Klager—wife, mother, gardener

Frank Klager—dairyman in Woodland, Washington; Hulda's husband

Klager children—Elizabeth (Lizzie), Idehlia (Delia, Della), Martha, Fred (Fritz)

Klager grandchildren—Delia's children: Irvina, Clara, Fred; Lizzie's children: William, Roland

Amelia and Solomon Strong—Hulda's sister and brother-in-law

Bertha and Carl Tesch—Hulda's older sister and brother-in-law (also Frank Klager's best friend)

Emil and Matilda (Tillie) Thiel—Hulda's brother and sister-in-law who lived next-door

Thiel children—Albert, Elma, and Hazel

Bobby—Klager dogs

Dr. Alice Chapman—family doctor in Woodland, Washington

Dr. Carl Hoffman—local family practitioner in Woodland, Washington, and surrounding areas

Laura Hetzer—lecturer, Lowthorpe School of Landscape Architecture for Women

*Nelia Lawson—a garden helper, formerly of Mississippi

*Jasmine—Nelia's nanny

*Ruth Reed—a garden helper

*Barney Reed—Ruth's father

*Cornelia Givens—a reporter

*Shelly and William Snyder—botanists from Maryland

*a fictional composite of people in Hulda's life

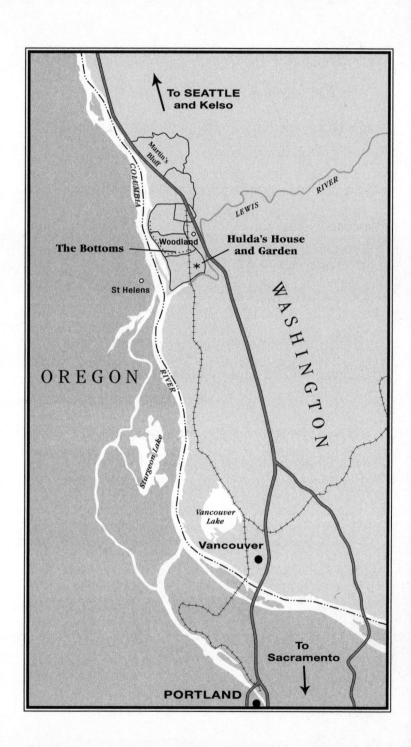

Hulda (left) in her garden with visitors.

In the dooryard fronting an old farm-house
near the white-wash'd palings,
Stands the lilac-bush tall-growing with heart-
shaped leaves of rich green…
With every leaf a miracle…

WALT WHITMAN, "When Lilacs Last
in the Dooryard Bloom'd"

Catch on fire with enthusiasm and people will
come for miles to watch you burn.

JOHN WESLEY, founder of Methodism

And out of the ground made the LORD God to
grow every tree that is pleasant to the sight.

GENESIS 2:9

I am thinking of faith now…
and what we feel we are
worthy of in this world.

DAVID WHYTE, "The True Love"

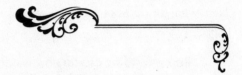

PROLOGUE

1948

It's the lilacs I'm worried over. My Favorite and Delia and City of Kalama, and so many more; my as yet unnamed double creamy-white with its many petals is especially vulnerable. I can't find the seeds I set aside for it, lost in the rush to move out of the rivers' way, get above Woodland's lowlands now underwater. So much water from the double deluge of the Columbia and the Lewis. Oh, how those rivers can rise in the night, breaching dikes we mere mortals put up hoping to stem the rush of what is as natural as air: water seeping, rising, pushing, reshaping all within its path.

I watch as all the shaping of my eighty-five years washes away.

My only surviving daughter puts her arm around my shoulder, pulls me to her. Her house is down there too, water rising in her basement. We can't see it from this bluff.

"It'll be all right, Grandma. We're all safe. You can decide later what to do about your flowers," my grandson Roland tells me.

"I know it. All we can do now is watch the rivers and pray no one dies."

How I wish Frank stood beside me. We'd stake each other up as we did through the years. I could begin again with him at my side. But now uncertainty curls against my old spine, and I wonder if my lilacs have bloomed their last time.

SELECTION

One

FOOD FOR THOUGHT

Hulda, 1889

Daffodils as yellow as the sun, ruby tulips, and a row of purple lilacs from the old country border the house I live in with my husband, Frank, our three young children (ages eight, five, and three), and next month, if all goes well, our fourth child. We are hoping for a boy. My parents live with us, but only for a few more months. They've built a new house near Woodland, Washington. We'll be moving too, to a farm of our own south of Whelan Road. We'll still be within a few miles of each other, a close-knit family of German Americans captured by this lush landscape between the Lewis and Columbia Rivers. We call where we live the Bottoms. It's made up of black soil that was once the bottom of those great rivers—and sometimes becomes so again with the floods. We hope our new places will be less prone to flooding, though it's the nature of rivers to rise with the spring thaws. We live with it.

My mother and children have dug daffodil and dahlia

bulbs, snipped lilac starts to plant, and my sisters and brother and neighbors will give us sprouts from their bushes once we move, which is the custom. A lilac says "Here is a place to stay," and how perfect that such promise of permanence should come from family and friends?

We can't move the apple orchard. But I wielded my grafting knife and wrapped the shoots, *scions* they're called, in sawdust and stored them in the barn earlier this year when the trees were dormant. Today I'll graft them onto saplings at my parents' new house, so one day there'll be an apple orchard there. I've also stepped into the uncommon for a simple house Frau: I've grafted a Wild Bismarck apple variety known for its crispness with a Wolf River, an apple of a larger size. My father encouraged such dappling with nature—and that I keep my efforts quiet, at least for a time.

It was April, and we tied the scions onto the saplings he'd started as soon as he knew they'd be building the house. I liked working with my father in the orchard, a misty rain giving way to sunbreaks, and the aroma of cedar and pine drifting down from the surrounding hills in the shadow of Mount St. Helens. So much seems possible in such vibrant landscapes. A garden is the edge of possibility.

He was a great storyteller and advice giver, my father, though this day his story surprised. "Don't tell Frank right away," he told me. "Let him think you're just grafting plain old apples to help us extend the orchard."

"Frank wouldn't mind."

"In time—when you have the final result in hand. But Frank discourages you. I see it, Hulda." I pushed at my frizzy walnut-brown hair and stared at him. "He dismisses your interests if they go beyond your children and him."

"It's a woman's duty to meet her family's needs."

"Meet their needs first. But you want a crisper, bigger apple too," he said. "Nothing wrong with that."

"I do. I get so annoyed at those mealy things that hang on to their peels like bark to a tree."

He nodded. "Some would say that meddling with nature isn't wise. Frank might agree—especially if the one meddling is a mother who should be content with looking after her family."

I stood, using my hoe to help me and my burgeoning belly up. I was nearly as tall as my father. He liked Frank; at least I always thought he did. My love and admiration for both men were rooted deep. It felt strange to defend my husband to my father. "You're wrong, Papa." I pushed my pointy straw hat back. "Frank's a good helpmate for me. And he'll like having more pies."

My father tied another scion onto a branch, making sure the cambium was fully covered in the slanted cut I'd made so the two would bond securely. "You have a gift, Hulda. You can see distinctive things in plants. You see the possibility, like a crisper, larger apple, and then imagine it into being." He lifted another scion as emphasis. "Those are gifts few have, and people can be envious."

My father had never granted me such a compliment, and I was both pleased that he noticed and humbled that he shared it. "Not Frank," I insisted.

"Not everyone understands that we are all created to have complicated challenges and dreams. We must honor our longings, then go beyond them whether others support us or not."

I wondered if he spoke of my mother. Did she resent my father's dreams that took us from Germany to Wisconsin, Minnesota, San Francisco, then back to Wisconsin, and then here to the Lewis River of the new state of Washington? My father had many longings: farming, becoming a brewmaster, investing in creameries and cheese factories before the landscape was dotted with cows. He'd done all those. Now logging interested him, and he'd built a big two-story house; yet another adventure that meant more change for my mother— and the rest of us too.

"My dream is to raise my family." I didn't see getting a crisper apple as any budding desire. I wasn't rising beyond my station. "These apples will make life better for them." I was merely an immigrant housewife wanting to save time peeling apples.

"Just think of what I've said." He wrapped his big paw around my hand that was holding a scion. He looked me in the eye. I swallowed. "Huldie, don't deny the dreams. They're a gift given to make your life full. Accept them. Reach for them. We are not here just to endure hard times until we die.

We are here to live, to serve, to trust, and to create out of our longings."

"Yes, Papa," I said, but it wasn't until after he was gone, years later, that I came to understand what I'd committed to.

Two

Secret Progress

Hulda, 1899

In the ten years after my father's caution, I accepted that I did have an eye for seeing what wasn't there, something formed out of subtle differences from the blending of two things. He passed on three years after our conversation. My mama's gone now too. Their big two-story house sits empty, though I keep the apple orchard under my wing, hoping for that crisper, bigger apple.

"I love making you pies," I told my husband of twenty years one morning, "but the apples are so mealy and small it takes a week of Wednesdays to get enough to bake."

"Ach, woman. You do more than the average mother, I submit, but there's not much you can do about the nature of an apple." Frank washed his sinewy arms at the sink, removing the barnyard stink clear up to his elbows before grabbing the towel and placing a peck on my cheek. He sat down for breakfast. I set the platter of biscuits and gravy, Frank's favorite—after eggs and bacon or pancakes and sausages or hot sauerkraut with spices and juniper—before him. Lo, that man can eat despite being only an inch taller than my five feet seven inches!

"Remember what happened to Eve and the apple," he said.

"Eve was being curious."

"See what it got her?"

I set hot coffee next to his plate. "Yes, but God gave us curiosity along with the ability to listen. That's where she failed. So it's natural to wonder about everything, even the nature of an apple."

"Wonder all you want, but nothing will change. Blooms come when they will. Rivers flow and flood regardless of our efforts. I submit, we humans can't do a thing to get an earlier bloom or extend the season either."

I reminded him that where a rosebush was set could change the blooming time and how it seemed to me the activity of birds and bees from one year to the next changed the colors of my daffodils. I love daffodils and have hundreds of them planted around the house, lining the walkway, perking their yellow heads up against the barn, marking spring as they push up beneath the water tower and windmill. I'd dabbled in changing plantings, not understanding how it worked until I read about Mendel's and De Vries's efforts and how they "bred" plants, though I've never told Frank of such readings. I'm not sure a wife should keep such things from her husband, though, so I took a deep breath.

"There's this Californian, Luther Burbank. He's extended the season of certain plants by having them bloom earlier in the year, bringing on the fruit before you'd think. He put thousands of french prune buds into young almond saplings, grafting them in June. With careful pruning, by December, he had nearly twenty thousand plum trees ready for orchard planting, enough for two hundred acres."

Frank looked at me. "What would you do with twenty thousand plum trees?"

"Nothing." I waved my hand to dismiss his words. "It's the idea of it. That grafting one plant to another can make significant changes."

"There certainly have been changes since I got grafted onto you." He wiggled his eyebrows. They had a touch of gray already.

"Frank. Listen." I sat beside him. "Where once was an almond tree, now is a plum, or at least it behaves like a plum tree. That's almost a miracle."

"I submit, you'll twist the minds of our children with all this talk of changing nature." He didn't sound cross, so I took it as a wary jest, but then he added, "You're a simple German housewife, Huldie. A good mother, my helpmate on this farm. That's enough for any woman, or should be."

I remembered my father's warning, brushed at the bun at the back of my neck and stood. I picked up an apple. It looked bigger, but it still didn't have the crisp I'd hoped for. I considered telling Frank about my grafting efforts as I sliced and placed apples in the bowl with the other soft little chunks. "Ouch!" I put my finger to my mouth.

"What?" Frank said, turning to me.

"I've cut myself. These apples! The peels cling like babies to their mothers." I sucked at the cut, then Frank, who had gotten up, handed me a clean cloth and held it to my wound, his big fingers warm and comforting around my hand.

"Guess I shouldn't sharpen those knives so often."

"It's not the knife." I pointed. "It's this apple!"

"No sense decrying its nature." He looked at me, must have seen the determination in my face. "I submit that if anyone can bring about a change in God's design, it'd be you," my husband lauded.

I took the strip of cloth from Frank, and he helped wrap it around my cut finger. It would annoy me all day having that cut.

"I guess every great inventor has to have a little pain in his life," Frank said. He still grinned about my wanting that better apple, but he kissed the bandage and returned to his oatmeal.

"Frank." I stood beside him.

"What?"

He turned and I popped a piece of the soft apple into his surprised open mouth. "Just remember this conversation on the day you have a big, crisp, sliced apple and pies more than once a week."

THREE

JASMINE AND NELIA

Old Fort Vancouver, 1900

The once-slave woman, old and worn, ambled up the hill from the river carrying the cargo she'd been sent to recover. "If I've told you once, I've told you a dozen times, you ain't allowed near that river. Too dangerous and deep, your papa tells you, and I'm telling you too, though Lord knows, you don't listen to either of us no more." She set the six-year-old down, heaving from the effort. Nelia, the child, turned and stamped her foot.

"I hate you! I hate you, and I hate Papa. I hate everyone!"

"Well, I suppose you do, but that don't change the fact that you ain't allowed near the river without an adult beside you. They's currents in that stream could suck you under. It ain't like that paucity, Leaf River, where you was born and growed."

"I want that river back," Nelia screamed.

"We don't get back what we lose." The old woman sighed. "We get what we got comin' to us. I 'spose, though, we can make somethin' outta that. God gives us tools, child, He does." She softened her voice. "You missin' your mama, and that's a worthy fret." She touched the girl's narrow shoulders. "It surely is."

"I hate it here. I want that river to take me under." The child stood defiant, but her arms no longer crossed her slender chest. Hair as black as oil splayed around the child's face like grass around a fence post. The child had found a pair of scissors and hacked at her curls.

"Come here, child. Let me put a little huggin' on you for a time. I could use some of that myself. We'll 'member all the good things of your mama. Then we'll catch the day, strengthened by our bit of honoring hope." They walked the lush grounds separating the buildings Mr. Lawson had called the Fort. "Let's count all these gardens, Nelia." The child used her fingers.

"One more than all my fingers," she announced. "Eleven."

"You're such a smart girl. Eleven gardens. Hmm-um." The old woman smacked her lips. "All them taters and kale. Those men eat well. And see them strawberries marching beside the paths there? They'll be ripe soon."

Jasmine wondered if their new home near Woodland, Washington, would look like this place, with chilly winds in the morning kissing squares of growing things. She wondered how her employer had found such a place for his tailoring business. She guessed the man wanted to go as far away from the memories as he could and had chosen a landscape and relationships so different only his accent—and the presence of a colored woman—would link him to his past. She hadn't seen many people like her in Fort Vancouver, though seeing a few Indians made her feel a little at home.

She watched her charge, Nelia, lean over the strawberries, poking with her small fingers at the tiny green stubs that if left alone would turn red and be ripe for picking. The child needed time and tending just like those berries, but she ought not be left alone the way Mr. Lawson did his daughter. Jasmine ached for the sadness of the child's life, a hole she could not fill. She watched the girl pull at the berry, toss it aside. To distract her, she shouted, "Look there." She pointed past the six-year-old child. "Over there, Nelia Lawson. Would you look at that!"

The girl turned. "I do believe that's a lilac blooming," Jasmine said. "Like the one your mama planted when you was born. Let's go take a sniff and then sit." Jasmine could use the rest.

Nelia didn't want to smell flowers. Flowers wouldn't bring her mama back and they wouldn't make her papa smile again and they wouldn't make her like this cold breezy air or those trees that made your neck ache as you tried to see their tops. This Washington was a strange place and she wouldn't love it, not ever! She crossed her thin arms again, pressing them against the ivory buttons of her dress. She kicked at the hemline of her skirt, didn't care about the mud collected there that Jasmine now brushed at.

Jasmine pushed up against her knees. It was the old woman's heavy breathing that finally loosened Nelia's arms. She worried over the woman. People you loved died if you weren't careful. Nelia must not have been careful looking after her mama. Now Nelia was in a strange place, her father distant as the Mississippi and as elusive as feathers floating on wind.

"If you don't want a hug, that's fine," the old woman said. "But I needs one real bad today, and I know yours is a tender heart, Nelia."

She didn't want Jasmine dying, and that breathing worried her, and so Nelia sighed and walked behind the old woman who lifted her heavy legs up the hill.

"Let's take a sniff. Where your papa is taking us, we'll find a lilac bush like that. Won't that be dandy?"

The child nodded, took the old woman's hand, and they sauntered to the shrub. Nelia gentled the pale lavender bloom in her small hand and inhaled. Tears formed and spilled. The scent brought back thoughts again of all they'd left behind.

Jasmine sniffed too, saw the child's tears. "Ah, Nelia, let's let the fine smell of this here flower be a hope for the future as well as a sniff to honor the past."

"Mama would have liked this flower?"

"I declare, she would have."

Nelia nodded, and before Jasmine could stop her, she broke a bloom from its stem and headed toward the big building she'd seen her father enter earlier. The stately man stepped outside at the knock of his daughter. He looked at the flower she held up to him, but he didn't take it. He scowled at Jasmine as she waddled up behind Nelia.

"She was just interested in the bloom, Mr. Lawson, sir." Jasmine puffed from the effort of her fast walk to catch up to the child. "Reminded her of Mistress Mary. A good memory, don't you think, sir?"

"There is no good memory of a woman who died before her time." He stepped back inside, away from Nelia.

Jasmine bent to inhale the bloom, held Nelia's hand. "Some folk can't face what is, child. Always make it harder to move forward."

FOUR

SWEPT ALONG

Hulda, 1900

It became important to me for Frank to understand my need to create, and daffodils were the perfect school slate. I tried to explain what I wanted to do.

"Really, Huldie." He called me Huldie when he was questioning my wisdom, making me sound like a young girl when I'm nearly forty. "You can tell such differences?" Frank—if he swept the floor—would sweep with a wide brush and not notice the little things that stuck in the corners. That feature of his nature allowed him to overlook a person's flaws, for which I'm grateful, as I have my share. But it kept him from seeing the world the way I did, full of small parts to puzzle together to form grand pictures.

"Yes, I can see traits. I notice which rosebush opens its blooms before the others, and I can see the slightest shade of color difference in a daffodil. They aren't all yellow as a canary."

"Show me," he said.

We walked outside into the March morning. The daffodils were planted in patches in the front and another in the back. Bobby, our dog, bounded past us as we stepped down from the porch. He was an inside dog for his meals (along with the cats) but out in the woodshed on his old quilt for sleeping. This meant more sweeping every day, but the children learned how to do that early on, and even Fritz, our youngest and only son, wielded a broom with aplomb by the time he was four, Bobby barking at the straw strands as our boy laughed and swept.

The dog with his swirling shepherd's tail bounded ahead as Frank and I walked to the closest daffodil patch. I had a hundred bulbs planted south of the house that year, and many were well up, nodding their yellow heads. A chinook wind warmed the air and teased those flowers open, slow and tender like a courting man's words to a young woman's heart.

"See, this one's slightly more yellow than…that one." I pointed to a plant a few feet away from the one whose bloom I held in my hand, two fingers separated by the stem, the bloom soft as a baby's bottom in my palm. I leaned my steady hoe against my knee as I squatted. "This one here has a hint of red."

Frank squinted, touched the bloom as though the feel of it would help him see the color better. He took a step toward the one I pointed at. "That one over there is slipping toward more yellow," I said. I walked the edge of the patch and checked for snakes before I reached into the flush of yellow, choosing another single bloom that had the shade of a male meadowlark's breast; such a brilliant yellow. "Now that one is even more golden than the first I showed you, can you see that?" He nodded, but I wasn't sure he really did. "That one is duckling down. This one, morning sun." I pointed to another. "Egg-yolk yellow." Frank squinted. I could tell he tried to see what I did.

"I'll mark that one." I took a strip of red yarn from my apron and tied it to the stem. "The sunlight is perfect to catch the slightest distinction. When I break the bulbs apart this fall, I'll want to plant this one right next to the other egg-yolk yellow, and that way, they'll fertilize each other. I might get an even deeper hue."

I inhaled their scent. I noted those differences too, marking ones with the most deeply satisfying smell with a white strand of yarn. I thought of my mama. She loved the smell of daffodils. Inhaling a soothing scent from a flower could take away pain, the kind of pain that comes with loss and longing. I urged Frank to inhale, and he stuck his slender nose inside the bloom.

"They're all individual to me, Frank. I see each one, unique and perfect as it is, but a few move toward more what I'm imagining than another."

I showed him a few more distinctive blooms, noting the size differences as well as color and then found myself kneeling and weeding, my mind soothed by the effort, inhaling scents of heaven. I pulled yarn and marked them for scent and color and hardiness and early or late blooming.

It would take time to change a tree's or flower's habit of being. My father used to say it took thirty days to change a person's ways. Much longer for a plant. But like people, they can be shaped if the qualities one loves the most are noticed and nurtured. In some ways, I think Frank knew that insight first, as he loved me out of my annoyances from the time I was sixteen and his new bride until now when we partner together to raise our family. I hoped he understood that daffodils gave me more.

"Where are you off to?" I asked him as he turned, began to step away. "I thought you wanted to know how I see things." I was irritated with him for flitting from one thing to another like a bee to a bloom.

He pulled out his pocket watch and looked at it. "I've been standing here close to an hour watching you seek and find. You just disappeared inside that patch, Huldie."

"No," I said. No to my not realizing he'd been standing there, and no to how much time could have passed. I looked toward the sun.

"Yes," he said.

"I just—"

"I submit you're lost in the blooms. Like once you got lost in me."

"Oh, Frank." I stood and kissed his cheek, the hoe against my shoulder between us. "I still get lost in you."

Frank gave me a wistful smile, and I swallowed no small level of guilt. I didn't devote myself to him the way I did to those flowers, but wasn't that in human nature too? We fall in love, our passions deep and moving, and then we go on to living, the love still strong but different, as babies come and cry and need our loving too. They grow older, and we seek nurture in new places, and what safer place can there be but in a garden?

Frank walked off toward the barn, and I didn't know what to say to keep him with me. A hummingbird vibrated past my head looking for sweets. I worked my way back toward the house, calling Bobby with a slap to my knee, hoeing out a few weeds as the dog came running. Was it wrong to find sustenance in creation, to feel pride in seeking those crisp apples? I put my hoe away, took off my hat and decided to bake fresh bread for Frank's supper. It was the least I could do when he felt my love for him wasn't as grand as it was for a daffodil. Or an apple. He was wrong, of course, wasn't he?

That fall we harvested the apples from my father's orchard. I gave each apple tree that same scrutiny I gave my daffodils so I could keep shaping and deciding which branches I'd graft where the following year. Baskets sat on the ground, and despite the work, it was a happy time with my children—all four here on weekends, the oldest two away in Portland attending school during the week. I looked for the largest apples, and on that day in 1900, I saw the fruit of my labors. On the ladder, I pulled a good-sized apple from the stem, rubbed it clean with my apron, then with anticipation, bit in.

Crisp as thin ice on a spring morning! "Frank!" I shouted, nearly spilling off the ladder. "Come here. I think I've got it!"

"Got what?" he shouted back. I watched him step back off his ladder.

"Just come." I scrambled down, lifting my skirts. On the way I grabbed two more apples, then three more cradled in my apron. "Here." I gave each child and Frank an apple. "Bite into it." I grinned.

"Tart," Lizzie, our oldest said. "But good."

"Good," Frank said. Fritz nodded agreement, and Delia and Martha rolled their eyes with pleasure as they chewed.

"Tart, yes. And big. And now the test." I took my knife out and began to peel the apple I'd bitten into. I managed a long, slender peel instead of the dozens of small, broken bits of skin that I was used to. "Would you look at that?" I held up the length of peel that wiggled its way into an S. "I've got my crisp, bigger, easier peeler. Right here in Papa's orchard!" I danced a little jig.

"Glad a good apple makes your day," Frank said.

"Don't you see? I bred these, Frank. Papa and I grafted

them. A Wild Bismarck and a Wolf River variety, and now I have the best of both in one fruit. Oh, I can hardly wait to make you a pie."

"You grafted these?" Frank raised an eyebrow.

"I did, and I've been waiting these long years to get what I wanted."

"Why didn't you say?" Martha, our youngest girl, asked. She's fourteen, and she sounded hurt.

"Oh, it was just an experiment. If it didn't work out, I didn't want to bother you all. I had no idea it might actually work."

"But you look so…happy," Delia said, she with the deep brown eyes.

"Is something wrong with that?" Their caution brought my spirits down. "I thought you'd like having more pies."

"That's fine with me," Fritz said. "Let's get them picked."

We returned to the work at hand. I heard geese chattering on the Lewis River. It made a wide loop not far from my father's house, and the birds liked stopping there on their way south. I set the apples from that tree aside and marked the basket too. I'd cut a dozen branches from that tree this winter and graft them in the spring to extend the number that gave me my perfect fruit. I heard my family call to one another, make jokes, and gather at the baskets to drink water from the jugs. I felt separate from them and couldn't name the feeling that settled over me. Frank caught my eye and sent an encouraging smile. Perhaps I should have shared my dream and effort along the way so that this moment of triumph wouldn't seem like mine alone.

It occurred to me that my father had been only half correct with his lessons in the orchard that day: it was important to dream, but sharing it with those you loved made achievement even better.

FIVE

SHELLY BERRINGER

Baltimore, 1901

S helly Berringer would arrive any time now. It was her first trip to Bill's home in Baltimore. She'd obsessed about what to wear, how much dust there'd be on the stage between Annapolis and Baltimore, whether she might change her clothes somewhere in between before seeing Bill. She carried an umbrella to ward against the June sun but wouldn't really need it. June along the Chesapeake Bay was never really warm so much as balmy.

Shelly wasn't impressed with professors, yet W. A. "Bill" Snyder, in his forties, had caught her fancy. She was surrounded by instructors at the naval academy where her father taught. One had to see through the fog of their academic words to find their true hearts. Bill was shorter than her father but carried himself like a general, which he wasn't. He was a man with a purpose, though, aware of his surroundings. Bill had brushed away the fog and shown that his true interest wasn't for teaching so much as the subject he taught: botany. Shelly had never paid much attention to the science of plants. It was the comfort of gardens that offered happiness.

The stage bumped along, and Shelly remembered Bill's description of his mother's garden and conservatory and how he'd planned an outdoor luncheon for them. She wondered what flowers he might choose for the centerpiece, hoping it wasn't chrysanthemums, because those made her sneeze. Had she told him that? Mums were his mother's favorite. She was glad now she'd chosen to wear what she had. She needed to be direct and let him know exactly who she was—his mother as well.

He'd shared stories about his mother—whom he obviously adored—stories that caused a stream of perspiration to dribble down Shelly's neck now, alighting at the collar of her dress. Bill loved his conservatory and the garden on the family estate where he said he "forgot about his loneliness in the company of stately roses, flashy peonies, and the ever-quiet sweet williams in season." His mother seemed unaware of her son's companionship with blooms, urging him to "let the gardeners do it; that's why we pay them."

Shelly shifted on the seat, put her feet up across to reduce swelling. She was glad she was the only one on this stage so she could lift her legs. Bill would meet her at the stage stop. She'd stay with her aunt that evening. Even though Shelly was twenty-two and had lived around the world, traveling with her parents, her father insisted she have proper escorts. At least he'd let her make the trip alone. Bill had told her he admired independent women but "it makes sense to accommodate your father until such time as you marry and would then be accommodating your husband." He used his professorial voice, and she'd bristled at that view of independence but kept silent. The relationship wasn't far enough along yet.

Shelly's poor father worried she might never marry, since she'd found happiness tending him after her mother's death five years previous and looking after the gardens she and her mother had both loved. "Putting down roots," her mother called it when they arrived at a new army base and she nestled petunia seeds inside squash hulls for spring planting or laid tulip bulbs they'd brought from the last military station into new soil. It was the sign they were home when her mother found the place where "the lilacs would grow and the soap would foam up in the nearest creek." She was from New England, and that was the story told about Vermonters staking their claims with soap and lilac starts.

Bill had invited Shelly to come to his garden for tea six months into their travels. Traveling was how they'd met, Shelly visiting her aunt in Baltimore and Bill coming back from his week of teaching in St. John's College in Annapolis.

"Why I'd be pleased beyond words, Mr. Snyder," she'd said when he invited her. "Beyond words."

"Excellent. Shall I send a cab for you?"

"That would likely please my aunt."

"Oh, of course, your aunt." He cleared his throat. "She must come too."

She heard the disappointment in his words and was grateful when he added, "She'll be most welcome."

"I'll do my best to convince her of the opportunity to see one of Baltimore's finest gardens."

But her aunt had not found the "opportunity" because Shelly hadn't given it to her. Shelly sent a note with just the tiniest of fibs expressing her aunt's regret but giving her blessing that Shelly come alone by stage. Now here it was, the important day. She would meet his mother, and she would see where the garden path would take them.

She felt the driver slow, and she pushed back the curtains when the stage stopped. Bill stood there in a white linen suit, straight as one of the four thousand cadets that surrounded her daily. He stopped to adjust the silver pin on his white tie, check for spots on the white linen suit. He took a deep breath and approached the cab. Why, he was as nervous as she was!

The driver leaped down, opened the door.

"Miss Berringer." Bill leaned into the dark cab and offered his hand before the driver could.

Shelly placed her fingers in his palm, and he closed his hands around the warm flesh. She hadn't worn gloves. "Welcome." His words didn't quell the look of surprise when Shelly put her foot out on the step and he saw the tops of her black high-button shoes and a hemline barely reaching the top of them. She exposed a portion of striped-stocking-covered leg the width of a mum above her shoes.

"Your...dress," Bill gasped.

"I hope you like it. It's the rage for casual wear, like picnics. Which is what we're having, isn't it, Mr. Snyder?"

"A picnic? Well..."

"I mean, we are having brunch in your fabulous garden you said. I'm sure it will be fabulous."

"As are you. I...I didn't expect—"

"The reform dress?" Shelly finished for him. She'd chosen a black-and-white skirt whose hemline came a good foot above the ankle now that she stood. She wore no bustle, no corset but a wide belt and a loose white blouse with a scoop neckline trimmed in two black rows of ribbon. She carried a small straw hat. It was the latest in women's fashion—suffrage fashion. Not at all the gossamer yellow he'd seen her in when they'd first met.

"I've never actually seen the garb on a person, but I've read of it."

"And the consternation it can cause in certain social circles." Shelly smiled at him. Would he meet her test?

"Yes, circles visited by my mother and friends."

"You said you liked an independent woman, Mr. Snyder."

"I do." He smiled then. "I'm glad to see you are one."

He put his elbow out for her to take, and they began walking toward the cab he'd hired for the drive from the stage stop to his estate.

"What are we having for lunch?" Shelly wanted to sing with joy that he'd so graciously accepted her uniform of the day.

"Watercress and cucumber sandwiches, a fruit aspic, and perhaps a chocolate mousse. Do those appeal?"

"They do, they do. Your mother will join us?"

"Alas, just as your aunt had complications, so did my mother. She was called away suddenly, so I didn't have time to let you know you'd be with me unchaperoned."

"My aunt didn't really have other plans today… I never let her know."

Bill squeezed her arm as he helped her into the cab. "My mother, too, had planned to be gone. I never let—"

"Ah, then another day they'll be introduced to our re-forming ways."

"They will indeed." He patted her hand, skin to skin. "I hope you like chrysanthemums," Bill said then. "I've a center-piece of yellow ones."

"I'm partial to lilacs myself." He had blue eyes that Shelly began to sink into.

She sneezed as they stepped out of the cab and approached Bill's garden. "Those mums just don't like me. They just don't like me, Mr. Snyder."

"Never mind about them. I like you." He leaned close

to her ear. "We'll move them. Better yet, we'll move the luncheon."

"But I want to see your garden."

"You will, you will," Bill said, and Shelly noted he repeated words just as she did. "To the front lawn. We'll have lemonade and sandwiches there and give the neighbors news to tell my mother when she returns."

"I like a man who can adapt," Shelly said.

"The strongest plants always do."

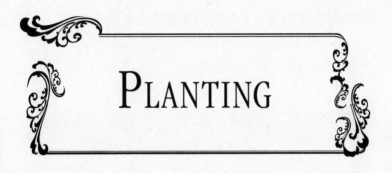

PLANTING

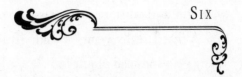

SIX

SALACIOUS JOY

Hulda, 1901

F rank painted a sign that said Daffodil Farm and stuck it near the road that passed the house. People often stopped by on a Sunday afternoon in spring to look at the wash of yellow. I'd cut stems, and the children would put them in water, and we'd give bouquets away. In the fall, people returned, and I'd give them bulbs to plant. I took such pleasure in walking past a neighbor's house to see yellow bobbing daffodils or tulips I recognized by hue as mine.

Delia, my middle girl, cut lilac blooms too, in season, and we gave starts away. The lilacs begged me to turn my interests their way. I'd always had a dream, one I never told my father; but after our apple conversation, I told Frank.

"I've always wanted to see a red lilac," I said. "And a creamy white."

"I like them the way they are. But I know you see them

different." It was the height of the season where the colors were true and outshined the glassy leaves.

"What I really want," I said, "is to have a bloom with many petals instead of just four."

Frank pushed his hat toward the back of his forehead. "Now, that's a challenge."

I shrugged my shoulders. "But I've had success with my apples and my daffodils. I think lilacs are next."

"So long as there's bread on the table," he cautioned. "And pies in the oven."

"I'll make time for you, Frank." I patted his hand. "And the children. You know I will. I just need to mark these bushes so I can pollinate next spring." I pulled marked strips of cloth from my apron and took out one with two stitches made with white thread, to mark the pale purple bloom as the closest to white as I'd seen. At another bush I had ruby-red thread to suggest that purple bloom headed toward a reddish tint. I had made up dozens of markers while I sat in the evenings watching Frank write up the creamery board meeting minutes.

"How would it be if I made metal tags for you?" Frank nodded toward my threads. "I could press in letters for codes."

"Why, that would be good. Wonderful. Thank you. Now I can spend my evenings looking at seed catalogs." I grinned.

"Would you ever consider selling some of your inventions to a seed company?" Frank asked.

"What would be the fun in that? I like being able to give them away, to see who they go to. It's just a little hobby, Frank. Nothing serious."

Frank nodded, but I felt a twinge of guilt again, that I devoted time and now Frank's energy, too, for tasks that had no financial return and actually took money when I ordered new bulbs. At least I was pollinating from my own plants, so we saved that expense.

"If you want, I can mark things in that book you keep too."

"Your penmanship is so much better than mine."

"You wouldn't want to breed a pale purple to a deep purple without knowing it."

I couldn't tell if he teased or not, but he was absolutely right.

⁓

On a still morning when cranes called to one another on the Lewis, and dew marked the day, I made my way with a magnifying glass, a crochet hook, a turkey feather, and one of the children's paintbrushes. I sought pollen on the palest purple bloom I'd marked the year before with Frank's tag. Lilac pollen is as tiny as beach sand. The day was almost sultry with the fresh smell of turned earth from the vegetable garden Frank plowed up for us. As though I carried a hot cup of water across a room, I first used the paintbrush to lift pollen onto the turkey feather, and then with the crochet hook, I placed a grain at a time onto the stamen pushing up from the center of a promised bloom on the plant I wanted to change. Before moving on to the next one, I carefully wrapped a cloth bag around the fertilized plant so no bird or bee would come along and try to interfere with my plans. It seemed brassy to think that what a bee did by nature was somehow interfering, but I wanted to control what happened as best I could. I soon gave up on the paintbrush and just used the turkey feather to lift the pollen and carry it. I couldn't get close enough to the plants with my Chinese hat on, so I took it off to bend closer to my work. With each transfer of pollen from one plant to the other, I held my breath. I did hundreds that first day.

"Look at you, Mama," Lizzie said, home for the summer. "Your face is burned to a crisp. The ladies at church will cluck their tongues when your cheeks turn brown as a bean." I'd forgotten how long I'd been out in the sun without my hat. Lizzie left, then returned to rub lard on the worst parts, her fingers cool against my hot face. "There's a recipe in my ladies' magazine for a face cream. Let's try it."

"They'll know I've been out in my garden, is all. And lard is just fine for the burn."

"But what woman forgets her hat, Mama? For so long?"

"Yes, yes, I know. I'll remember tomorrow."

But I didn't, and I caught the looks of my church friends at the Bible study on Wednesday evenings when Woodland's faithful of many denominations gathered. With raised eyebrows, they'd ask what I was working on now.

"Lilacs," I said. And yes, I noticed a frown or two that I didn't think was just about my tanned face. I was doing something simple housewives didn't do and, even more salacious, taking pleasure in it.

SEVEN

LOST IN SEEKING

Hulda, 1902

My girls grew up, despite my wish to keep them at my side. So, when they were all three together, it was a festive time, even though we had work to do. I hated ironing and was glad when my girls reached an age where I could convince them that ironing shirts and sheets would develop their characters. At least that's what my mother always told me while she heated the flatiron for me. On a spring afternoon, I heated the irons for Lizzie and Delia and Martha as they worked their way through the baskets, while I perused seed catalogs for ornamentals. I already had my kitchen garden planned. My girls had apparently been planning events as well.

"We'd like to have a double wedding, the way you and Aunt Amelia did," Delia said.

"You would? Have you chosen your intended, or are you still piddling around with your travels?"

"I'm not piddling." Lizzie held the iron midair. "I climbed Mount St. Helens because I like the challenge."

"I can understand that. But challenging your brain is a better use of your time."

"She's had college, Mama," Martha said. "She needs a body challenge more than a mind one." Martha was the only one of our children who didn't have pearl-pale skin. Hers had that wholesome look of warm sun, but of course that wasn't the fashion then. I think it made her self-conscious, adding to her quiet ways.

"I guess you're right. Mountain climbing is a challenge that never appealed to me."

"It would build your character, Mama," Delia said. She left her ironing board to pour kerosene into the one modern iron we had. She took her time.

"I have other things to do," I quipped. "Like surviving three chattering girls avoiding ironing."

"We're doing it." Lizzie's clear voice rose above the groans of her sisters. "I'd rather entertain you on the piano." Lizzie had a lot of interests, including music. I was proud that Frank and I could afford to send her off to Portland for schooling and music lessons and a piano. I'd graduated eighth grade at Lee Lewis School and wished I could have gone on further. But I met Frank, married him at sixteen, had Lizzie at seventeen, and that was that.

"Ha," Delia said, coming back to task. "I should be baking."

"Your father likes his collarless shirts pressed well. See how important you are."

"You've been waiting years to have us do this," Lizzie said. She had the same oval face of her sisters and cocoa brown hair like them too.

"If you're going to have children, make them be girls. A mother can always use the help."

I thought back to when I had only daughters. With Martha's arrival two years after Delia, I had three young girls underfoot. I set aside a plot where the two older ones could make their mud pies while Martha slept in her basket beneath the cedar tree. I kept the sun from her face, but she still looked suntanned even in winter. She took after Frank. They all had big brown eyes, though, taking after mine, I guess. Inside the house, the room heated up with the irons and the hot cotton. As much as I disliked housework, this afternoon of ironing and conversation was turning out to be a fine time. I was glad Fritz was with his dad somewhere with the cows.

Martha finished her basket of clothes and picked up a book. She was our studious one, always studying, thinking, even writing some to express what lay inside her. We shared that too. Fritz we indulged as the only boy. At thirteen he was already taller than Frank and fine looking. He helped Frank with the chores and freed me from some of that work, though I liked moving the cows to new pastures near the river, listening to their moos and such, getting in a good walk on a spring day. But a boy needs to know what his father's work is so he can step into it when the time comes.

They were good children. I like to think Frank and I gave them those good qualities, but we just provided the soil for the planting. Oh, we tended and pruned when they got too wild, and we watered their spirits at the right times down the street at the Presbyterian church where Lizzie played the organ now that she was living back home with us. I didn't openly brag on my children, at least not in front of them, for that can harm a child as much as no words of praise at all; and I had to keep them in line.

"Will you make our wedding dresses for us?" Delia broke into my musing.

"Knowing you could do it just fine yourselves, I'm honored to be asked." I'd have to fit it in between plantings. I watched my apple grafts, added more each year. I made up nicotine tea to spray on invading insects. Now, daffodils consumed me, and my lilac efforts needed encouragement too.

"You girls should think twice about a double wedding," I said.

"Didn't you and Aunt Amelia have fun?"

"Yes, but it wasn't just my day. We shared the limelight, and that can be humbling, which is a good thing, mind you. But a girl only gets married once, and it's nice to think she'd have it be just her and her husband's special time."

"You always celebrate your anniversary with Aunt Amelia.

And she's your best friend. Like Lizzie and I are," Delia said. I looked over at Martha, but her expression never changed as she turned pages in her book.

"An anniversary might be nice to share just with one's husband too," I said.

Ours was a big, jovial German family. My brother lived down the road, my two sisters and their husbands also close by. Every birthday meant a gathering. Every holiday saw cousins saunter in, sit and chat, offering opinions. It was an opinionated family, I can tell you that. I liked that kind of family camaraderie, but it made for times when I wished I'd been an only child. I sometimes think if Amelia hadn't been marrying, Frank and I might have waited, and I could have gone on to high school in Portland.

But that was wishful thinking, past its prime, just like I was, my girls talking about marrying and moving away. I was fortunate my girls wanted my seamstress skills to decorate their weddings when they could do it themselves.

"So have you picked a date for this double wedding?" I asked. Lizzie hung up Fritz's shirts and started pressing on her skirt, the last in the basket. She took a mouthful of water and sprayed it across the linen to dampen it, then began to press.

"Just the year," Delia said. "Nineteen-o-three."

"Next year?"

"Do Nell Irving and Fred know of your intentions?" Martha asked.

"Not exactly." Both girls laughed at a private joke. "But that's never stopped us before. We'll let them know when the time comes."

"Don't you always say you have to plan ahead?" Lizzie added.

"Some things you can't plan on your own." I shook my head. "So much for ironing building your characters. I think you're using this time for plotting against unsuspecting young men. They should know what you intend."

"They will, Mama. We've planted the seeds. We're just letting them grow."

EIGHT

CORNELIA GIVENS

Sacramento, California, 1903

Cornelia Givens wrote wretched little poems when she was eight years old with titles like "I Threw a Dead Flower Away Today" after tossing out a handful of weeds she'd picked for her mother. She cried when she passed the trash bin and saw again the once pretty blooms mixed in with breakfast gruel scraped from the pan and last evening's egg noodles covered with a red sauce neither she nor her sister enjoyed one bit. Her mother was creative when it came to fashion but left much to be desired in the kitchen, which is where Cornelia found her own creative bent, mixing up roux and sauces that piqued the palate and brought deep inhales from her sister. But writing was her passion.

Still single at twenty-five and living at home, some mused that she might remain so with her strong-willed ways. She didn't care. What she did care about was getting a byline—

writing feature stories with her name attached—and it looked like that was going to happen at the *Sacramento Bee*. The paper's motto upon printing its first edition in 1857 was "The object of this newspaper is not only independence, but permanence." Cornelia liked the idea of things that would last forever. She'd written a short piece about public ownership of the water company, and her editor, Charles Kenny, had penciled "good writing" before handing it back. Later there'd been an editorial about the value of public ownership of things citizens depended upon, and Cornelia felt she'd aided in that view, even though he hadn't printed her piece.

"Might I have a word with you, Miss Givens," CK said. Everyone called him that, and she followed him into his office that overlooked the Sacramento River. She liked working for the man. He was wise and fair. Her job at the paper was to answer the phone and act as a secretary, so she brought her notepad. "You've heard of Mr. Tidings's untimely death." She nodded. "I realize I'm not giving you much time to grieve, but I'd like you to take over his Common Woman column."

"Oh." She was astounded, but Cornelia prided herself on her quick thinking. "Women don't take advice well from other women," she said. "I thought I might get a feature post, attend city meetings, and be a reporter as my advancement past being a secretary."

"Women don't take advice from other women?"

"My mother said it's a proven fact. She ran a millinery,

and she told me it took time and lots of trust before a customer would accept her opinion of how a hat looked on her. They get defensive and jealous." A stack of papers fell from the edge of his desk as he stepped back, pondering, and Cornelia quickly knelt to retrieve them. She set the papers on the walnut desk and poked her long hairpin back into the knot of blond hair that graced her head.

"Women will accept your advice if you write it well. That's what the paper needs. You want to do it or not?"

"Oh." It didn't look like he was going to let her write features. Would she be stuck at the desk bringing in scones for the reporters her whole life? Maybe she should take what she could get, see if she could turn it into something more.

Before she could concur, CK said, "I just can't see how a woman could get jealous about food questions or how to get fly stains off a wall without ruining the paint. Or how to decorate for a child's birthday party. Or the best way to fumigate a room without damaging the lungs unduly. Have you seen any of the letters, Miss Givens?"

"No, I haven't." Cornelia didn't know the answers to those questions, but she doubted Mr. Tidings had either. He probably asked his wife for suggestions, and she could easily ask her mother or neighbors. Her editor was right—they claimed they always were. What mattered to the common woman might well be better answered by one, rather than a common man.

"I thought you wanted a byline?"

"I do. I just thought, well…"

"It's this"—he pointed to the pile of letters—"or you keep answering the phone."

"You think women would still ask for advice?"

"Certainly. Might as well get people used to the idea that a woman can write."

"That's very progressive of you, CK. And if a feature presented itself, one that women might find interest in, I could—"

"Let's take it one step at a time. For now I need you to write an answer to the question of what to do about a maid who I think—I mean who a reader thinks is stealing. She's a favorite maid, and the matron of the house doesn't want to lose her."

"Why, be direct. I've always believed that people are doing the best they can, that they are usually cooperative and helpful and worthy of trust until proven different. The matron should tell the maid that things are missing and solicit the maid's help in determining what might be happening to those things. Ask her advice and implement suggestions, then see if things improve. If they do, perhaps you've found your culprit, but the problem is solved, and she gets to stay. But more likely you might discover other hands that could be dipping in the till, and the matron now has someone else helping her solve that problem."

His eyes narrowed. "My cousin. I knew we shouldn't

have let him stay in the guesthouse. Have that column on this desk in the morning."

"Yes sir."

"And say it just like that, you know, that it might be someone else, a cousin, perhaps."

Cornelia nodded. He handed her a stack of letters. She had her byline.

She stayed late to write the column, then picked up her purse and fairly skipped home. Tomorrow she'd bring the reporters and her editor fresh-baked croissants to say thank you. She hoped it wouldn't mean the men would come to expect it. But then, maybe one day she'd write a piece about food and how people use it to express their feelings. There might be a byline in that.

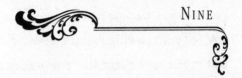

NINE

LONGING FOR LEMOINE

Hulda, 1903

I sat by the fire and read my seed catalogs, especially noting the lilacs. I must have sighed out loud because Frank looked up from the notes he was working on for the cheese cooperative and said, "What?" He served as secretary for that group, his penmanship like artist's drawings, the letters so perfectly shaped. He learned his lettering in Germany, where he was born and lived and attended school until he was eighteen and came to America.

"Oh, just these Lemoine lilacs Cooley's says it can import upon request," I said. "They have to come from France."

"Now I suppose you want what, a more purple lilac?"

"Well, that. Or one that could withstand an early frost. Or better yet, that cream lilac." I closed the catalog. I could just imagine the color of snow blooming against black stems cradled with shiny green leaves. It would take years turning a pale purple into cream, especially without a lighter lilac to breed to it. Lemoine had a white. "Can't you just see bushes covered with creamy-looking flowers?" I could. They were as real to me as the rain that fell outside the window. "Why, I bet people would actually come by to see a creamy-white double lilac with twelve petals."

Frank grunted, but he put his pen down. "Why would you want people tramping through your garden?"

I shrugged. Maybe that was prideful, but sharing beauty isn't bad. "I'd give them starts if I was fortunate enough to develop a new variety."

"Twelve petals? Pretty ambitious, I'd say." Then after a pause, he said, "What would they cost, your French lilacs?"

"Oh, way more than we have money for." I scratched Bobby's neck as he lay at my feet. "It's just a daydream, Frank. A girl likes to have her dreams." I thought of my father.

"You'll make gains with the lilacs you have."

"True. But you can only go so far with mediocre stock. Lemoine are well regarded, and with careful hybridizing, I'd love to see what I could do with them." I picked up the catalog again and found the drawing of hydrangeas Cooley's carried.

"How many would you need?" Frank said.

"Oh no. It was just a daydream, Frank. Truly."

We really couldn't afford expensive French plants just for pleasure like that. Fritz outgrew his shoes and needed new ones, and the girls planned a summer wedding, and we never knew how much milk the cows would give or what price the cheese would bring, even with the cooperative's stabilizing help. Besides, we'd just bought the house my father had built, closer to Woodland proper, away from the Bottoms. We didn't have money to spare as we planned to move into that house and have the wedding reception there. We were raising Papa's house up three feet to weather the floods. No money or time to spare for hybridizing. And I'd be transplanting from our Bottoms farm to the house on Pekin Road so that was plenty to keep me busy.

"Could you get enough starts that if successful, you could sell them in a catalog?"

"Oh. No. I don't think so. No. I...I wouldn't do it for money. Just forget it, Frank." I turned the page. I didn't know why he was being like this, suddenly promoting my interest in plant breeding. Had I spoken too often out loud about my girls leaving home and the emptiness I thought that would bring?

He got up and stood looking over my shoulder, reaching down to push back to the page I'd been perusing. "So, how many would you need?"

"Fifteen," I said before I could stop myself. "You couldn't do much with fewer than fifteen. And I'd have to order a white one, hoping it shades to cream along with ones known for hardiness and a few with a heady scent. Five of each kind would do it." I caught my breath and my senses. "No, Frank, we really can't afford—"

"Yes, we can. I bought a new bull two years back; I guess you can buy a few posies."

"But the cost—"

"We'll sell a cow," he said. "Carl's been wanting that heifer from Daisy and the bull. She promises to be a good milker. If he still wants the heifer, you can order your lilacs. All the way from France." Carl's my sister Bertha's husband and Frank's best friend.

"Oh, Frank, you are the dearest man alive!" I stood and kissed him, then over my shoulder I saw the boxes I'd gathered to pack up for our move. I stepped back. "No. I can't justify the expense and neither can you. I won't have it."

His neck colored red with my pronouncement. The wife isn't supposed to have the last word, but I spoke the truth.

"You may be right." Frank shrugged. "You usually are. All right. I won't talk to Carl."

I felt a twinge of regret with my certainty. My persuasive powers sometimes worked against me.

That night I dreamed of a creamy lilac, the color of pale butter. And when I awoke, I knew that's all there'd be, just the dream of one.

TEN

JASMINE

1903

"Y ou gots to let this child go to school, sir," Jasmine told the tailor in his Woodland shop. "She need brain work. Missing that's why she behave so bad. She coming up with things to trouble you and me and her too." Jasmine knew she ought not speak up to the man who had been her employer for years, but his head was buried in cloth, worryin' over competition of store-bought goods, and she feared he'd forgotten about his Nelia. She had to stand for the child. She couldn't stand well with her aching hips, but a body must do what it must for the happiness and well-being of children.

"There are plenty of books at the house for her to read," he said. "She'd probably be asked to leave school by the second day anyway, since she behaves so badly." He glared at the child. "Cutting up perfectly good clothes. The child's possessed."

"No sir; ain't no possession. There a smart girl inside, and she need ways to challenge her mind so it can get out without harming her. Or us."

"Then set her to work cooking. Mrs. Runyan can use the help. You too, can't you?"

"Yes sir, we needs help. But that don't free that mind to find a path that take it to good things, higher things. You not getting her schoolin', that same as neglecting a tree and letting it die for lack of watering."

"Well, what do you suggest?" The man stood, scissors in hand. Nelia hovered beside Jasmine, her shoulders pressed into the woman's fleshy side.

"Maybe see if they's a place she could board in town. Stay there and go to school 'stead of boarding with the Runyans way up the Lewis River." Mr. Lawson had moved them to a faraway logging outpost with a single boarding house, while he stayed in Woodland, sleeping in the back of his shop. He rarely saw his daughter. Jasmine supposed this was as safe a place for her as could be with Mrs. Runyan being the only white woman around, the rest being Indians and loggers who weren't all that talkative, but not hurtful either. But the time had come for change.

"She start cutting up other people's things, and we have to move anyway, then what?"

"All right, all right!" he said. "I'll see what I can do."

Jasmine and the girl began the long walk back home, smelling the sweet scent of lilacs coming from the west. "I sure like them smells," Jasmine said. "Can you smell them, child?"

Nelia shrugged. She took the woman's hand and clung to it. "Yes, child, you just hang on to me. I be your tree till your daddy find someone to help you get you some roots of your own."

He needed to do that fast. Jasmine didn't think she was long for this world with age and ailments ready to settle on her wide shoulders.

"Let's take a walk toward that lilac smell, child. See what else might grow in that garden. Maybe we take that heavy cloak of sadness you wearing and lay it flat, plan a picnic on it with lilacs blooming all around us. You like that, child?"

The girl nodded as Jasmine stroked her hair. The past held Mr. Lawson hostage, but Nelia still had a chance to heal.

ELEVEN

THE CHANGE

Hulda, 1903

I didn't relish all the adjustments necessary to turn a new landscape into the comforts of home, but my parents' yard was a canvas I could paint with flowers. I set rows of lilac starts to add to theirs as soon as I knew we were moving. A ginkgo tree already flourished there, planted years ago. I pictured an umbrella tree and magnolias to grace the property. I tried not to think about this having been my parents' house. I tried not to think about the fact that my girls were going to be married at the Presbyterian church and celebrate in this yard and how much I'd miss them afterward. I'd have my birthday in May, and I would be old. I tried not to think of turning forty.

We packed with the goal of moving in April. On Saturday, moving day, all the relatives and neighbors planned to load furniture and whatnot onto wagons and transport trunks and farm equipment the few miles from the Bottoms to the house on Pekin Road.

It rained the week of our move, cool, shivery rains that didn't mist like some springs but pelted down with the wind, pushing wet through wool. We watched the Columbia and Lewis, and when the water hit a certain spot on the banks, we started moving cows to higher ground. Most of the farmsteads flooded, and all the farmers had to wait until the water receded before beginning to plant. We had to.

When the water disappeared, life along the river settled down. The air was thick with the scent of newly turned earth and the flutter of pink and white from apple and cherry blossoms that farmers and house Fraus would plant. The high water never lasted all that long, but there'd been major floods in the late eighteen hundreds that ravaged a few weeks. Floods could make a misery of a garden, not to mention be deadly to people and cattle. Rain, which is our constant companion in the Northwest winters, fell as hard and steady as usual on moving day. All our goods were loaded, so we drove them to the new house where we sloshed through foot-deep water carrying things in. Lizzie's piano had to wait.

I thought all the rain on moving day was a bad omen, but Martha, our studious one, said the ancient Greeks wished for foul weather on an important day so that the gods wouldn't notice mortals being hopeful and happy. "It's why people do silly things to couples on wedding days," she advised me.

"Oh, is it?"

"Yes, because the gods don't want mortals to be happy on their own; they might come to believe they don't need the intervention of Zeus or Aphrodite. They'll get too proud and independent, suffer from hubris." She looked solemn.

"Hubris."

"It means prideful, Mama."

"Lucky for us, then, that we don't believe in those kinds of gods," I told her. I held the umbrella over her head as she stepped inside our new home carrying an armful of her many books to the second floor.

Water pooled on the flat areas around the house, but we'd raised it the right amount. There'd be muck and mud in the yard and a darker canvas than I'd imagined.

The sounds that came from outside that first night—the wind in the apple trees, rain pattering on the roof—and the sounds of Bobby, allowed inside, rolling on the carpet instead of a wood floor, were all new. I'd need to integrate them with sounds from memory, of when we'd helped Papa build the house or been there for Mama when he'd died. Frank turned over in our double bed and laid his arm across my belly. "Does it feel like home yet?" he asked.

I was glad the room was dark and no full moon shone through the glass transom above the door.

"Not yet," I told him. "But it was the right thing to do, I know that. I think the soil is better here, and we're higher."

"Can you find peace in this place?"

I patted his hand. "I think I'll go back and take a look at the old garden tomorrow. Say good-bye to what I've left there before I really dig in to this soil."

"All the important things you brought with you."

"I know, I know. And the Lord knows my lot. He makes my boundaries fall on pleasant places." I paraphrased the psalm. "But leaving is…difficult. I put roots into that soil, Frank, deep roots. And it's like I've left a limb behind, but I can still feel it with me."

"Don't know anything except you that might make me feel that way."

"I appreciate that, Frank."

He put his arms around my shoulders, tugged me to him. I hoped he wouldn't feel the wetness on my face. "You'll be my wife and mother our children here in this big new house. Make it your own place doing what a woman needs to do."

"Yes. That's what I'll do."

That's when the melancholy began.

Twelve

Like Water

Hulda, 1903

Melancholy seeped in like water filling footprints on a soggy lawn. It was always there beneath the surface that year but didn't assert itself until pressure was applied.

The children slept in two rooms upstairs, Fritz having his own, the younger girls sharing a bed, with Lizzie sleeping on a small cot in the same room. Frank and I occupied the large south bedroom. From my bed, I could look out onto the yard, a yard that needed a lot of work. The kitchen was bigger, and the dining and living room settled around the six of us just fine, giving us room to play Parcheesi at the round table that had been my mother's. The china hutch held favorite things like my grandmother's silver tea service and a valentine from each of her grandchildren and the Haviland china with the green cloverleaf pattern daintily painted around the edges. I was prepared to feel comforted by the memories that surrounded me in our new home.

"Expect a little nostalgia," my sister Bertha told me as she dusted the hutch after I mentioned feeling sad.

Maybe the sadness began with thinking of my parents too much. They were everywhere in that house, memories like cobwebs catching me unsuspecting. The flood didn't help my mood either. It wasn't as bad as it could have been, with just a foot of water blanketing the fields, pushing up against the bottom steps of the house. We dug and buried bulbs and moved sludge and debris from around the peonies I'd planted. I saw progress and even decided to shape a garden plot at the front of the house and make it like a flatiron.

"That way when I'm working in that plot, I'll imagine I'm really getting my ironing done," I told Amelia who laughed with me as I thought she would. "This planting will be as close to a flatiron as I ever hope to come. Poor Martha," I added. She'd be left to iron, with her sisters married off soon.

But the usual satisfaction I experienced from my hands on a hoe was missing.

The actual physical pains began right around my birthday. We Thiels usually gathered on a birthday for feasting and storytelling, and this year everyone planned to come to our yard. I had the bright idea to try out new recipes that we might use for the weddings. I'd begun baking early in the week, trying to disregard the discomfort that settled beneath my stomach. I thought I did a good job of it and knew that soon the kitchen cupboard would be stuffed with cakes and cookies, jams and jellies, fresh bread and cheeses too.

"Mama, you're holding your side funny," Martha said. She rolled pastry dough and spots of grayish flour stuck to the frizz at her temples. Martha always looked like she should be Bavarian royalty with her huge piercing eyes, olive skin, and a regal bearing that settled on her shoulders whether she was reading a book or rolling out pastry. "Are you all right?" she'd stopped her work and just stared. "You look so pale."

"Oh, just a female complaint, I suspect. Nothing to worry over."

By the end of the week, I couldn't get out of bed because my side and stomach hurt so. Frank called Dr. Alice Chapman, the only doctor we had. I didn't like doctors and wasn't sure about a female one. Frank insisted someone see me. The short woman arrived with her black leather case. It helped to know her husband doctored people too, in Kelso, down the road, so she might have gotten medical information from him. She pressed and prodded at my abdomen as I lay on my bed where I could look out over the flatiron planting. Frank stood beside me, holding my hand.

"What do you think, Doc?" he asked.

"Not sure what to think," Dr. Alice told him. She asked us to use her first name. She was young, but she carried herself like one with years of experience. She wasn't much older than Lizzie, I guess. "Has your flow stopped?" she asked directly.

Frank's ears turned red as a rose, but he didn't make his escape as I thought he might and should have.

I frowned. "Perhaps so." Though until she mentioned it, the thought had not occurred to me. I wasn't that old.

Dr. Alice thought surgery might take care of the problem, but I would have nothing to do with that. No cutting. It was bad enough I was here in my own bed with a visiting doctor seeing the cobwebs in the corners.

She gave me potions, but as the summer wore on and I didn't get better, the girls decided to postpone their weddings. I felt terrible about that, and it added to my malaise. I couldn't seem to shake the feeling that this was my ending, that forty was as old as I would get.

"Don't think like that," Frank told me as he sat beside me on the bed. The log cabin quilt I'd pieced lay folded across my feet. Outside the window I could see the end of the daisies from my mother's old bed, but I couldn't view the lilac nursery from my window, all the new starts I'd transplanted lined in rows. I didn't even have the strength to rise and look after the bushes I'd started. I think that worried Frank more than anything, that I had no energy even for flowers.

"Maybe my time has come." I wiped at tears. "The children are almost grown. They'll be leaving this nest before long. Perhaps this is all the Lord has allotted for me to do."

"You don't have the creamy-white lilac yet." Frank brushed damp hair from my forehead. "And I thought you wanted one with a bunch of petals, not just a measly four."

I smiled. "You remembered that boast."

"I never thought of it as a boast. I submit, when you say

you'll do something, you always accomplish it. It is just a matter of fact—and time."

"I haven't accomplished anything without help, and now I never will." I was so weary of looking at the flowers on the wallpaper, so disheartened by the aching and needing Martha's or Lizzie's or Delia's assistance for everyday things like using the chamber pot. I was so weak I couldn't even make the privy.

I looked back over my life, and what had I accomplished? I'd shaped an apple toward a little more crisp. I'd produced a brighter yellow daffodil that only I could really see the difference in. I'd seen a happy smile on a child's face when they inhaled a rose. But what were these moments in the scheme of things, when people devoted their lives to curing disease, to living in foreign lands looking after the less privileged. "What have I really done with my life, Frank? And now, it's likely over."

I saw the worry in Frank's face, the way his eyes pinched. I guess he'd never seen me discouraged. I didn't know what discouragement would look like either, but now I was it, discouragement in the flesh, facing the reality of a life lived with little meaning except for giving the world four fine people who might go on to do great things even if their mother hadn't.

Frank said he didn't call Amelia, but someone must have because she arrived from Vancouver, the whirlwind older sister ready to set things straight and get me out of bed. It was a few days after I'd spoken with Frank and admitted the paucity of my life, the failure to contribute to the betterment of mankind. I'd done nothing "to do justly, and to love mercy, and to walk humbly with my God," as Scripture challenged us to do. If anything, I'd been prideful thinking my flowers contributed to a hurting world in a healing way.

"What's gotten into you?" Amelia punched at my feather pillows, sniffed. I knew they needed cleaning. "You've sprawled in that bed long enough."

"I can't get up. I'm so weak. And nothing seems worth doing. Seasons come and go whether I do anything or not."

"Well, of course they do. But that doesn't mean you don't do it too."

"I've given what I had to give. Martha and Fritz practically take care of themselves, and they know what Frank needs, and they tend to him. The girls will marry. What is there left for me to do, really? And now I can't even have any more children—"

"Did you want more?" Amelia asked.

I shrugged. Frank and I hadn't wanted any more than four, but now, knowing that I couldn't have any more children just added depth to my confused weariness.

"No sense crying over spilled milk," Amelia said.

"I'm not crying," I said, although tears spilled from my eyes and I wiped them with the handkerchief Frank replaced each morning.

Amelia plopped on the side of the bed. "What you need is a new project. Something to consume you again, the way your daffodils always did. And the roses. Don't you want to check on your apple hybridizing, try something new? Your lilacs?"

"What does it matter?"

"Dr. Alice says it's your mind keeping you down now, not your body."

"That's why I don't like doctors. They talk too much."

"It's what she told Frank, and it's what he told me. We're worried about you, Hulda. I try to imagine what Papa would say to get you up. Or Mama."

I did too, but they were silent.

She patted my hand, stood for a moment, then left. She'd thrown out her lifeline, and I'd failed to grasp it.

Nearly a month passed, and I still hadn't died. I had strange dreams, though, and more than once I looked out my window and could have sworn I saw a small child, a girl, slipping in between the magnolia and the cypress, crouching beneath a lilac bush. But I was likely daydreaming myself into a garden I didn't have the energy to walk to. I had an appetite, which grieved me sorely since any self-respecting person who had admitted she'd given all she could surely didn't need to respond to the smell of fried potatoes or the aroma of apple pie rolled out at Delia's hands.

I heard Amelia's voice in the hall, then the sound of her

footsteps. I noticed that everyone had a distinct sort of walk, and I could name them now, even before Fritz stuck his head in the room, or Amelia as she did now.

"Still think you have nothing to offer?" My sister offered a cheery smile.

"Don't." I just wanted to be left alone.

She stepped into the room. "I found this book, written about that famous plant man you so like."

"Luther Burbank?"

"Yes. That's his name." She handed me the book. Inside she'd stuffed a sheaf of papers titled "Proceedings: International Conference on Plant Breeding and Hybridization, 1902," published by the Horticultural Society of New York.

"Where did you get this?"

"I wrote to them. Or rather Frank told me I ought to. We thought...that is, we decided it might be of interest to you. There's a paper there, presented by Luther Burbank himself."

"About his poppy work?" I sat up in bed. "His daisy efforts?" I'd read of his crossbreeding a *Chrysanthemum leucanthemum* that grows wild in the West with *Bellis perennis*, a small English daisy with larger flowers and shorter stems. He'd written of his work, rejecting, sowing, rejecting, and finally crossing a newer generation daisy with a German daisy, the *Chrysanthemum lacustre*, that produced a huge flower, but still not a blaring white like the kind he said he wanted. It made me think of my creamy lilac that would never be. Some of the articles of his efforts were printed in the *Los Angeles Times,* and later I would read a few others in *Popular Science Monthly* magazines. But his real interest was in developing foods that would ship more easily, bloom earlier so we'd have longer seasons. He hadn't been interested in flowers much, except how they could teach him what to do with vegetables.

"I have no idea what he wrote about," Amelia said. "I just know he presented a paper of some kind. You read about it."

I picked up the papers she handed me and sighed as I paged through until I saw Burbank's name. Even that didn't inspire me.

"I'll read it later." I put the pages on the bedside table. "I'm just so tired."

But later that evening, the book sitting there called to me. I read about Burbank's efforts and that he had at last found what he looked for. He'd named the daisy for the California mountain, Shasta. "He's going to sell the seeds himself." I sat up straighter, called out. "Frank?"

"What? Do you need something? I'm just about to put the dog out in the shed."

"When you come back in, come right up." I kept reading, and when Frank arrived, I told him, "He says it's the perfect flower as it's simple, modern, inexpensive, easy to grow, and yet has international ancestry. He used Japanese daisies and

English ones and good old American ones that are considered weeds by many. They just grow wild in the meadows. But see here." I pointed to a drawing included in the Horticultural Society paper. "Look at the size of the bloom. It's huge, bigger than your palm. And he'll sell the packets for only ten cents each."

"We could order them in and have them in the spring. For the girls' weddings."

"Of course. They're getting married next..." I realized there was no date set. They were waiting for me to be better. "Let's say...June."

I realized what I'd said and leaned back on the pillow. Weariness returned, but Dr. Alice had been right. What kept me low wasn't my body, but my mind. I knew my girls were entitled to begin their lives with their husbands, to have what Frank and I had. Luther Burbank's successes with flowers— not just for food production—inspired me. Even he could see that ornamentals carried as much dignity and usefulness as tomatoes, kale, or corn.

"Good to see you thinking the girls can send the invitations." Frank undressed for the night. The window was open, and I could hear sandhill cranes making cooing noises in the field between the house and the Lewis River. Soft and settling-in noises.

"It's time." I pushed myself up and with his help arranged the pillows so I could continue reading the paper and saw that Mr. Burbank had written a new book about his efforts and the role of the environment in addition to the natural characteristics of a plant. "Can we spare a dollar for Burbank's book?" Frank nodded, happy I think that something interested me at last. "Mendel doesn't hold that the environment has much influence at all," I said, "but Burbank disagrees. He thinks everything can be changed." I looked up at Frank. He was smiling. Lizzie and Delia had come in, Martha behind them.

"Your voice; it's stronger. Are you all right?" Martha asked.

"Not yet, but I will be. Listen." I patted the bed that the girls might sit. "Burbank thinks how we behave toward plants makes a difference in their growth, their future, their very features. He thinks plants can be convinced to change, that it's part of their God-given nature. Not something Darwin believed in at all."

Frank's eyes shone with tears as he said, "That doesn't sound very scientific of him."

"Science isn't about only university training or conducting research in sterile laboratories or even keeping notes in certain ways so others can replicate your work. That's not what Mr. Burbank is about, Frank. He's about...well, here, let me summarize." I took a deep breath and had enough air. "He wants better fruits and flowers, not just crisper vegetables—and he says that the work of creating better plants will help people think of nobler efforts in life, bring richer foods to people around the globe, instead of bullets or bayonets. All things are connected. His work touches the soul as well as soil." My children looked dazed by such scientific words spouting from my mouth after so long a time of tears. "Don't you see? He knows flowers are important too. He does the Lord's work."

"So do you, Mama." Lizzie patted my hand. "So do you."

I sighed and sunk back onto the pillow. "And it's time I got around to do more of it. Just as soon as you girls get married off! I hope June sounds good to you both?"

Lizzie and Delia looked at each other. "That's perfect," they said in unison. "Will you be strong enough?" Delia asked.

"I will be."

That became the promise I made to myself.

THIRTEEN

FOREIGN INFLUENCE

Hulda, 1903

Burbank's newest work in California made me want to get better—that and the weddings. Then Frank did something I wished my father had been alive to see.

"I sold a couple of cows," Frank told me in November. Rain poured down the gutters, and the patter on the roof at times drowned out our words. I washed up the evening dishes, the first time in a long time I felt strong enough to stand that long. In the evenings I kept my feet up, quilting, reading, looking at seed catalogs. I couldn't do much real creating with the same varieties I always had. Crossbreeding demanded new life.

"To cover the wedding expenses next year? Two cows? Well, we can give each of the couples a nice gift to help them get started."

"I submit, that's not what I had in mind."

I looked at him. "What, then?"

"You're most alive when you're in that garden of yours. That's where and how I want to see you. So let's just say I want to buy them for self-preservation: mine."

"Buy what? I thought you were selling cows?"

"Those lemon lilacs."

"Lemoine?" I could barely catch my breath.

"Whatever they're called."

"But, Frank." I sat down at the table, my hands still wet with dishwater. "They're so expensive and so... I mean breeding them won't result in better food for someone. They're... ornamentals."

"I watch how flowers make you feel. I don't understand it, but I don't want to get in the way of it either. So I've sold two cows, and we'll invest in...beauty."

"I don't know what to say." My father had said Frank couldn't support my efforts, but he was wrong. Maybe Frank wasn't encouraging my work for the reasons my father would have, to pursue a dream, to meet a challenge; but he was willing to risk with me.

"Just tell me how to find that catalog with the lemons in it. I looked high and low for it. Thought I'd surprise you and order them myself."

"I'm so glad you didn't." I held his face in my soapy hands and kissed him. "Now I have the pleasure of choosing them and anticipating their arrival. Oh, Frank." I hugged him, kissed him hard. "You are a good, good man."

"So you say," he said, then kissed me back.

"How did you even know about it?" I asked my oldest sister, Bertha. She and Carl had come in to town to pick up supplies, and we shared a cup of tea. Later we went out to the flowers and talked as we weeded.

"Frank spoke to Carl about a heifer. So much expense," Bertha said. "Think what that money could do for the Johnson family or that Smith child or the tailor's girl who looks like a waif. I can't believe Frank would let you spend that kind of money. On flowers, for heaven's sake."

"You should be happy my husband wants to indulge me so your husband can be indulged. He bought the cows."

"I don't know what Carl was thinking. That money has a better place to go. The whole point of having a herd is that you grow it from your own animals." Bertha plucked a dried leaf from my hair. "The same is true for flowers, or should be."

"Yes, but occasionally you have to introduce new blood. That's all I want to do with these lilacs. I still have others I started from the bushes Mama brought with her. I'll be using them to pollinate with too."

"But all the way from France! What would Mama think? That you're getting uppity."

Uppity? *Mein Gott im Himmel.* This is what my sister thought of me?

I weeded a bit more, then said, "Beauty matters, Bertha;

it does. God gave us flowers for a reason. I think so we'd pay attention to the details of creation and remember to trust Him in all things big or little, no matter what the challenge. Flowers remind us to put away fear, to stop our rushing and running and worrying about this and that, and for a moment have a piece of paradise right here on earth. God offers healing through flowers and brings us closer to Him."

"Oh, Huldie, really? You think that? It doesn't sound… Christian at all."

"When those Johnson young people died in the pond last summer, don't you think the bouquet of flowers we brought gave some small comfort to their parents? And when I planted tulip bulbs on those young people's graves after the parents asked, don't you think imagining those blooms covering their loved ones each spring gives them hope?"

"Maybe. But such expense on frivolous—"

"Living things offer solace, Bertha. I can't remove the poverty of the Smith children, though I try, I do. Frank and I support the deacon's fund. But when I brought Mrs. Smith fresh-picked vegetables last summer and included a bouquet of my lilacs, it was the flowers she went to first. She inhaled their scent, and for a moment as she buried her face in them, I think she forgot about the misery of her drinking husband and the rags on her children. She needed that moment to gain strength from those petals to face her life as it is. A moment of joy is no small thing to give another."

I couldn't always talk Bertha down, but I seemed to this time. "It's no different than how you feel about music," I continued. "A song sung that fills a heart with gratitude or splendor or wonder is as good as food at times. Flowers do that too, and I think it's worthy work to bring a more unusual flower for others to discover, to somehow weave that special scent into the memories of their living. Why it seems to me when I smell sauerkraut, my mind immediately goes to Mama."

Bertha laughed. "Mine too."

"And when I smell a daffodil, I think of Frank and a day he watched flowers consume me. And lilacs remind me of a time he offered to make my metal marking tags. It was his way to be a part of what I love so much. He will always be there with me when I smell a lilac, no matter what might happen to him. And if I die first, then he'll have the flowers to remind him of what we did together. Or maybe it's the smell of cows that will remind him of our lives together. I don't know." Bertha wiggled her nose and smiled. "I just know that I feel closest to heaven when I'm out here in this garden, and if, as a result, someone finds comfort in what they see or take away, then to me, that's not an indulgence, it's a…calling. A passion, Papa called it."

I felt my face grow warm.

"Papa did?"

I nodded and stood. Bertha and I are the same height, and she nudged me with her shoulder then. "It's all right. I shouldn't have said what I did about the Johnsons and that Lawson girl. I do feel the same about music," she said. "It's just that Carl would never pamper me the way Frank does you, and I guess I'm a little, well, jealous."

"Carl loves you to death." I put my arm around her waist. "There isn't anything he wouldn't do for you."

She shrugged. "Maybe I'm afraid to ask, in case he wouldn't."

Frank and I settled for seven Lemoine. Seven was really all we could afford of the *Syringa vulgaris* variety. We placed the order, then waited. It's what a gardener does.

They arrived on board the steamship *Toledo,* a new competition to the *Mascot* that had ruled the Lewis River for years. The cranes warbled in the fields and sunbreaks pierced the clouds that Friday, March 4, 1904. I will never forget it.

I paced, barely able to keep my hands at my sides as Frank picked up the bundle wrapped in burlap and carried it to the wagon. The horse stomped his foot and twisted at the smell, I suspect, earthy and moist and all the way from France. Once home, we slowly removed the burlap as though laying open a treasure recently found. There lay seven spindly lilac stems with a few leaves flattened like winter's leaves.

"Don't look like much." Frank frowned.

"No, they don't. But neither did our babies when they

arrived all bare and pink," I said. "Let's get these heeled into the ground." And we did, the roots taking hold in this new land that had been my parents'.

When the buds opened a few weeks later, I realized that two of the Lemoine wouldn't work; the leaves and buds were too small. "Those will have to go," I told Frank.

"They will?" He looked grief stricken.

"I need to start with the strongest and best. We have to cut our losses." He nodded, swallowed hard.

That left five to pin my hopes on.

I made my way with magnifying glass, crochet hook, and turkey feather, moving the first pollen from the Périer to one of my own lilacs that I'd noted was the closest to cream. Such a tiny hope, that pollen. I wondered if Luther Burbank felt such anticipation wrapped inside anxiety and caution as he did his work. "Please don't let me make mistakes," I prayed. "Please, let me do this right." Then to the plant, I said, "Come on, tiny pollen. Give Hulda Klager the best you've got."

I knew that it would take years before we knew if what we had invested would bring anything more than hard work and hope.

One pollination down, turkey feather and crochet hook; hat back, holding my breath. France to Washington State. Dreaming.

Hundreds more to go.

FOURTEEN

RUTH REED

Woodland, 1904

Eleven-year-old Ruth Reed watched her father walk a fine line, and he expected Ruth to walk there too. By day her father worked at the cheese plant. On Wednesday evenings Barney Reed led Bible classes at Woodland homes. A Seventh-Day Adventist, their Sabbath services never turned away people from other persuasions who came to the meetings he officiated with his bushy mustache and tiny glasses he adjusted often on his nose.

Ruth liked it best when they met at the Fred Lewis homestead on Whelan Road and combined their study efforts with Baptists, Methodists, and others. She listened to the banter and discussion, and afterward her father often told her mother that he'd "get converts yet out of those confused Presbyterians."

It was Mrs. Klager that Ruth fancied the most. The

woman stood tall, and straight up and down. She always noticed Ruth, asking important things like how the tulip bulbs she'd given her were doing rather than commenting on "what a big girl she was becoming" like some of the other mothers did. During the discussions, Mrs. Klager asked probing questions of belief, especially about science and how faith informed it, or vice versa. Ruth didn't always understand the questions, but she saw how they made her father's face get red, and he talked faster than normal. Ruth heard that Mrs. Klager had been ill a long time, but she didn't sound weak at their classes.

Ruth got another education after classes were over and he had a second piece of pie after they were home. Her father finished Mrs. Klager's apple pie. Ruth didn't tell him that Mrs. Klager had made those apples herself, or so she'd heard. Crumbs dribbling on his chin, her father took issue with most everything Mrs. Klager said. "She doesn't have the slightest worry about messing with Eden," he told her mother one February evening. "She accepts as gospel the writings of people like Darwin and now this Burbank fellow. She says she gives all that glory to God, but then she messes with plants trying to make a better daffodil or rose." He chewed the apple pie with his front teeth, like a rabbit might. Her father's back teeth hurt him when he chewed.

Ruth didn't want to see her father more upset. She and her mother had something to tell him, and she didn't want him saying no.

"The Baptists and Latter-day Saints and others claiming the Christian faith seemed to have no concern about what Mrs. Klager was saying," Ruth's mother said.

"Yes." He jabbed the air with his fork. "They apparently like the idea of larger flowers, or in the case of that Burbank, bigger plums and even spineless cacti."

"Isn't that for cattle?" her mother posed. "Perhaps they see it as a way of subduing the animals and earth as God intended man to do."

Her father frowned, and Ruth thought right then and there she might as well forget lessons. But he surprised her. "I suppose spineless cacti could mean the difference in places like Australia where cattle needed feed and there wasn't enough water to grow it. And certainly not having to scrape off those barbs means an easier life for those farmers. But still," he cautioned her mother, pausing to chew with his front teeth, "it interferes with Eden. Cacti aren't even mentioned in the Bible. The Burbanks and the Klagers of the world take God's creation and turn it into naked cacti, and somehow expect the world to accept it as better than what God Himself placed on this earth."

"Papa?" Ruth cleared her throat, wanting to stop him before his rant raged on for hours. "Mama and I have something to tell you."

"What? What is it, Ruth?" He towered over her like an unhappy teacher.

"I have a job. Later this spring."

"You do? Well, that's resourceful of you."

"I'll be able to pay for my own piano lessons."

"Piano lessons, eh? You have a talent for that?" He didn't wait for an answer. "There's no better lesson than learning to give your best to your employer. So what will you be doing?"

"Helping Mrs. Klager," Ruth said.

"Mrs. Klager?" He glared at his wife.

Her mother said, "Two of the Klager girls are getting married, and she needs additional workers. Mrs. Klager was awful poorly last summer and nearly died."

"God punishes when we're wayward," he said.

"But not all trouble is punishment, you said that yourself," her mother said. "When you lost your job in Ontario and we had to come to America, you said it was God's plan."

He squinted at Ruth. She stepped back, swallowed, let her mind drift.

Ruth saw Mrs. Klager's garden as shapes of color just as she noticed the shapes of most of her world.

She'd been attracted to the Klager yard the very first time she rode with her family past the picket fence. "Look there," she'd pointed.

"It's not polite to point," her mother said.

"But see? That garden in front of the house is shaped like a flatiron."

Her father had slowed, and the vibrant colors clustered inside that household shape made her wonder what the names of all those blooms might be. She saw a woman bent to the tall grasses and three other girls with hats and gloves working silently together, backs up, then down; kneeling, then standing; hoes digging, then offering a leaning post. A wind chime of laughter floated toward Ruth and her parents as the horse plodded by. Ruth twisted to watch the women as their buggy rolled past. Imagine, people working together without hearing, "Keep your head up; don't look down so much. Pick up your feet; you walk like an elephant. Take your fingers out of your mouth. Straighten up." These were daily admonitions from her father, and her mother repeated them when he wasn't present, adding a few of her own. Her mother spoke more softly, but the piercing felt as painful. She knew they wanted the best for her; she trusted that. She thought this might be how they expressed their love for her, wanting to shape her into the perfect girl. But she wasn't, would never be, the shape they wanted.

"Get your father a cup of coffee." Her mother's words brought Ruth back. To Ruth's father, her mother said, "Perhaps Mrs. Klager having a need our daughter can meet is part of God's plan as well. And it pays for the lessons."

"She's not a good influence, eh?"

"I can think for myself, Papa. It's being charitable, helping another. You say we should. That way I can stay and go to school here in town. I won't have to—"

"No, no, now that goes too far. You'll continue to go to

school as we plan for you. What would people say if you worked and lived in town instead of on Martin's Bluff?"

"But I can't work the Sabbath," Ruth said.

"She needs more experiences." Her mother poured cream into her husband's cup. "And staying with the Klagers is a way to do that."

"What'll you be doing? How does all this happen without my knowledge?"

"Watering plants, Papa. Carrying buckets. It's good work. I'm strong."

Her father sipped his coffee. "We'll see. Let's go home now." He put the pie plate in the sink. "A snake to worry about, eh? Right in my own backyard."

Ruth didn't know if he referred to her or to Mrs. Klager.

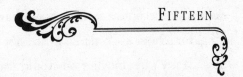

FIFTEEN

BOTH VEXING AND PRIVILEGE

Hulda, 1904

The future sons-in-law stepped forward to help put finishing touches on the yard where they'd be married. Fred Wilke, who would wed Lizzie, farmed for the Goerigs but he had a passion for travel, something Lizzie loved too. She took pleasure in visiting faraway places, and Fred promised he'd take care of that wish.

Nell Irving Guild was Delia's choice. A farmer like Frank, he had the kindest eyes, and he treated Delia as though she were fine china. She did at times look fragile with her tiny waist, which she didn't get from me with my pickle shape.

Both girls planned to wear white, another difference from Amelia and I at our weddings where black or lavender was the acceptable color. Neither girl would wear jewelry, and both dresses had sections of lace at the throat that let the skin show peekaboo through. They were going to be beautiful, and the men in their lives knew it.

Then there was Martha. At eighteen, that girl had already decided to become a teacher. She'd leave soon after the weddings for school in Portland. I tried not to think of the emptiness all my girls moving on would leave behind. Instead, I thought of Martha's dreams too and had no doubt she'd be a fine teacher if she could keep herself from "di-gress-ions" as she's prone to stretch out that word.

Ruth Reed helped us too, a young girl taking piano lessons from Lizzie at the Presbyterian church instead of here— some condition her father placed on her. I was just pleased she had time with Lizzie at the church and was allowed to help me out after school. She was so thankful her father allowed her to attend school in town, and so was I. She was a big-boned girl, the buckets were heavy, and my, we had so many plantings to tend.

On a May morning, serenaded by goldfinches and robins, we pulled weeds and planted alyssum to line the wood-chipped paths where guests would wander with their punch and the men their ale (carried to the barn) following the Presbyterian service. Roses bloomed in June. I hoped for sweet-smelling daphnes bobbing their blue heads.

"Let's be sure we pull the weeds beside the barn," I told Fritz.

"Ah, Ma, no one's going to even look at the barn."

"You don't know these neighbors." I shook my finger at him. "They have good eyes. And that's where you men always end up with your brew." It disgusted me the men drinking, but so long as they didn't invade my house with liquor, I turned a blind eye to it. After all, my father had been a brewmaster, so I couldn't very well join the teetotaler society. They smoked there too, but at least I collected the butts and used them for my nicotine tea to poison insects.

"Let the daisies stand out against that brown barn as the backdrop instead of gangly thistle," I told Fritz. "Ruthie will be here before long to help water. I'll be glad when her parents decide to let her stay here. Poor child. It makes quite a trek for her to walk the distance."

"She's a good kid," Fritz said, and he sounded like an old man, which made me chuckle since Ruthie's but four years younger than his fifteen years.

Lizzie and Delia were busy on their knees, pulling weeds in the peonies' plots. I hoped the blooms would hold from their usual May into later June for the wedding. Laughter rose as the girls chattered, and I was both delighted that they were such good friends and at the same time saddened knowing after next month they'd be gone from this place.

"Don't look so sad," Martha said, coming up beside me.

"I'm not. Just wistful watching all my charges grow."

"The ones with green stems, or the two with purple skirts and aprons?" she teased.

"All. But this morning, the skirted kind." With our hoes we walked the wood-chipped paths toward the apple orchard.

I heard the distant whistle of the *Mascot* as it steamed down the Lewis. "It'll be new and different for you with them gone, won't it, Martha?"

"Yes," she said after a pause. "I'll miss them. But in some ways, they've been gone for a long time already, their lives wrapped up in Nell Irving and Fred. All that courting, sitting in the lamplight in the evening on the porch, then telling each other what was said all over again afterward. Don't say I said this, Mama, but sometimes I think they're daft they get to giggling so."

"It's love, honey. That's what makes us laugh at the slightest hint of joy. They'll settle down once they're married and likely be more open to their younger sister's and brother's lives, not so taken with their own. Especially now, with the wedding. It'll happen for you too, one day, Martha."

"I'm not so sure." Her brown eyes looked deeply into my own earth-toned eyes. "You and Daddy aren't much different now than I imagine you were when you first married. You laugh and tease each other, and he puts his arm around you for a squeeze, even when your hands are full of flour dough."

I laughed. "That's when he's most likely to give me squeezes." I leaned into her as though to share a secret. "Your father is a joker, and it's my surprised squeal he likes the most. Did I tell you about the time he exchanged one farmer's entire herd of cows with another farmer's? On Halloween? Can you imagine those two farmers' surprise at their morning milking?"

She laughed. "It's what I'd want if I ever did find a man to love. I like a sense of humor, and I like surprises."

"I didn't realize that. I'll keep that in mind." I thought then I should plan a surprise for her on the girls' wedding day.

I walked the orchard, checked on new grafts I'd made, then on to the lilac nursery. We had five acres here, and I imagined one day every inch might be covered but for the paths weaving through the ornamentals and trees. Cross-breeding was tedious. I might get only one plant out of four hundred that was reusable for breeding. The rest would be thrown out. Frank said he didn't mind the work or the toss-outs so long as he had three meals a day and my hand in his for a time on the porch at dusk. "One day I'd like to get an automobile," he told me, "but other than that, watching you work toward that cream lilac or the one with many petals is enough wealth for me."

"One day." I felt a little guilty spending so much money on the Lemoine. An auto would have made his life easier.

I looked over the petals on an amethyst-colored lilac to see if there might be even one bloom with more than four petals.

"Mother!" It was Lizzie. "Can you please forget those lilacs? You haven't heard a word Delia and I have said to you, have you?"

I might have blushed. "No, now, well, I was tending my plants for a minute."

"It's been two hours, Mama. There are other things that need tending."

"I know, I know. Come along, then, let's see what might be ready for your bouquets and the table dressings too."

The girls led me back toward the tulips where Martha knelt, then stood, the three girls "filling me in" as they called it, the way I filled in an open garden space with new plants. "Just stay here now, Mama," Lizzie said. "Don't go off with your hoe. What about lavender for our bouquets?" I nodded. Whatever they wanted would be fine. I owed them that.

I had humbling to do about being as attentive to my children as I was to my flowers. Mr. Burbank wrote a book professing that raising plants was like raising children. Both were vexing and a privilege. He didn't have family as far as I could tell, besides a mother who he brought out west to visit now and then—but otherwise, he was alone with his workers and his plants. That was enough for him. I wondered if one day it would have to be enough for me if I outlived my Frank.

Sixteen

Nightmares and Daydreams

Hulda, 1904

In early June, just two weeks before the wedding, I startled awake. "Frank. Your horse must be out."

"Huh?" He woke groggy from my elbow poke. I heard a horse whinny, and Frank said, "That's ours, in the barn."

"Cows, then," I said. "Can't you hear them?"

I rose and grabbed my robe, tossing my long braid outward, feeling the pressure of it along my back. "They're running around the house," I said. Bobby—we named all our dogs Bobby—our new dog, had started to bark from the potting shed, and I shushed him through the open window. No need to rile those bovines any more than they were.

"Not our cows," Frank said as he pulled on his pants and slipped the suspenders over his bare shoulders. "They're on the Bottoms where they belong." He peered into the dawn. "Not our horses either."

"Horses?" Our neighbors had horses. My brother, Emil, living next-door, he had horses. I headed down the stairs, grabbing a broom from the kitchen before scampering out the door. Frank followed with a lantern, and I guessed he had bare feet just as I did, the wet grass matting at my toes and swishing against my nightdress. I couldn't see them but could hear the thundering hooves. Or it might have been my heart wondering when they'd come out of the darkness toward me, rush right over me. Horses could do that in their confusion.

Where are they? The lilac nursery!

"Frank, try to push them away from the lilacs!"

"I don't see them," he shouted back.

How many were there? Three? Five? A dozen? The earth shook.

Where had they come from? "Hayah!" I shouted when Frank's lantern cast a quick light across what looked to be a sorrel's back. They headed to the nursery! "Push them out, Frank! They'll destroy the Lemoine!"

The sound and the smell of them swished by as they galloped toward my brother's home, but the herd kept going, so I don't think they were Emil's. I hoped they weren't, because I'd be giving him choice words if he'd failed to keep his barn door closed.

"Maybe they bypassed it." Frank's breath came in short gasps. He held his lantern high as he approached. I knew what he was talking about.

I hopped through the tall grass onto the path, tears already forming. All that work...

"No. Look."

Frank set the lantern down beside the Lemoine where I knelt.

"Look what they've done. Just look."

"What?" Frank said. "I can't see well enough."

But I could. The horses had destroyed two more Lemoine lilacs, the roots ground into nothingness by their massive hooves. "They're gone. Two more French lilacs dead, and dozens of starts trampled too."

"We'll see if we can salvage them, Huldie. Don't cry now. Don't fret. Things will look better in the morning."

I held my head in my hands. "Frank. Three. That's all that's left." I lifted the oblong metal labels that marked the survivors: Mme Casimir Périer (Lemoine, 1884), a beautiful double white; President Grévy (Lemoine, 1886), a double blue; and a splendid purple labeled Andenken an Ludwig Späth (Späth, 1883) made up the triumvirate. All that was left.

"I'm not sure I can do anything with three." I'd wondered if I could do anything with fifteen, let alone seven, then five. But three?

"Now, now, I submit that these are three more than you had two years ago at this time," Frank said. "All is not lost. You've already cross-pollinated a few from the others, the wrecked ones."

"Not enough to even notice." I shook my head. "All I can introduce as new now are these three. I so wanted to see a creamy white with many blossoms in my lifetime, Frank. And now…seven years for a bloom after I've crossbred…"

"You'll keep busy." Frank patted my shoulder. "Waiting isn't done alone. There'll be work to do. The time will fly, you'll see. Right now, there's the wedding. Think about that." All I cared about was my lilacs and how I hadn't saved them.

Frank was right, of course. That Sunday I thanked the Lord for saving me three—Frank called them my Magical Three—and I asked for patience. It's what I would need to produce the bloom I imagined in my heart. I could envision a sea of white each spring. I'd just have to be patient in my crossbreeding and learn better how to wait. And I'd fence in the nursery areas. I ought to have done that before.

"Not sure asking for patience was a good idea," Frank said after I told him what I'd prayed for. "Seems to me as soon as you ask for patience, you get something coming down the pike that requires an extra dose of it."

"I figured I was safe. After all, I've already had the misery that spurred the request."

"Maybe. But misery loves its company, and I don't want it settling in with you. I want that special place next to you, not a plant or two."

The next morning we walked home from church with

our children in front of us, the girls squired by their young men. Those children were my petals, every one of them. I wiped my eyes and took a deep breath, sliding my arm through Frank's.

"Let's get a better look at how the rest of the yard fared," Frank said when we arrived home. The girls rustled up dinner, and we could hear their chatter with their beaus through the open windows as Frank and Fritz and I walked the paths.

Irises had been clipped by the shod hooves. They'd missed the peonies, though they were already beginning to splay out. A few daylilies looked as though a fat cat had squatted in their midst. Horses hadn't had time to rip off an oriental poppy as they fled through the yard. Most of those blooms had already faded, but they still lent a color point for the eye. I spied the break in the neighbor's fence on the other side where they'd trashed through. A flash of words spewed from my mouth, and Frank cautioned me. "Now, now," he said.

"I'd like to say those things to my neighbor." But I wouldn't. Not until I'd had time to think it through. Instead, I told Frank, "As soon as we can afford it, let's think about one of those automobiles where the horsepower is contained inside metal. And offer the neighbor a ride now and then so he might be inspired to rid himself of those horses."

Frank grinned. "Who would have thought that horses trampling lilacs would lead to such a windfall for me!" Then he looked contrite and added, "Course it's a terrible thing they did to your lemons, Huldie. But you'll make lemonade of it, after all, I submit. Yes, indeed, that's what I submit."

We could not have asked for a more glorious wedding day, even if the gardens could have been in a little better form. I'd tried to save seeds from the two equine-destroyed lilacs, but to no avail. I would have to focus on the three remaining. But that would be later, after the wedding, after things had settled down in my daughters' lives, and I could concentrate on the lilacs.

On my daughters' wedding day, the sun shone bright and birds twittered in the magnolia and the holly trees. The flat-iron garden plot was awash with blooms of many colors. Pansies and petunias bobbed their heads. Marigolds trotted around the perimeter of that iron-shaped planting. Lavender lent its sweet smell and promise of abundance to the occasion. I would carry a nosegay of lavender, and we handed out small bouquets to women as they arrived for the ceremony, at least those who didn't have a flower already on their person.

I looked out at the gardens the morning of the ceremony while ironing the girls' dresses. Delia's dress was satin, and it showed the wrinkles more than the linen that draped Lizzie's slender frame. Both girls had cape bodices and ragamuffin sleeves, though Lizzie's sleeves were lace and Delia's all satin.

I finished ironing and hung the girls' dresses from the top

railing of the stairwell, so their long gowns fell as though a waterfall. Martha and I worked in the sunroom with the lavender, and she reminded me as we created our bouquets that supposedly lavender represented a "woman in her prime, someone devoted."

"Really? I guess I knew that flowers had certain meanings, just not what they are."

"Violets are what Jupiter tossed into the fields for his beloved Io to graze upon after he turned her into a cow."

"A cow," I said. "Not a horse?" I shook my head, remembering those lost lilacs. "What are they teaching you at the normal school?"

"Greek and Roman mythology. Jupiter's wife was jealous of Io, so Jupiter gave her up, but he wanted her to have royal grazing. Thus the violets. The Greeks used to line their graves with violets, Mama."

"I'll keep that in mind when some horses I know meet their Maker," I said.

Martha laughed. "Lavender is fitting for Lizzie and Delia, don't you think? Modest yet mature; full of devotion. The Egyptians used lavender for both perfumes and embalming and the Romans for medicine."

"I like the perfume and medicine part." I twisted a sprig of lavender. "And lilacs? What does your Greek mythology say they mean?"

"A nymph named Syringa captivated Pan, the god of the

forest and fields, and he chased her. To escape, Syringa turned herself into an aromatic bush."

"Inventive of her."

"But purple lilacs mean 'first love,' and white ones stand for 'the innocence of youth.'"

I rather liked Martha's flower meanings. They were different from the old books I had in which the sentiments of flowers often contradicted each other.

I wished lilacs had been in bloom for my daughters' weddings; the sentiment was perfect. Instead, they carried mums mixed with baby's-breath and lilies, and of course lavender. Martha and I would later mix an egg white and paint the bouquets with it, then dip them in sugar to preserve them. "The girls will love having the bouquets from their wedding day on their first anniversaries," Martha said, and I agreed.

Our neighbors came and all the uncles and aunts and cousins within the region. I loved having children rushing around, a fiddle player in the backyard, and glass lemonade pitchers holding down tablecloths lifted by the afternoon breezes. My brother, Emil, clapped the grooms on their backs and told them stories of Lizzie and Delia that I know the girls wished had been kept in the family.

The wedding photographer set up his camera in the parlor for the official photographs once the girls were dressed. We didn't hold with the opinion that the girls shouldn't be seen by their future husbands until the ceremony. Instead, they saw each other as they stood before the camera lens and then would together head to the church for the ceremony.

Frank surprised them each with a pair of white leather gloves as soft as Bobby's ears with special stitching—different for each girl—along the top of each finger.

"Oh, Papa, these are beautiful," Lizzie said and hugged her father. Delia did likewise, rubbing her fingers across the stitching.

I looked at this man I married all those years before. He never ceased to surprise me with his attention to little things that matter to someone he loves.

"Mama, you put him up to this." Delia wagged the gloves at me.

"No, I didn't. I've been so busy getting the garden up to perfect. Your father never even mentioned a present." I'd thought the wedding and all the fixings of it would be present enough, but Frank thought otherwise. "I'm sorry I didn't think of it. They're lovely." I felt the soft leather.

"It was Martha," Frank said. "I asked what she thought a father ought to give his daughters, and she said, 'Something to keep their hands comforted.' Course you don't have to wear them just for today."

Martha stood in the doorway so as not to upset the camera arrangement, and she moved aside when the photographer said, "Are we ready, then?"

"What made you think of gloves?" I asked her as I stepped

out into the hallway. I could hear my sisters in the kitchen putting final touches on the cakes. They'd shooed me out some time ago, and I realized everything was as ready as it would get. "Gloves seem like such an unusual wedding gift," I offered.

"It's to keep their hands warm when their husbands are gone." I turned to Martha thinking then what an odd thought that was. I must have frowned. "When they travel," she said. She rubbed her own gloveless hands together.

"Yes, I suppose. Well, the girls love them, and your father was a dear to get them made in time."

"That tailor, Mr. Lawson, had them made up. But he doesn't work with leather, so Papa got him to order in the gloves special."

"Lawson. Yes, I heard about him. Moved here from somewhere south. With a daughter."

Martha nodded. "She's a scowling thing. Nelia, he called her. She never smiled the whole time Papa and I were there. Not when I picked up the gloves either. But when I scratched my hand on the edge of a table, she rushed right over to tenderly pat my wrist."

Her description of the girl found a little place in my memory that day. I always have been partial to children and wondering what swats of life turned a naturally loving child to one that frowns their days away. Made me ever grateful for my own children and the happiness I saw in their eyes.

"Your father's a good man. You find one like him, Martha, and you'll be the happiest girl in the world." I whispered that last part since the photographer had turned to shush me. I looked at those two couples and felt tears well up. I couldn't have been happier for them, such a good life they had ahead of them.

The Reverend A. W. Burholder officiated, and I never saw two more beaming brides than our girls...except the day Amelia and I spoke our vows. Frank walked them down the aisle, stepping carefully on the white cloth the flower girl sprinkled rose petals on. The day was warm, and we fanned ourselves with stick fans Fritz had fashioned over several days out of cardboard and glue. Reverend Burholder reminded the couples of the sacredness of this service and that their vows were spoken not just before their relatives and friends, their new husband or wife, but before God as well. "It is a three-way promise," he reminded them, "in sickness and in health."

Frank squeezed my hand at the mention of sickness, and I leaned into him to let him know I remembered too, that time of trial last summer. I was so grateful to be feeling better.

After the ceremony, we ate. Oh, goodness, how we ate! My sisters had each baked a layer cake that took three hours to complete. I'd been grateful for cool mornings when we fired up the cookstove. White frosting covered the cakes, and we'd decorated them with lavender sprigs and tiger lilies. My brother, Emil, made a big to-do over bringing each cake out to set on the tables, and the crowd erupted in applause when the girls cut into their own cakes and then fed their husbands. Such an odd custom, yet one that Amelia and I had indulged in ourselves all those years before.

The couples left on what would be a short honeymoon trip, each to different locations; I guess they decided they didn't need to do everything together. Fred and Lizzie left for Portland; Delia and Nell Irving took the steamboat up to Kelso, not as far away since Nell Irving had cows to tend to after the weekend. Frank and Fritz would milk their herd along with our own until they got back.

"Just leave things for picking up until tomorrow," I told Martha who had already begun scraping plates into the chicken's bucket. Ruthie had left with her family and would be gone a few days before they allowed her back to help with the watering of my plants.

"What?" Frank said. "You never want to leave things unsettled."

"Today is special. I just thought...you and Fritz better get to those cows," I finished.

"I don't mind, Mama." Martha sounded wistful, and I put my arm around her, leading her toward the house. I hadn't thought of anything special for Martha on this day, even though that had been my intention. Those horses and lilacs had taken my mind from planning a surprise.

"At least change your clothes first," I said. "We'll miss them, won't we?" She nodded. "But there they go, off onto a life of their own. You'll be off too before long, finishing your studies. But until then, I'll need you more than ever if I'm to get any goodness from those French lilacs."

"Oh, you and your flowers," Martha said.

"It's always good to have something to look forward to." I tried for cheerful in my voice. "Especially when you have to say good-bye to something you've loved and had daily in your life for years."

I picked up lavender twists left on a side table and inhaled. They'd been cut all day, and they still had a fragrance that filled my head. "It's true, I always have my flowers to bring me comfort," I told Martha. "But they can't bring anywhere near the comfort of you."

Martha didn't say a word.

We walked past the parlor, and with the photographer gone, I stopped, hung the framed photographs back onto the wall. We'd removed them to reduce any clutter in the background. Now I held the picture we'd had taken at Mama's funeral. I hung it back up as Martha headed upstairs. I walked into the sunroom then to check on my starts, the "other children" in my life. I pressed my fingers in the soil, calculating moisture levels, checking on the lilacs I'd brought inside after the fiasco with the horses. All was well, and I was anxious to begin tomorrow seeing what I could do with what remained of my imports.

I heard Martha upstairs, changing clothes, I imagined. Her silence when I said she brought me more comfort than my plants still haunted.

SEVENTEEN

SHELLY SNYDER

1904

Shelly Snyder." She said her new name purposefully, standing in front of the oak mirror in the room her husband said had always been the guest room and was now the master suite in their Baltimore home. The wedding had been held not in the garden of his fine estate but at her parents' home in Annapolis, which suited her fine. She had few friends to invite since her father had traveled so much in his military position and they never stayed anywhere long enough to make real friends. Bill's mother provided only a very short list of guests, so having the wedding "close to your home, dear" had proven a wise idea.

But that was nearly six months ago, and since then Shelly had shared her husband with his mother, his students, the Baltimore estate, and yes, his garden, which thankfully had been cleared of chrysanthemums despite her mother-in-law's protests that mums were her favorite flower. This was how she knew her husband truly loved her. This, and because he'd succumbed to a few of her other wishes, including finding a home they might live in, just the two of them. The mums had gone, and she knew that had been a huge sacrifice for him.

"Mrs. Snyder," she said to the mirror. No, that was her mother-in-law. Then, "Mrs. William Snyder." She couldn't decide which sounded more...sophisticated. She was going for sophisticated this day, anticipating conversations beyond children and food.

Shelly winced at herself in the mirror with that thought. She had nothing to contribute to those subjects. At her mother-in-law's social gatherings, Shelly wanted to talk about Emmeline Pankhurst's founding of the Women's Social and Political Union or comment on the growing popularity of the reform dress, or even that Mr. Ford had started his own motor company and soon they could all be driving rather than taking cabs or walking or riding on trains. But those were not deemed "appropriate." She hoped at least they might talk about books. She'd recently read one set in the American West called *The Virginian*. She'd been to Virginia and had never seen anything like the author's description. She guessed the Virginian had been changed by his environment out there in the sagebrush. Bill was always telling her how the environment could change his posies. She picked up her yellow beaded purse, straightened her hat. Her skin looked white as porcelain, and that surprised her too. She'd always looked robust with pink cheeks, without rubbing geranium leaves on them; a hint of suntan. In Annapolis, the sun warmed her face as she removed her hat and sat on a bench near the bay. These past six months she'd been quarantined in the house with Bill's mother during the weekdays, reading her way through the library books, attending the occasional teas, but otherwise lonely. Quite lonely. Until Bill arrived home on Friday evening. Even then she had to share him with his mother.

She'd decided to create this day of independence after a fretful argument she had with Bill.

"I simply can't stay cooped up inside this…mausoleum," Shelly whispered her outrage. Keeping her voice low so as not to alert his mother to their arguments frustrated her almost as much as the clipping of her wings. Shelly wondered if the woman listened at their door. She wanted to open it quickly and catch her at it so Bill could see what she had to deal with. But he'd likely just invite her in and comment on how wonderful it was that she cared so much about making Shelly's life pleasant. He was so blind when it came to his mother!

"There are three acres of grounds here," Bill whispered back. "New blooms appear each day. Why, I suspect the—"

"Don't start with the litany of that garden," she hissed. "You know it better than you know me." Tears pressed against her eyes. She swiped at them. She would not let her tears speak for her!

"I want to know only you, Shelly." Bill reached for her. "You are the love of my life."

Shelly stepped back, arms across her chest. "Then why is it I rarely have any time with you? Why is it we do nothing on the weekends except 'check in on the garden' as though what I've dealt with all week is no concern of yours."

"If there were problems, you'd tell me, or Mother would. So when I see you walk out to the carriage, I am the happiest man alive assured that all is well. Until we come inside and you...you..." He searched for words.

"I argue with you. I argue. It's the only way I can get you to actually see me."

"That's not true, Shelly. It's not. I thought you'd be happy here. Everything taken care of. No worries. You have an allowance. You can visit your aunt. Why don't you do that more often?"

"I visit her every week. It's the only time I leave here. I'm a captive."

"That's nonsense."

"Let me come with you to Annapolis. We could stay with my father during the week. It would save you the expense of a room. And we'd be together."

He'd considered that; she knew he had. His hands had twisted back and forth as he did when he walked and was deep in thought about his posies. But then he'd shaken his head. "No. I spend my evenings preparing for classes, grading papers, all things that would bore you, and you'd find me even less a social creature than what you long for. I...I thought you understood what my life was like."

"I did." She dropped her arms to her sides. "But I thought you'd allow a change in your life with me in it. It's as though I'm another potted plant and that you just shifted a few others around so you could make a place for me in the hothouse. Just a pot in the hothouse."

"Oh, Shelly." He'd come to her then and held her, but it hadn't been enough to silence her. She pushed back.

"If I can't come with you to Annapolis... If I can't go out—"

"Mother takes you to her club meetings."

"I don't need an escort," Shelly snapped. "I need a husband. I need...a life."

"I've given you the best one I have." There was nothing negotiable in his voice, and she knew then that her thought of making him change, of getting him to be the man she dreamed he was, wasn't going to happen.

"Then I will simply tell you now, before your mother tells you later, that I will be going out on my own, despite the 'impropriety of my independence,' as your mother calls my desire."

So today she was doing just that. She took a cab, noting the lush estates along the cobbled streets. Shelly thought it odd that people of wealth built lavish homes with gracious gardens, then hid them behind iron grates covered with clematis and ivies as though they didn't want anyone to see what they'd built.

"Mrs. Shelly Snyder is pleased to make your acquaintance," she said to herself inside the cab. "Mrs. Shelly Snyder is pleased to make your acquaintance," she repeated, but emphasized the word *Mrs.* Yes, that's how she'd say it at this first meeting of the horticultural society, without her mother-in-law to escort her. If she couldn't change Bill, she would have to change herself. This was the best way she could think to do it: learn what she could about flowers and hope she could get her husband's attention with more of her own attentiveness to what he truly loved.

EIGHTEEN

NEW BEGINNINGS

Hulda, 1905

I walked to the tailor shop to buy new needles, past the mercantile, then the Independent Order of Odd Fellows lodge that housed the dentist and Dr. Chapman's office. It was a balmy spring, nearly a year after the girls' weddings. I'd filled the empty space of their leaving by cross-pollinating, growing seeds from plants. Martha was away at school, so I only had Fritz and Frank to spoil and Ruth when she worked in the garden. I bravely wrote to Luther Burbank, expressing admiration for his work, and he'd responded months later, though the letter was more a pat on my head than evidence he actually understood I shared his enthusiasm for hybridizing. But even his letter didn't fill the hole I couldn't name.

I loved watching my daughters turn into sensitive, joyful wives. Lizzie had a few complaints about being alone when Fred traveled, and I'd urged her to intensify interests that didn't require his presence. "You always liked azaleas," I reminded her. "Why not think about hybridizing?"

"I don't have the same passion for plants as you, Mother."

"Well, let's get that piano out of here and move it to your house," I said. "I hoped one day you'd give me lessons, but that'll have to happen when I'm old. I'll come to you for them."

"That would help," Lizzie said. "I didn't realize how much I'd miss teaching. Wish being married didn't put a stopper at that door."

Delia had no complaints at all. That surprised me, because she did have her share of issues growing up, whether a stitch was too wide and needed to be taken out or whether the way a cake rose—and fell—was the result of something she'd done in the mixing or just the nature of that cake. She was fussy like me that way. But with Nell Irving, she was happy as a clam, or so she told me. She worked side by side with him, with the cows and hogs and sheep on their acreage, and said she could see now why I liked to work beside her father so much. "We're just good friends, Mama. Isn't that nice?"

"It is." I started to tell her how to keep it so by careful tending and by bending now and then to his wishes, but she just smiled.

"I have a good teacher, Mama. Not to worry. I was watching."

Frank had tilled a section for the vegetable garden, and it

was planted so we'd have beans and beets and peas to eat and can. But now the lilacs were coming on to that perfect time for cross-pollinating, and I had needles to replace for my evening sewing, so I trekked to the tailor. There I saw his daughter, and the idea struck me, the hole I needed to fill.

"Do you ever let your daughter walk out on her own?" I asked Mr. Lawson. "My garden's not that many blocks from here."

"She's a handful."

The child appeared quiet, shy.

"I've raised three girls and a son, so I think I can handle a little thing like her. What's your name, child?"

"Nelia," her father answered for her. "I suppose I've not done proper by her since her nanny passed." He faced his daughter. "You want to visit Mrs. Klager's garden?" The girl nodded, and when she did, I saw something familiar in her profile. She'd snuck around the picket fence once or twice, flitting in beneath the shrubs. She did no harm, but I'd wondered who she was. Now I knew.

"Perhaps she could help me. I'd pay her, of course."

He seemed relieved for the invitation, and the girl walked out with me, beginning a summer of her assistance. She'd come early as I'd requested, when the air was still and the bees and birds weren't yet stirring. I confess, I loved an audience, having people ask about what I was doing and why. Maybe it was the teacher in me that hadn't found students until the garden. I liked seeing their eyes light up with under-standing, especially if the concept was foreign to them as cross-pollinating usually was. Maybe Martha got her interest in teaching from her mother.

"Here are the parts of a flower," I told Nelia. "These are sepals." I pointed to the complete outer leaf of one of my lilacs.

"Are they always green?" Nelia asked.

"Most often a shade of green, yes. But that's a good ques-tion. This inner leaf is called a petal. They usually aren't green, and they're flashy. They like to bring attention to themselves. It's what we often notice first. Now see here." I had her lean in close. "That area there is called the stamen. It holds a secret powder."

"Fairy dust?" Nelia asked. The child had huge blue eyes, as blue as a summer sky, and they looked at me in awe with the possibility that I'd just shown her magic.

"Not fairy dust, no. But still magical. The tiny case is called the anther." She repeated the word. "And inside of it is the dust. We call that pollen. Now this other part here"—I pointed to a feature next to the anther—"that's the pistil. The stamen gives the pistil the pollen, and then the sepals and petals protect it so it can produce a seed. If no pollen makes its way to the pistil—"

"Is that like a gun, a pistol?"

"No, no. The word is *pistil,* p-i-s-t-i-l, and unless pollen reaches it, there can be no seed. Usually birds and bees bring the pollen from a plant they've visited, and then they drop it onto the pistil of another plant, just when it's ready. But I'm doing that with my turkey feather and magnifying glass so I can see it better. It's so small. I used to cover them, but those I didn't pollinated just as well, so I gave that up in...oh, nineteen aught three, I suppose. I'm trying to pollinate this one in such a way that one day it will produce a bloom that is creamy white."

She nodded, but I suspect I'd already given her too much information. She watched, and with careful hands—her fingers were so small and delicate—she helped me place a metal tag at the base.

"Can't you just plant a seed next to the plant you want it to be like?" Nelia asked. "I see yellow and white corn kernels covering the same cob."

"You're a good observer, Nelia. Something every horti-culturist needs to be. And it's true—nature will just pollinate and make its own individual plant that has a mix of this and that. But I want specific things to be different. Color. Whether the plant will be stronger and can resist diseases or will maybe even have a better smell. We have to...select for that." I was going to say breed for it, but I wasn't sure if her father would approve of my use of the word and her possibly repeating it. "That's all we're doing, really, selecting what nature has already put there for us, and seeing if we can enhance it."

"Diseases are bad," she said.

"Yes, yes they are." I wondered what disease had affected her life. Bobby whimpered, lying on his side, his bushy collie tail lifting.

"Is he hurting?"

"No. Likely a rabbit dream."

Nelia seemed satisfied, but I saw her compassion turning toward wounded things.

The morning had slipped away, and I looked up surprised to see the sun high overhead. "Goodness. Frank and Fritz will be in for dinner. Quick as a lamb's tail, let's see what we can rustle up for them and ourselves."

I sliced ham and made sandwiches, put out pickled beets from last season, and filled big glasses with milk. The men ate heartily while Nelia picked at her sandwich. She eyed a platter of cookies on the counter.

"In this house we clean up our plates in order to get dessert," I told her.

She lifted her eyes to me, to the cookies, and then formed new interest in her ham sandwich, which she consumed, though I did think I saw a sleight of hand at her side where Bobby assumed a position next to her chair.

"No feeding the dog. Or cat," I said and made it stern. I'd done that with my own children early on and found I didn't have to repeat it as they got older. "They get fed in the kitchen, next to the stove, after we've eaten."

"Yes ma'am," she said.

"When did you make these, Huldie?" Frank asked, eating his cookie and rescuing the child from my words, though he knew my routine of spoiling after a period of stern. Nelia had a cookie now too.

"Early this morning, while it was still cool."

"They're good," Fritz offered.

"Didn't think you'd have time what with your lessons going on out there," Frank said. "Is she a good teacher, Nelia?"

The child nodded. She wiped her face with the back of her hand, and I gave her a napkin. "Jasmine liked lilacs," Nelia said then. Her words were soft as the breeze breathing through the wind chimes hanging on the porch.

"Did she? Do you know what kind she liked?"

"Purple. We came by your garden and smelled them. Then she died."

"Mrs. Klager has lots of purple," Frank said.

"I'm sorry about Jasmine. She must have been special."

"Maybe we can make one even purpler," Nelia said. "With that pollen brush. My mama liked purple ones too."

"We can try," I said, pushing a wayward curl around her ear. "We can surely try."

I stood up and went to the sun porch. Ludwig Späth, an excellent purple. "Let's check Frank's tags and see if we can find the most purple lilac in my garden, and we'll pollinate dozens, see what we come up with next spring."

"Or the spring after that," Nelia said, bobbing her head, her cookie going up and down with her nodding. Bobby's head followed her cookie's every move. "Making flowers takes a long time."

"Yes, it does," I said to this plant of wisdom before me.

"So does forgetting," she added, and I knew there was much healing left to do in the life of this precious bloom. I believed that lilacs were just the plants to do it.

NINETEEN

CORNELIA GIVENS

1905

Cornelia Givens raised her hand to tap on her editor's door. She checked her attire. She wore a white blouse and gray linen skirt with a whisper of a raised hemline that came to the tops of her high-button shoes. A dark belt emphasized her small waist. When she patted her hair, she felt the pencil sticking out from the bun at the top of her head. She pulled it out, held it in her hand with the card. A watch hung from a gold necklace, stopping modestly well above her breasts. It was her professional dress, and it rarely varied in the two years she'd worked for the *Sacramento Bee* as a columnist with her own byline. She held a plate of cookies. She took a deep breath and knocked.

"Come in," CK said.

She handed him the plate, and he sighed as he picked up the maple sugar cookie. "What can I do for you that is in any way repayment for these priceless gems?"

"I've received yet another question for the Common Woman column about flowers and plants and gardening in general. I know nothing about these things, especially flowers." Cornelia tapped the pencil on her card. "I feel I deprive our readers by choosing to ignore these kinds of concerns about the mold on leaves or bugs that eat their rosebushes for lunch. I answer baby questions and indulge myself with recipes I personally love. I get requests for more, but I'm failing the gardeners out there."

"Go on." His eyes gave her their full attention, something she'd seen whenever anyone addressed him. She always felt listened to.

"I want to make an excursion to improve my understanding of all things horticultural," Cornelia said.

"The library is free," he said, and he grinned.

Cornelia had studied books about horticulture and botany and recently read an article in *Popular Science Monthly*, written by the Dutch horticulturist Hugo de Vries, who had come all the way from Holland to visit the Luther Burbank gardens in California. "I'll keep going to the library, yes. But I'd like to meet real experts and also cover the agricultural exhibit at the Lewis and Clark Exposition in Portland. There will be dozens of exhibits from around the world related to plants, new crops. We could fertilize two bulbs at one time, so to speak."

CK munched on his cookie, a man in thought.

"I've had contact with one exhibitor already, and did you

know that the organizers pump water into a marsh to make it a lake to enhance the exposition site and—"

"You're wrangling for a feature."

She took a deep breath. "I think I'm ready. Some exhibitors support programs of more public gardens." The *Bee* devoted many column lines to stories about the betterment of public life, favoring taxes to support it. "While I'm in Portland, I could also interview Thomas Jefferson Howell. He wrote *A Flora of Northwest America*." The book had taken the botanist years to complete, and the illustrations were magnificent, but he was somewhat of a recluse. Cornelia was beginning to think most gardeners were—Luther Burbank's flamboyant promotion of his efforts being an exception.

"That has possibilities. You've contacted an exhibitor? From California?"

"Not from California."

Cornelia handed CK a business card. "Miss L. L. Hetzer," CK read. "A woman?"

"Indeed."

"Looks to be quite the artist, if she drew this sketch herself."

Cornelia leaned over to look at the card with him, noting the fine ink drawing she guessed might be the garden the woman worked at back east.

"She's a renowned instructor at the Lowthorpe School of Landscape Architecture for Women. In Massachusetts. Apparently all the women learn to draw and do surveying and so on, so they can design estate gardens or public parks." Cornelia emphasized the public part.

"I don't like to be an easy editor. Makes reporters lazy. But I like this idea. And you're right; you're ready for a feature piece. Maybe we can emphasize how good landscape architecture brings the country to the people, and that brings people to a city. How it's a good expenditure of public money to maintain parks. The exposition appears to be on the road to making money by bringing people from back east and all."

"That could be another aspect of my feature, the economics of the exposition—as well as gardens. An interview with a woman from an all-women landscape college would be quite unique. I have a few other ideas as well."

"Yes, yes it would. All right, you have my blessing. And if you can get Howell to see you, make that happen too. And hopefully"—he shouted after her as she backed through the door—"you'll get something for your Common Woman column. You can always add the recipe for these cookies."

Back at her desk, Cornelia read the letter that had inspired her to suggest the trip to the exposition in Portland in the first place. She intended one of her features to emphasize the importance of nature in memorializing those we love, and what better place to do that than at a worldwide exposition featuring plants and trees?

"I have leggy lilacs planted by my mother in 1860," the

letter began. "I lived apart from my mother for most of my life, and upon returning for her funeral three years ago, I made the decision to remain in her house. Her lilacs haunt me. The top of the foliage is over six feet high now, while the bottoms are bare as rooster legs. They bloom for only a few days in the spring, and some of the scent has faded. I seek a way to make them pretty, like they were when my mama was young and vibrant and alive. They need to be a memorial for her, and it saddens me to see them disappear the way she did, with faded blooms and the aroma of neglect."

Aroma of neglect. The letter-writer's words haunted Cornelia as she thought about her sickly mother. She never intended to neglect her, but only rarely thought of what her life was like when she'd been young and vibrant.

She donned her hat over straw-colored hair and grabbed her bag. She'd buy her ticket on the way home, make sure her sister looked after her mother. But first she'd pick up a celebratory bouquet of flowers at the stand outside the office to cheer them all.

TWENTY

FAIR

Hulda, 1905

How would you like to go to the Lewis and Clark Exposition in Portland in June?" I asked Lizzie, Delia, and Martha. I knew Fritz would want to go. We were at the farm, working in the beds. I'd planted rows and rows of lilac starts, and they needed mulching and monitoring, even though they'd long passed their bloom. Nelia and Ruth carried buckets and dippers, walking along the aisles between the rows, pouring life-giving water onto the young roots. I'd acquired the help of a few boys I called my "bucket boys," so I didn't have to do so much heavy lifting. Some of the sprouts I'd pollinated had bloomed within two years, but most would take three to seven. The ones that bloomed were finished by Mother's Day, and a June trip to the fair seemed like good timing, without the rush of pruning, marking foliage, or even harvesting the vegetable garden. Besides, I wanted to see the Japanese exhibit because of their reputation for unique iris bulbs, and I heard that Chile was giving away monkey puzzle trees.

"What fun!" Delia said. "I hear there are interesting foods being offered there from places like the Philippines. Where is that, anyway?"

"In the South China Sea," Martha told her. "More than three thousand islands in all."

"I love having a sister who can answer questions like that off the top of her head." Beneath her straw hat, Martha grinned at the compliment.

"Speak to your respective husbands about going." I stretched my back. "Call it an anniversary present. We'll take you all. Ride the steamer to Portland. I hear there's a train or streetcar that will take us from downtown to within a block of the exposition."

"Or take the train all the way," Delia said.

"We'll let the men decide." I loved the banter the girls engaged in.

"Nell Irving's been teased some by his friends because the fair is at Guild's Lake." Delia brushed at a bee. "But he tells them his name is pronounced *guild* like the skilled trade associations in the old country, and the lake in Portland is spoken like *guile*."

"Is Nell Irving certain he's not somehow related?" Lizzie asked her sister. "Maybe he has wealthy ancestors he didn't know about."

"If that's so, we're probably the only relatives without electricity."

Electricity hadn't arrived in Woodland yet, and I'd heard that the exposition featured a display of over a hundred thousand light bulbs that surrounded the exhibit buildings, making it like day when it was night, man's efforts diminishing the glow of the stars. I couldn't imagine starlight being drained by electric bulbs. I hoped our community never suffered such a bleaching of the night sky, though I'd be happy enough to have light bulbs illuminating my seed catalogs on a rainy winter night. The thought of how man transforms God's creation brought Barney Reed to mind. We had our fair share of disagreements about man's—or woman's—role in changing creation at this week's Bible classes.

"Oh, look at this!" I told the girls. "Look! Come here! It's got five petals! Five!"

My daughters hovered around, staring at the bloom I held in my palm. "So it does," Lizzie said. "Is it from one of the Lemoine?"

"Yes, oh yes. I can't believe it. It's better than the apple. Just look at that!" I inspected every single bloom on that bush but only found the one with five petals. I marked it, then moved to several others. "I'm just amazed. Five. If I can get five, then six, seven." I turned to them, tears brimming. "Twelve petals *is* possible."

They'd moved on, Lizzie looking at a dahlia, and the

other two chatting about what they'd wear. I felt separated, apart.

"Imagine that. Five petals," I repeated as I approached them.

"You sound surprised, Mama." Martha turned toward me. "It's quite a feat."

"I know I raved it could happen, but I didn't really know. It's all experimental, so nothing is certain." I could hardly wait to tell Frank when he came back from the Bottoms where we still kept the cows. "I should write to Luther Burbank and tell him."

I caught Lizzie rolling her eyes and corrected myself. "Oh, I'm just piddling around with that idea. Now, what will you girls wear?" I said, hoping to be invited back into their conversation.

"Will you please dress in something fashionable?" Lizzie pulled her garden gloves off. "I'll even make it for you." She grinned.

"Fine. But nothing requiring a tight belt or a too-big bustle. I like loose, and remember, I'm shaped like a pickle."

We chatted about what we'd wear, what we'd take with us, how long we might be gone, and I kept my mind with them. After all, the fair had been my idea. But my thoughts kept slipping back to the five petals on the purple lilac and my wish that my daughters understood my enthusiasm for my success.

Fred worked for the steam company, having started there shortly after he and Lizzie married, so he'd have to arrange his schedule. Nell Irving needed someone to milk their cows for a couple of days, as would we. Bertha's husband, Carl, would probably do it. We'd have to move the cows up to Martin's Bluff before we left. The trip meant additional work, and I suspect that extra work was a reason we didn't let ourselves do entertaining things much. It took so much energy to get to bliss.

Frank teased that our intimate moments were limited by the same philosophy. In Frank's mind, whatever it took for hugs and kisses to be the result was well worth the effort. I believed that too, but practicality and fatigue often ruled my roost.

June 20 opened with the usual mist over the river. We congregated at five o'clock in the morning on the shoreline, ready to board the sternwheeler *Mascot*. We could come back to Woodland on the same day and arrive home in the dark, but we'd decided to spend at least three days at the exposition and would have two nights at a Portland hotel.

Once on board, Fred reveled in his passion—steamboats. He began explaining everything about the sternwheeler to us, providing intriguing details as though the boat were a character in a book. "One hundred thirty-two feet long. Beam is twenty-four feet, and the depth of the hold is five feet five inches." Fritz listened intently. Our son hadn't shown much interest in steamboating, but he did love the river, loved to fish, loved to take a raft out and let it drift him like a leaf on a lazy stream, and never complained about the trek back up-river tugging his raft along the bank.

"We'll approach a riffle before long." Fred pointed to an area ahead where the early morning sun shimmered over water wrestling with rocks beneath the surface. "The captain knows how to maneuver around it."

I stood with Fritz, listening to Fred Wilke wax about the ships and the excitement of work on the river. His eyes lit up as he spoke, and Lizzie, standing off to the side, smiled in admiration of her husband. That's as it should be. A husband needs his partner to take pleasure in his interests, to know that he provides. Her generosity of spirit adds to his confidence and to her own security.

Nell Irving and Frank talked of cows, and the girls soon carried on with their own conversations inside, with other passengers sipping tea at tables covered with white linens. They sat out of the breeze so they didn't have to hang on to their hats, but I liked the feel of the wind on my face, breathing in the river smells and all the emerald foliage along the banks. It calmed me. All the organizing to make this trip happen had frazzled. And truth told, I missed Bobby and my plants, even though I had all the flesh and blood that should have been enough to fill me up right here beside me. Finding five petals spurred me on, and I wished I could be there working for more.

Mallards scooted their way near the shoreline, and I watched an eagle swoop over the steamer, making a wild dash to the water, then slowly skim the riffles, gaining lift to help carry his cargo, a small steelhead. I turned to signal Fritz and bumped into Frank, who'd apparently been leaning against the wheelhouse door.

"Did you see that eagle?" I asked him.

"I did." Frank walked to me, patted my shoulder, then leaned on the rail beside me. His silence was a comfort. We were like two old oaks growing up next to each other, basking in each other's shade, making room for the acorns that will come after us. "This is nice, isn't it? All the *Kinder* here, whole family. On an outing."

"It is," I agreed.

"We don't do enough of this. We work together, but to just play? I'm not sure you really know how to do that."

"I relax." I adjusted my hat. "I thoroughly enjoy my time in the garden."

"But you make work of it. Dozens of details to tend to, notes to make on plants, starts to dig and plant or toss out, what all. Do you ever really just smell your roses and dahlias and lilacs that you work so hard to grow?"

"I get satisfaction when I can clip blooms and give them

to the girls or the neighbors or someone else," I said. "Or when I discover that extra petal. Did I tell you that one of the Lemoine-crossed lilacs had a bloom with five petals instead of four? Oh, surely I told you that."

"More than once."

I felt my face grow warm. "That's a joy I can't find in watching a baseball game or even going to a Fourth of July celebration."

"I submit, I like having us all together here, the whole family without any plants. It's good to have cheer more than only once a year at Christmas." He grinned.

"I did think of it, this trip. Don't I get credit for that?" Frank patted my hand. "Though I did wonder at the trouble caused by my suggestion."

"I thought Emil and Tillie said they'd come over, do watering and whatnot."

"Yes, they will, and I wrote out what I wanted them to do. But, oh, I don't know. I feel bereft away from them. What if a storm brews? What if the river rises unexpectedly? I won't be there to rescue my charges."

"These next few days you'll have to let the good Lord look after them," Frank said. "He's in control of them, anyway, despite all your effort."

"Now you sound like Barney Reed."

"Never. Barney's mixed up God-given creativity with a view that everything man-influenced is somehow bad or wrong."

"Everything woman-influenced too," I said.

Frank laughed again. His good disposition was contagious, and I kissed him, a quick peck on the cheek so as not to embarrass the children. "Now see, I'm capable of a little fun now and then."

"That you are," Frank said. He grabbed me and kissed me, a sweet lingering touch.

"Oh, for heaven's sake." I pushed back, but not far. "What will the children think?"

"That their parents love each other. The best gift we could ever give them, better even than lilac starts for their own gardens." I punched his shoulder. "That and a good time with us all together in one place."

Twenty-One

So Little Time

Hulda, 1905

The Agricultural Palace, as the building was known, looked like something out of *Arabian Nights*. Spires and fountains and greenery marked the edifice that Nell Irving said was built of sticks under plaster and not meant to last. Inside were examples of produce from the Northwest, how the industry hoped to meet the Orient's needs, touting that we were closer in Washington and Oregon to Asia than producers back east.

Several nurserymen showed off their wares, and I picked up catalogs to see what new varieties of bulbs and starts they might have for sale. Copies of *Sunset* magazine were available for a nickel, including older issues from 1901. I skimmed a series featuring Luther Burbank's work, saving this deeper reading for my winter's pleasure. In another section of the palace, the United States Department of Agriculture handed out seed packets for free, and I took one of everything they had. I thought it a good use of our tax dollars that the government encouraged people to grow their own food, take pleasure in plants. Mr. Burbank and I had this in common, a belief that the more experimenting done by individuals, the more information we'd all have about how plants mutated or crossed and what that might mean for bigger melons or broccoli that could be shipped more easily to areas where it didn't grow well at all. I imagined the nurserymen didn't like it that individuals had free seeds to experiment with, but it was less expensive than having universities do all the research, and it allowed amateurs like me to make discoveries. I accepted with glee the latest pepper seed and a new variety of tomato. There were few flower seeds, and that saddened me.

Our family separated during the day so each could take in the pavilion that most interested them. I cooled myself with a fan Frank bought me, a lithograph advertising the exposition pasted onto a stick. In the evenings, we all met at the bandstand illuminated by electric balls that arced out like a bouquet held by a child's hand. The band played four times a day. The view was spectacular, looking over the lake toward the Bridge of Nations and the Government Building. As the sun set and evening like a slow violin song eased into darkness, we hardly noticed because of the massive light displays.

"It's true," I whispered to Frank. "You can't see the stars."

We listened to the band and looked out over the lake,

then meandered to the Fairmount Hotel, where we sank into plush chairs in the lobby and told stories of our day.

I listened to my children and our two sons-in-law talk of what had impressed them. I wished I'd asked for permission to bring Ruth and Nelia along that they might have seen this extravaganza.

My children and their husbands discussed the economics of the exposition and whether it would make money for the investors or be a blight on the reputation of Portland. I failed to see how anything so grandly designed could possibly be a black mark on a city. But most of all, I saw that these young people had interests and wisdom. They were discerning people who assessed facts but also had passion for dreams. I couldn't have been prouder. I felt grateful for their lives and the happiness I saw reflected in their faces. Tears pooled, and I blinked them back. I looked across the room at Frank, and he winked at me. I swear that man can read my mind.

On the last day we visited the Japanese pavilion again. Nell Irving said he'd read that the Japanese had spent more than a million dollars on it, but it wasn't as large as the Italian display that included marble statues. The Japanese exhibit was certainly impressive, with its pagodas and women dressed in costumes of vibrant-colored silk. They had a silk exhibit with displays of flowers, some varieties I'd never seen before. I wandered one last time into the Agricultural Palace and was stopped by a sign: Lowthorpe School of Landscape Architecture for Women.

"Look here, Martha." The two of us walked arm in arm, with Fritz and Frank keeping pace behind us, my husband carrying the two-foot tall monkey puzzle tree we picked up at the Chilean exhibit. I pointed with my fan. "There's a school about horticulture for women. Imagine that."

Martha read the brochure. "They haven't been around all that long. It opened in 1901. Two women run it."

"Still, just imagine working with plants all day long, inhaling the smells of the potting sheds." I sighed.

"You already do that."

"You should go to that college, Martha." She shook her head. Plants were my obsession. A curriculum identified the names of instructors and lecturers, a few of whom were men; the rest women. Photographs of the grand estate in Groton, Massachusetts, suggested professionalism, with the female students in the hothouses wearing long wrappers to protect their clothing, and a surveyor's transit on a tripod overseen by three women staking out a new planting area. I could see shovels and how they'd cleared an area hoping for the best drainage.

"I would have loved to go to such a school."

"We take women of all ages," said a soft-spoken woman standing behind a counter and holding greenery. Behind her were flowering plants on wooden stands and more photographs revealing life at Lowthorpe School. "I'm one of the lecturers. Miss L. L. Hetzer." She held out her hand, and I shook it like a man. "You have a special interest in landscape architecture?"

"My mother is quite an enterprising horticulturist," Martha said.

"Oh, let's not go that far." I looked at the brochure. "I've had no special training. Just an eighth-grade education finished north of here in little Woodland."

"But she developed a crisper, bigger apple," Martha said. "And she can spot a lilac bloom turning toward cream and the following spring can pollinate it with another, hoping to achieve the perfect creamy white one day."

"I adore lilacs," Miss Hetzer said. "Of course, Massachusetts has quite a different climate than your tepid Northwest."

"Rainy, tepid Northwest," I said. "Lilacs are a favorite across the country, though, and I've always longed for creamy white or one with more than four petals. I'm working on it. Just this year I had a bloom with five."

"That's wonderful!" I loved her enthusiasm. We discussed varieties then and how I'd crossed the plants. We must have chatted for half an hour or more. I lost track of time. Martha had wandered off, or maybe she went to get Frank because I heard him come up beside me, showed me his watch, the monkey puzzle tree riding on his hip.

"Looks like I'm wanted." I introduced Frank.

"I wish you well. Perhaps you'll visit us."

"Oh, that's not likely. I don't go too far from my gardens. This is the first outing we've had in, oh, ten years or more. But I'll keep your card, and when I get that perfect bloom, I'll send you a letter. Perhaps we can share notes on pruning."

"Speaking of pruning," Miss Hetzer said. Frank raised an eyebrow.

"Just one second more."

"We're heading off to the dock," Frank said.

"I'll be along, I will. What did you want to say about pruning?" I asked Miss Hetzer.

"I wonder if you'd care to share with me what you do with older lilacs, to prune. A young woman who writes a column for the newspaper asked me about that, and I told her of our approach, but of course, we're in a different region in Massachusetts. She's in California."

"I prune after the bloom, but before July Fourth. I've also heard that in late winter, February or so, one can cut the entire plant back to six to eight inches above the ground, especially with older shrubs. Hardest thing I have to do is cut something back, but it's a reminder of the nature of a garden, teaching us about life. To grow healthier and larger, we have to be pruned now and then. Lilacs too." I spoke too much to this stranger, but she nodded agreement.

"What, then?" she asked.

"With the lilacs? Or life?" I teased.

"Lilacs. I'll extrapolate from that about living."

I vowed to ask Martha what *extrapolate* meant but continued. "The pruning will result in many new shoots, so during the second season, you'll have to identify the hardiest ones and retain those, while cutting back the others to ground level. And head the lilacs you've decided to keep just above a bud. That will encourage branching." I spoke with my hands, showing a horizontal cut through the air and holding an imaginary bud in my hand as precious as a newborn. "If it's an old hedge, it'll feel like you've exposed them to the elements pruning them back so far, and if they've become a windbreak, well, what's behind it will be battered by the elements for a time too, until the plants emerge to take their place as sentinels once again."

I thought of the hedge my mother planted and how I'd pruned it once we moved into the house. "Now, you can also prune over a few years, taking a few of the old branches out each year. It might feel less exposing, and it would allow some blooming every spring. But I prefer the first method. May as well get it over with."

"That's very informative. I'll be sure to tell my friend Cornelia. And really it's not much different from what we'd do in our cold climate."

"Flowers have a way of reducing differences," I said. "I love restoring old lilacs, but my goal is working with entirely new varieties."

"We confer often with horticulturists around the country and would be pleased to have you on our mailing list. If you'd care to sign here, I'll be sure you receive our catalogs and news."

Martha was back. She signed for me. Her penmanship is so much better than mine, and it felt strange to put my name on a list as a horticulturist. Martha looked at her watch. "We should be going, Mother." I started to thank Miss Hetzer, accepting more papers she offered for a winter's evening, when another young woman approached.

"This is Cornelia Givens, from the *Sacramento Bee,* the woman who asked about pruning lilacs. Your name is…"

"Hulda Klager. From Woodland, Washington," I said, putting out my hand to her gloved one.

"This woman could answer your regional gardening questions," Miss Hetzer told her.

"Really? That would be swell," the young woman said. She wasn't much older than Lizzie. "Could I ask you a few more questions now?"

"Certainly." I liked the idea of being interviewed by a newspaper reporter, but Sacramento didn't share the same climate issues as the Northwest. The reporter gave me little time to mention that.

"Do you heat the soil you bring in during the winter before you plant seedlings in them?"

"I do."

Martha tugged on my sleeve. "Mama, the boat. We'll miss the boat."

"And what about slugs?" The girl had a notepad.

"They're universal, aren't they? Sweet pickle juice or beer. Best use of beer I know of. They'll drink themselves to death if you put a bowl out for them. And you can compost them."

"Moles?"

"Traps."

"Mother…"

"I really can't talk now. My daughter's right. I have so little time. My family waits for me."

She handed me her card. "Would you write your name and address here for me? Then I can write to you. That would be lovely, if you wouldn't mind."

"I wouldn't." I scribbled our address. I asked her for another of her cards so I'd have her address too, and then we hurried away, Martha holding my elbow as we fast-walked to the dock.

"And we were just getting started."

"Nearly an hour and a half ago," Martha said. "Good thing Papa always tells you a fake time, or you'd miss every boat."

The rest of the family waved us forward as we rushed toward the gangplank. I was short of breath. Just before we boarded, the fireworks began. I'd forgotten there would be a display. We watched the explosion of color out over the water as I looked at my family's faces reflected in the rainbow colored light, so grateful we had taken this time to be together.

"We're blessed, Frank. We planted good seeds in our children and tended them well."

"I submit, we truly are."

It was what I'd hang on to as the pruning season began.

PRUNING

Twenty-Two

The Beginning of Endings

Hulda, 1905

M ama, you've got to come! Now!" Lizzie's voice sounded tinny over the phone line we'd just installed. It was two weeks since we'd all been together at the exposition, just around the corner from the Fourth of July.

"What?" I had to stand on tiptoes to reach the mouthpiece, as Frank had installed the contraption too high. I held the black piece that looked like a small trumpet to my ear, adjusted it yet again. "Say again."

"It's Fred. Something's wrong. Dr. Alice is on her way."

Lizzie and Fred lived just north, close enough for us to see one another every day, but far enough away we couldn't hear their disagreements. From the stories Lizzie told and from seeing them together on the trip, they had a good solid marriage for barely a year since their vows. They'd done the discovery, as I thought of it, adjusting as they had to. Fred liked his shirt collars starched more and preferred that her flannel nightdress stay in the closet—though she said he was fine with her wearing linen to bed. He didn't like carrots. She'd gotten him interested in a new sewing machine, and he'd had one delivered for their anniversary. He'd added a bouquet of flowers too, knowing that a woman likes to receive things that are fleeting as well as everlasting. I'd chuckled at her tales of adjusting to married life and was pleased to know that they worked on the kinks.

I'd never heard her this frantic.

"Lizzie, calm down. What's happened?"

"Fred's been complaining about his stomach hurting for the past week, but he didn't want to take time off work to go to the doctor. I thought it was what he ate at one of the pavilions, something he wasn't used to. This morning, he collapsed on the steamship. They're not sure what it is. The doctor there said… Oh, Mama, he looks awful, all pale and clammy and moaning. He's in so much pain!"

Tears thickened her voice.

"Dr. Alice is on her way?"

"Yes, yes, but you come too."

"We'll be there as fast as we can."

I rushed out to the barn where Frank sanded new stakes for my starts and told him to harness the horse, we had to go to Lizzie's. The zinnias had made their debut, dotting the greenery with yellows and pinks.

Frank dropped what he was doing to harness the horse, while I went back out to cut dahlias and the willowy cosmos for their purple color and a few of the zinnias, whose blooms would last a long time. I wrapped the stems in a damp cloth, finishing as Frank brought the buggy around from the side of the barn, and I stepped up into it.

"Now I wish we'd gone ahead and gotten that vehicle," I told Frank, "so we could get there faster." I lifted the flowers to my nose and inhaled, the aroma inviting an exhalation of prayer in the covered buggy. "She sounded so upset." I reassured myself. "Dr. Alice will have good words for them." I inhaled again. "It's probably minor. Food poisoning, maybe."

Frank looked at me. He knew me as someone who spoke the truth, but when it came to my children, I sought optimism even in the face of challenging facts. The sound of Lizzie's voice haunted.

I let my mind wander. The horse trotted along the Lewis River, which was running strong from spring freshets. Clumps of riverbank slipped into the water as the river looked to undercut the banks, the water moving ever closer to the road. I wondered if one day that road would just disappear, consumed by high water and the dredging done by the government to allow more and larger steamboats to come farther up the river. We watched a steamboat dock, and I could see the bank give way, ever so slightly, but it would happen with every steamer docking. So much good soil going to waste. I could do nothing about it now, but being incensed about it took my mind from my child's painful voice.

As we approached Lizzie and Fred's home, I noted Dr. Alice's car already there along with another buggy. Frank tied the horse to the picket fence and helped me out, and we rushed inside.

Fred's brother, Edmond, stood with Lizzie in the hallway.

"Lizzie." Frank opened his arms to our daughter.

She raised her eyes and moved her crying from Edmond's shoulder to her father's arms. Edmond's eyes were red too, and he rubbed at his nose, his eyes not wanting to make contact with any of us.

"So…how is he?" I laid the flowers on the table and removed my hat, scanning the room for the doctor.

"He's gone." Lizzie said.

Edmond nodded toward the bedroom, and I approached the door.

"Gone? You mean he's—"

Before I could knock, Dr. Alice stepped out, pulled the door shut behind her. She shook her head at my questioning eyes, hugged me briefly as she walked to Lizzie and Frank. "I'm so sorry, Lizzie," she said. "So sorry. Appendicitis. Must have burst a few days ago, and he's been fighting the infection ever since."

"If only he'd gone to see you when I told him!" Lizzie said, anger her first visitor in grief.

"Don't blame yourself," Dr. Alice said. "We never know with these things. It might well be that the first sign of the burst was when he mentioned the pain, and by then it would have been too late. I'm so sorry." She touched my daughter's shoulder, but let Lizzie's family be her comfort in this storm.

"Can't you do something?" I asked.

"Nothing, Mrs. Klager." To Lizzie, she said, "If you want to know for certain, I can perform an autopsy, but—"

"It won't bring him back," Lizzie wailed.

"No, it won't."

I opened my arms to take my daughter in, wrapping her with love scented with my garden's blooms. Her crying renewed, and I held her, prayed it would bring her relief, that I'd know what to do, what to say.

"I'll let Tom Chatterson know," Dr. Alice said, clearing her throat.

The sound of the undertaker's name was my trigger. "We can take care of things," I said, then asked, "Can't we?" Lizzie nodded, wiped at her eyes with the handkerchief I handed her. "Edmond, I'm so sorry. You'll let your parents know." He nodded, and I watched grief take hold of him, his only brother gone. "He'll lie in our parlor," I said. "I'll contact the reverend. The women's group will bring food. What's that girl's name with that lovely voice? She could—"

"Huldie—" Frank touched my shoulder.

"What? Things need to get done."

"In their own time." Frank pulled both his daughter and me into the steadiness of his arms. "Lizzie needs time," he said. He kissed the top of Lizzie's head, then mine. "She has to do this on her own."

I nodded. But what mother doesn't want to relieve her child of suffering? It was easier to bear my own loss of a mother and father than to watch my daughter endure the anguish of a lost friend, lover, husband. She'd turn twenty-five on July 6. So young to be widowed.

"Do you want me to let Delia know?" I asked her.

She nodded yes. "I tried to call but couldn't reach her. Jennie said she'd keep trying her."

I slipped from the safety of Frank's arms and went to the phone. I knew as soon as I put the call through that Jennie, the operator, would know, and so would the others on the line. But that was a good thing too, because neighbors could begin helping as they did: bringing food, doing chores; praying for Lizzie as they washed their dishes, fed their cows, dug in their gardens. People would come to sit with my daughter, speaking little, but being present. They'd do whatever they could; but nothing would bring Fred back.

Our new pastor, Angus Kenzie, performed the service. He spoke of a plant's cycle of life, from seed to sprout to bloom, then fading away to nurture the soil. I loved the image and thought I might return to it often as I helped my daughter grieve. He spoke of youth—Fred was but three years older than Lizzie—reminding us that death comes to all, and who is to say that a shorter life on this earth is any less abundant than one who has lived many years. Frank squeezed Lizzie's hand; I had my arm around her as she sat between us. We were two old stakes propping up our delicate sprout, hoping we'd be enough to bring her toward her next season of blooming.

TWENTY-THREE

A TIME FOR EVERYTHING

Hulda, 1905–1906

We invited Lizzie to move back in with us, but she said no. She had to find a way to live without Fred and returning to "grandpa's house," as she called it, would only delay that journey. Lizzie turned down an invitation to move in with Delia and Nell Irving too, which in a shameful way made me feel better about her declining to live with us. My daughter wanted to be strong, and I was proud of that; just disappointed that I couldn't buttress her when life's winds were clearly tossing her about.

Fortunately, Fred had purchased a small insurance policy, something people didn't always do in those days, giving Lizzie resources and time to make decisions about how to go on.

She had her garden and her music. As the days turned into weeks and months, I'd come by her house, and we'd garden together. After pulling weeds, it was time to harvest, to can beets and snap peas and pick apples and make sauce. We chopped cabbage for sauerkraut, the cabbage heads as big as basketballs and with fall, picked squash and pumpkins, some of which the neighborhood children used for their Halloween parties. Fritz helped pull the pumpkins and predicted an early winter from the cold autumn winds.

Her garden was bountiful, and she spoke one day as we stored potatoes in baskets in the shed behind their house about how strange it was that so much life should come from such a small plot of ground.

"It doesn't take a lot of space to grow enough to feed a family." I regretted in an instant that I'd brought up family. Delia had just told me that she carried a child due next July. She didn't know how to tell her sister and asked if I would. I'd put it off too.

"Delia has lovely news." I picked up a potato and studied it.

"What would that be?"

"She and Nell Irving are expecting."

I thought there was a hint of hesitation, but then she said, "Are they? Why didn't she say?"

"She didn't want to upset you."

She nodded. "I'm happy for her."

"I know you are. You can tell her that. She didn't want to—"

"Fred wanted a family, Mama. We just ran out of time."

"Yes, you did. You'll love again, you know."

Lizzie shook her head. "No, I think I'll be all right alone. I could take in a girl so she can attend school in town. But I'm not sure I could live through the death of another husband."

"Grief is the price we have to pay for loving," I said. "I hope one day you'll discover that it's worth it." I thought how easy it was for me to say that. I'd lost my parents but none other with whom I was close. Comforting Lizzie, I felt like I walked on lily pads and could sink to the bottom of the lake with one misstep. But at least she accepted the news of Delia's pregnancy well, and that's what I told Delia when I saw her later in the week.

Rains began in earnest in mid-October that year, 1905, the heavens crying with us for Lizzie's loss. Lizzie allowed us to be with her in her small home, but she never came to the farm. In late November she joined us at Delia and Nell Irving's for Delia's birthday celebration. I saw that as progress. Nell Irving had developed a cough with the rains, though I suspected barn mold. Frank often coughed in the winter months too. Lizzie smiled as Delia spoke of the baby and offered to sew up a baptismal gown, if she'd like. Delia was delighted. I heard Lizzie chuckle that evening at something her uncle Emil said, the lilt in her voice giving me hope.

As weeks wore on, it worried me that Lizzie still found reasons not to come to our home, not for Sunday dinner, not for celebrations. She visited her uncles and aunts, spent a weekend in Kelso with an old school chum, taking the stern-wheeler that Fred had worked on. But she had not entered our home since the day Fred was buried.

I told Frank of that concern as I brushed my long hair, then braided it before slipping beneath the quilts. The temperature had dropped below freezing, and I shivered beside my husband. "I wonder if the memories of Fred's courting, their sitting on the porch swing, brings too much pain," I said. "Even her wedding memories are woven into our home."

"It takes time, Hulda. Give her that. You're so patient with your plants. You just have to be patient with people." Frank yawned.

"I'm patient. It's been almost six months. I just want her back, the Lizzie I knew. She didn't talk about that stern-wheeler trip. Do you suppose that brought back bad memories of him getting sick? Or good memories of our family trip? What do you think, Frank? Good memories or bad?"

I spoke into silence, listening then to the even breathing of a man sound asleep.

"I submit good memories," I spoke for him. "I submit that's what you'd say if you'd stayed awake to speak, and one day those memories will bring her comfort. They must."

In the spring of 1906, I came by Lizzie's after shopping in town. We had tea. I told her they'd begun construction on the railroad that would run between us and the Columbia

River, with a big dike built up to run the track on. I'd sold them the right of way three years before. "We'll be craning our necks to see the cars when they roll on by us," I said. "That roadbed will be fifteen feet high." But I thought the train bed could well keep out the Columbia River water when it rose, too, and I hoped my lilac bushes would be tall enough by then to block any ugly view of transportation progress. We'd still have to weather the annual high water from the Lewis River to our east in a wet year.

"That'll change your view, won't it?"

"I suppose. We won't be able to see all the way to the Columbia from the upstairs window, but change is inevitable," I told her. "Oh, here, I brought you this." I handed her a store-bought bar of soap that she sniffed.

"Lavender."

I thought she winced at the scent. What was I thinking? She'd carried lavender on her wedding day.

"Ruthie's mother makes soap too, but these came from Seattle. I like the heart shape, don't you?" I cursed myself again for my mention of hearts. "Can I fry up an egg or two for us for an early supper?" She shook her head no.

She stood, and I saw that her clothes hung from her frame like a dishtowel over the back of a chair, shoulders so bony.

"You should go home, fix supper for Papa and Martha and Fritz. While it's still light out."

"Oh, they're fine with my being here with you. Fritz does

his homework by lamplight, so I suspect he doesn't mind eating by it. And after I clean up, there's just enough time to do a little quilting or look at my seed catalogs before bed. I'm still reading the material I picked up at the fair." It seemed that everything I said today could be a fuse to a painful explosion.

"I'm so glad we did that, Mama, went to the exhibits and all. You can't know."

"Are you? Good." I brushed a curl off of her face, as I did when she was young. "Good memories are essential when we've lost someone. After your grandma Thiel died, I couldn't even garden, my heart was so empty. Your father helped me out by reminding me of little things we'd done together: wash eggs, shuck corn, boil rhubarb into sauce until I thought I'd faint. She always whipped up soups and took them to neighbors whenever there was need. And she told wonderful stories, like about her mother and the flannel-wearing geese."

"Oh yes, when she'd plucked them all thinking they were dead, and they were just under the influence of mash. I can just see her sewing up red flannel to get them through the winter." She sighed. Even that image didn't bring relief.

"I'll always remember Fred sitting on that porch swing at our old house," I said. "How shy he was about putting his arm around your shoulders."

"You and Papa were staring out the window!" From the icebox, she took an eggless cake I'd made and brought over earlier in the week. We often had to cook without eggs through the winter until the chickens took the spring light to heart and started doing what they were supposed to and began laying again.

"Yes, we did watch. It was our duty."

She smiled then.

"And I appreciated his help in the garden the year I was so sick. Oh, I know he came to be closer to you, but I did like the effort he put into the mulching."

She laughed at that, then fiddled with her fork. "It's been nice, your visiting these past months, Mama. I know you've had to neglect your garden."

"It's what a mother does." I'd stopped asking her to come to the farm, as doing so brought a rush of tears pooling in her brown eyes.

"It's taken me some time, Mama, and I'll need more, I know. I have good memories. But what I lost were the dreams Fred and I had together."

I imagined for a moment—just a moment—the emptiness I'd feel if I outlived Frank. We'd accomplished so much of our dreams—to have a family, to work side by side on the land, to give to our community. We had more things to do, and I thanked God we were still well enough to do them.

"The best way for me to help Fred live on is for me to do those things." She looked out the window of their kitchen, and I felt her leaving me, going away. "We were going to travel to New York or London or even Shanghai."

"It'll be different, but you can still feel his hand at your elbow, helping you along, by accepting what the rest of us want to give you."

She turned to look at me. "Those are perfect words to say to a woman's grieving heart."

My face grew warm. I was pleased to have brought comfort to my daughter.

But then I wondered if she prepared me for a journey away from us, that her distance from the farm these past months was prelude to a longer separation that might take her to the real Shanghai, away from Woodland forever, because the memories here eclipsed her soul. My heart pounded.

"I've something to ask." I held my breath. This was it. The last leaf to fall from the branch. "Could I come to the farm tomorrow and help you winterize the garden, dig up the tulip bulbs, spread straw over the plots?"

"What? Did I hear you right? Do you think you're ready?" Oh, what a foolish thing to say! "Yes! Yes, of course. I...I thought you might never. I mean, it seemed you've been avoiding it."

She nodded. "I have been. But the lavender soap made me realize I can't ignore the past. I have to incorporate it, breathe it in, then take it with me. 'There is a time to weep and a time to laugh.' Isn't that in Scripture?"

"Ecclesiastes," I said.

Her smile wasn't as wide as a rhododendron bloom but more beautiful. "Well, I think it's time to start laughing again," she said. "Besides, I want to breathe on the rhodies, make them bloom, and I want to see how the purple lilac crosses are coming. It's been too long since I've looked at the apples of my mother's eyes."

"That would be you." I squeezed her hand across the table. "And Delia and Martha and Fritz and your father. Don't let my time with those blooms ever convince you differently."

I hummed to the horse on my way home. It was Lizzie's rhodies and the lavender that would bring her back, and that was as it should be. A loved garden blooms hope above all.

Twenty-Four

Ruth

1906

Ruth's figure, even at thirteen, was like an hourglass with too much sand. All the Klagers were tall people, shaped straight as porch posts. Ruth was stocky. Her father used the word, and it made her feel like the pony who ripped at grass in the Johnson's field when she walked by to take her piano lessons. Stocky. Still, she had the strength to carry the buckets all day, if necessary, and some days it was. Mrs. Klager had a million bushes and bulbs. Well, maybe not a million, but enough to fill two circus tents, not that Ruth had ever been to a circus, but she'd seen the tents in the distance.

What she loved about the Klagers is that they listened when she spoke up, which wasn't often. If she followed Mrs. Klager's directions for the day, she was left alone in silence to do her work. She loved the feel of earth in her palms and never minded putting cuttings into piles or later loading them by the armful into the wheelbarrow. She could eavesdrop, being curious without being nosy. No one asked her what she was thinking or suggested there was anything wrong with her silence. At first Mrs. Klager dictated her rules, but soon there was no stern, only serene. This garden of the Klagers was the safest place she'd ever been.

A place of refuge was worth the grilling she endured when she returned home on the weekends. Her father worried that she was being "shaped" in ways that took her from Scripture.

"We never speak about religion," Ruth told him the very first weekend after she'd stayed with the Klagers. Her father had consented to her living at the garden only because the teacher at Martin's Bluff had gotten married at Christmas, and they hadn't yet replaced her. Ruth's mother insisted Ruth be allowed to continue her studies in Woodland, and her father had given in.

"Maybe not overtly." Her father pointed his fork, with a piece of ham stuck on it, directly at her. She decided she'd have to ask Miss Martha what *overtly* meant. She certainly wasn't going to ask her father. "Do you talk with her about how she changes those flowers, how she can do it better than God did, eh?" Her father glanced at her mother, and Ruth noticed that her mother's face was the color of roses.

"She says we are created in God's image, and that means our interest in how things work is normal, necessary even. You bring sheep into the yard to keep the weeds down, but they weren't weeds before you built the house. They were pretty wildflowers."

"What are you saying? You have these conversations?"

Ruth swallowed. "She's unlocking secrets, and doesn't Scripture say there is 'nothing new under the sun'? She's just trying to find what's already there."

"Finding out what's already there." He grunted.

The Klagers didn't speak much about pollination and whatnot, but one day as Mrs. Klager hummed a tune, Ruth said, "You like flowers as I like music."

"Yes, I guess that's so." Butterflies dipped and fluttered around the woman as much as her plants. "How are your piano lessons coming? I hear you practice at school, during your recesses."

Ruth shrugged. Her father decided he didn't want her at the Presbyterian church anymore. She was grateful he still let Miss Lizzie instruct her and that her schoolteacher allowed her to remain inside to practice her scales while other students played Pom-Pom-Pull-Away outside. Ruth dreamed that one day she'd play on a stage in front of a pyramid of seats, filled with people brought close by the notes she played. Imagining the pyramid shape of a stadium gave her pleasure, and she knew that the dream was worth the cost of schoolgirl teasing if they eavesdropped on her practices. And maybe, just maybe, her father might one day find in her the shape of a child worth listening to.

Mrs. Klager didn't push further on the subject. Nelia

might have told her that she practiced during recess, but it didn't matter. The woman accepted her shrug.

There'd been changes in the two years that she'd been helping the Klagers, the most recent being the day Miss Lizzie returned. Everyone joked and laughed when the daughter carried in her suitcase, and Fritz—such a nice-looking boy, that Fritz—brought in a trunk of personal items from the house Miss Lizzie had sold. The sun shone on all the glassy green lilac leaves shaped like spears. It was a sunny February day. Miss Delia visited too. She was the shape of a snowman, as she was just starting to show she carried a baby. Her husband, Nell Irving, was still ill, and he'd been told to rest. Delia said he might have to go away to a sanitarium to get his coughing under control. Edmond Wilke, Lizzie's brother-in-law and a nice-looking man, tall with broad shoulders, helped Delia milk her cows now that she was pregnant.

Ruth brought in a bag of Lizzie's shoes and belts from the wagon and carried them upstairs. Ruth and Nelia had already moved their own things out of the north bedroom into the smaller room across the hall. Nelia had been living there for the past year too. Fritz would live in the barn tack room. He'd share the building with the horse and the men when they gathered for their liquor and smokes on Saturday night. Martha and Lizzie would settle into the north bedroom, while the senior Klagers continued to occupy the south. Ruth didn't mind the change, but she wondered how Martha felt about not having her own room when she'd had it for almost two years.

"You girls stop and have a rest," Mrs. Klager told Ruth and Nelia. They'd been digging up a new bed for more lilac cultivars. "There's still plenty to do, you know. But we all need little breaks now and then."

"Yes ma'am," Ruth said. Nelia nodded.

"Your father's coming by at five, isn't he, Ruth?" Ruth hadn't known this, and a lump the shape of a rock grew in her throat. Maybe they didn't need her anymore with Miss Lizzie back home. She wondered if Nelia was worried. She looked over at the dark-haired girl with a hair ribbon the shape of a wide smile. She was in the process of talking Mrs. Klager into a cup of hot chocolate. Ruth would have preferred the cocoa herself, but it never occurred to her to ask for it. She lived with the philosophy that if she didn't expect anything good to happen to her, she would never be disappointed and she'd occasionally have a nice surprise. Like her parents allowing her to work for the Klagers and now stay with them too, except on weekends. But what did Mrs. Klager want with her father?

The afternoon pulled taut as a rope holding a ship to the Pekin dock as Ruth waited for her father to appear. When he did, Ruth stood straight, prepared for the worst.

"I'd like to speak with him in private," Mrs. Klager told her. "Would you please wait a moment before joining us?"

Ruth wiped her wet fingers on her wool skirt and watched as Mrs. Klager approached her father.

Mrs. Klager would invite him in, and her father would refuse.

Ruth heard the horse stomp at the buggy, wiggle his flank to annoy the flies, and then Mrs. Klager stepped aside and motioned to Fritz, who signaled his father and several other men who had been working on the railroad line going in behind the Klagers' house. Ruth wasn't sure why the men were needed now, since the buckboard with Miss Lizzie's things stood empty at last.

But now another wagon rattled around from behind the barn. Ruth squinted, stared. Could that be? A piano!

The tall, black rectangle bumped along in the wagon, pulling up outside the picket fence. "Good thing it has wheels on it." Fritz winked at Ruth and she blushed, even though he often winked at her and Nelia. They were like sisters to him.

He and the other men, Mrs. Klager's brother and Frank and Edmond, helped too. The Tesches, from Martin's Bluff, and their oldest boys put two boards up to make a ramp be-hind the wagon. Then with grunts and groans and cautions of "Don't split your gut" or "Hang on to it!" the men began to push the piano down the makeshift wagon ramp.

The piano, with its white, smiling rectangular teeth rolled along the path toward the house, digging up bark chips with its weight. Ruth stood off to the side.

"Close your mouth," her father said. She hadn't been

aware that he'd stepped inside the yard and stood beside her, watching the piano parade. "Not ladylike to look as though you've lost your wits." Then he added, "I've lost mine letting that woman bring a piano right to her doorstep and bringing the teacher to you too."

Ruth turned to him. "Mrs. Klager isn't upset with me?"

"Why would you think that, eh? No. Mrs. Klager wants you to practice here evenings and to have your recesses free for playing and talking or whatever it is young girls do, or so she tells me. And your lessons are to be here. Seems Mrs. Klager wants to learn to play, so that expands your piano teacher's duties. Letting you have lessons here is a favor I'm granting. She says it's a mighty help. I imagine before long that other girl"—he nodded toward Nelia—"will take up the instrument as well. She'll have a regular music school here." He growled, but Ruth could tell he wasn't all that upset. Her father cleared his throat, then turned his head to spit.

"The woman could negotiate with the fire and talk it out of burning." He looked at Ruth who bore a confused expression. "She's gonna pay for your lessons, eh?" He stuffed his hands in his pockets. "A frugal man can hardly turn that down."

She couldn't believe her good fortune. She'd remember this day, and she promised herself in the future she would look for the shape of hope in her life instead of the shape of disappointment.

TWENTY-FIVE

PLANTING FOR THE FUTURE

Hulda, 1906

Dear Mrs. Klager,

Thank you so much for your kindness in responding to my naive questions about the nature of gardening. My readers were so pleased with your comments about a garden having a spirit of its own. This proved quite an encouragement to at least one Sacramento resident who had wondered whether a garden could thrive even if its caretaker only watered the plants when the spirit moved her. Another was pleased with your answer about plowing and how good and regular mulching can prevent the need to hire a horse and plow master.

I must tell you that this year, for the first time, I planted a small box garden on my back porch. Just a few tomato plants and a row of lettuce. I planted pansy seeds and look forward to their happy colorful faces greeting me on a morning.

As spring brings new questions, please know how grateful I am to have a competent source of answers so that my readers will not be led astray. Also, should you care to receive a copy of the column, to ensure that I in no way misquote your guidance, I would be happy to send it to you. Again, thank you for your generous assistance.

Yours sincerely,

Cornelia Givens, Columnist

I felt guilty receiving such accolades from Miss Givens when all I did was write a letter to her now and then, answering her questions. I liked the writing part but the real thrill was helping people become better acquainted with the landscape they surrounded themselves with. It also gave me courage to write again to Luther Burbank.

I'd sent the latest letter before Lizzie moved back with us, which was good because once she arrived, my days were focused on making her comfortable here and preparing for the spring rush that my dear plantings required. I pushed the season by planting dozens of seeds in my sun porch, taking great pleasure in checking several times a day to see how a thin line pressing against the dirt ever so carefully would unfold, curling open to a nubbin of green, and make me squeal, inviting Ruth and Nelia to "Come see!" They tired of this after a bit, and that's when I decided to write to Mr. Burbank to ask about his work with roses and lilacs. He'd responded kindly, treating me as someone with knowledge this time, which I appreciated. But he also told me that his greater interest was in hybridizing plants that would help feed the world. I felt a little put down by that, as though working with flowers was a frivolous task. He might not have meant that, but it's how I took it.

Still, I wrote back, after a reasonable pause. I didn't want to presume on his time. I told him of my lilac passion and mentioned something I hadn't told even Frank: I had a dream that people would one day come to Woodland to see my lilacs, and I'd not only share my garden with them—just as people came to visit Mr. Burbank's Experimental Farm in Santa Rosa—but I'd give them starts of my new varieties and spread beauty to a wider world. Perhaps that thought went beyond my station, but sharing my garden truly added a dimension to the hybridizing. I suspected that was so for Mr. Burbank too.

Mr. Burbank wasted no time in responding to me:

My dear Mrs. Klager,

Your generous spirit is admirable, but you must also consider your purse. Selling to a nursery or two so that your varieties—should you stumble onto one—

will bring in a measure of income will not only please your husband no doubt, but it will also enable you to give flowers away, as you choose to do. Nursery sales extend the outcome of your painstaking work to new markets where you will discover from gardeners in other climes just how well your varieties travel. This will compound the work we do in ways that individually giving a start here and there simply cannot. I give visitors various starts myself, but then I receive thousands of visitors each year, something I suspect will not be the case in your little Woodland. Our work is worthy of its pay, Mrs. Klager. Do not underestimate your efforts.

I read that last line, "Do not underestimate your efforts," and yet right before that, it seemed he had underestimated mine. His words stung. I might not have thousands come to see my garden, but that didn't prevent me from imagining it.

March roared in with heavy rain and spits of snow and hail, the latter threatening to shred the rhododendron leaves on the more than a dozen bushes I'd planted in strategic places throughout the garden. With the rain and cold pelleting the sun-porch windows, I drew a garden plot plan, deciding where I'd move what plants, where I'd transplant the seed starts from my sun-porch nursery. This was a hopeful time, knowing I'd soon have hands in dirt, and blossoms would brighten the garden and my world. I liked having Lizzie back home. She seemed happy. She liked talking with Ruth and Nelia in the evening; she and Martha baked together, and I often heard laughter from the room next-door when Frank and I prepared for bed. I didn't like Fritz living in the tack room, but it was all fixed up nice for a young man, and he had books on steamboats that Lizzie had given him from Fred's collection. Fritz said he liked the privacy without hearing all the "giggling girls." Frank said he had pictures of girls up on his wall. I didn't ask for details of how he'd gotten them or of what they might look like. I never went in there.

My chicks were all settled on an afternoon, with Lizzie stitching, Martha teaching, and the girls and Fritz in school. Delia had looked healthy when we'd moved Lizzie back home. When we saw them at church on Sunday—well, just Delia came because Nell Irving had been moved to a sanitarium. She said how glad she was that her morning sickness had moved on to another poor pregnant soul. But I could tell she was worried about Nell Irving.

"A sanitarium?" Fritz said.

"Nell Irving is doing better, I think." Delia didn't use the dreaded word *phthisis* and covered her worry by saying, "It's a better place for him to get well. I hate it that I can't see him now. They're worried about me getting ill or the baby, so it'll be a bit before we can speak face to face. But by the time the baby's due in July, he'll be back. I'm sure of it."

I didn't tell her that the Presbyterian church had discontinued communion with a common cup after Nell Irving became ill. I hoped he hadn't contracted the disease there, but so far no one else had become ill with tuberculosis.

As a family, we walked with her to the buggy she'd driven to town. "How's Edmond doing with the milking?" Fritz asked. "I could come do that for you, if you want."

"Fine. Edmond used to help Bertha and Carl, you know." Delia shrugged. "He's good conversation over coffee before he leaves for his work and someone to cook a light supper for when he finishes the evening chores."

"Just so you know," Fritz told her. "I'd help."

She hugged her younger brother and brushed at his hair. "Don't you have a girl to court to keep you occupied?"

He blushed, looked sideways at me. "Mama frowns on me courting much until I'm old enough to vote, I guess."

I thought of our Sunday afternoon conversation as I worked on my garden plan. I surely hoped Delia was right about her husband's health. I'd heard of lots of people coming back from sanitariums, and I prayed Nell Irving would be yet another. I'd plant a flowering crab-apple tree near the gate in honor of his homecoming. I'd written to cheer him. It was a small thing I could do. With the Lemoine-bred lilacs looking good, perhaps I'd name a new variety for him. I planned to name my new varieties for special friends and family, when the time came. But right now, a flowering crab would give an array of color year-round but begin each spring with those vibrant pink blossoms that always spoke of good health to me: a blend of beauty, robustness, and sweet fragrance, all in one!

That's what I was doing when the phone rang, drawing a circle on my plot plan to mark that tree. The brazen sounds of two long rings and two short ones still caused me to jump a foot.

"I'll get it," Lizzie said.

I heard her cheery voice say, "Hi, Delia." A pause then, "Are you crying? What's wrong?" followed by silence, then, "No, no. Oh, Delia, no."

"What is it?" I rose from the sun porch and stepped up into the dining room. "Is it the baby? What's happened?" I was beginning to dislike that phone machine always bringing bad news.

Lizzie gripped the mouthpiece of the contraption. "We'll come right now. Oh, Delia, what can I say?" A pause and then, "We'll be there soon."

Lizzie's face was white when she hung the receiver up on its holder. She still gripped the mouthpiece as though if she released it, she'd collapse.

"What? Is it the baby?"

Lizzie shook her head, tears already tracking down her

pale cheeks. "It's Nell Irving, Mama. He's...he just died. Of tuberculosis."

My breath escaped. I sank to the chair, my eye drawn to the calendar hanging on the wall. It was from the Domestic Sewing Machine Company. A mother oversees a daughter's work on the newest machine, offering guidance and protection to the child. Protection. I looked at the date. March 8, 1906. Not even a year since our family moved as one to grieve with Lizzie so exposed and unprotected from a terrible loss. Hurt came without protection from any earthly source, no matter how much we loved.

"I...I can't believe that Delia...and you...widows... Both my girls..." I couldn't seem to finish a thought. "Come." I opened my arms. Lizzie fell into them, the call from her sister renewing the wounds from the loss of her Fred.

"Oh, Mama. Delia's going to hurt so much!"

"I know, I know." I patted her back. No words formed. A sister's ache was different than a mother's, but no less painful; no less deep a hole to fill.

"Call your father," I said after a time. "He's at the creamery talking to Mr. Reed about the latest report. Tell him we'll harness the buggy and pick up Fritz from school on the way to Delia's. We'll let Martha know at her classroom."

Lizzie nodded, wiped at her face with a lace-edged handkerchief. She turned to the phone, and I stepped outside. People needed tasks in grief, and I was good at giving them but less wise at finding distracting work for myself. Tears swelled in my throat. The air felt clear and fresh with scuddy clouds chased away by spinning winds. Cranes chattered toward the Columbia while I longed for a breeze to blow away Delia's loss, our loss, the absolute helplessness I felt. I was old, so old, and yet none the wiser for how to give my daughter and her baby the strength they'd need in the months ahead.

The horse was gentle and took well to the harness. Lizzie came out to help me finish, and then I scanned the yard. It was too early for my tree peonies with their flashy blooms. Tulips weren't up yet. A few lavender crocuses stood at attention. We'd planted them on Fred Wilke's grave. I didn't want them to be a reminder for Delia. I snipped three daffodils with their yellow heads, not yet in full array, but at least they offered bright color. A sweet aroma as I passed the shady side of the house caught my nose. I planned to leave my apron and don my hat, but instead I marched to the bush that had begun blooming on Valentine's Day, pulled the clipper from my apron again and snipped some of the pink-throated, alabaster blooms. I pushed my nose into the flowers and inhaled. Once long ago Frank had brought me a corsage of daphnes, when first he came to court me. I was so young, so uncertain. But Frank made me laugh, and he promised he would be there with me always. If I lost him, what would I do?

My throat opened with the aroma of daphnes, and the tears found their way to escape. I thought of Nell Irving and

Delia's baby. That poor child who would never know his father. I inhaled again and breathed out a silent prayer. *Have I done enough to protect my children? Have I covered them like I would a plant threatened by a late-season frost? Two of my daughters, widows. Are You trying to tell me something? Have I not listened?* I hadn't brought a handkerchief, so I wiped my face with my apron, then cradled the blue and yellow blooms in my arm.

"Let's go, Mama," Lizzie said.

I went inside, put the flowers in a Ball jar with water, removed my apron, settled the hat onto my head, and grabbed my coat. The mist was familiar as air and nothing requiring an umbrella.

I handed the jar of flowers to Lizzie. I inhaled once more.

"The flowers will have to be the cheer today. And many a day ahead as well," Lizzie said.

TWENTY-SIX

SHELLY

1906

At first, Shelly looked forward to the horticulture meetings merely as respite from her mother-in-law's dominance. Soon, the camaraderie of the women and their enthusiasm for all things horticultural won Shelly over. Oh, Bill had enjoyed making her his student in the greenhouse, but at these meetings, she found a different kind of eagerness and perhaps competition for creating the most fragrant garden or choosing plants that attracted the most butterflies or hummingbirds. Shelly had her own ideas about a certain kind of garden plot, and she'd even picked out the section of the green lawn on their estate that would house the first one. But the occasion that would begin her garden campaign had not arisen. She still had not conceived. She was saddened by that and discouraged, deeply, an emotion she could not share with Bill as it was too revealing of the loss within her life.

At a meeting in May of 1906, the entire club had been invited to tour the gardens on the Hampton estate and view the exotic plants heiress Eliza Ridgely had brought back from her world travels. It was to be a two-day event, with the women riding in an autobus and spending the night at an inn in Towson, Maryland, just north of Baltimore where the estate lauded over the surrounding countryside. Shelly had never ridden in an autobus. Anticipation mixed with anxiety framed her morning.

As they waited for the vehicle to arrive, Shelly considered her mother-in-law and her pervasive influence over Bill. The woman couldn't see that her son liked spending his weeks away in Annapolis just to avoid his mother. At least that was Shelly's belief. His mother didn't even call him Bill, his preferred name. He was always "William" to her, with an uplift at the end as though his name was just the beginning of a request, which it usually was. "William? Would you please bring me that lap robe? You know how cool it is in the evening" or "William? Don't forget to take the documents to the attorney, you do remember I asked you to do that today." And on it went.

The horticulture meetings were one of the few places Shelly was able to attend without her mother-in-law beside her—or often between her and Bill. At fine restaurants, Bill sat beside his mother to assist her, of course. The woman was a tactician who could plant a twelve-foot tree by herself but had Bill convinced she might need help lifting her silver spoon to her mouth at supper. *Egad, egad!* Shelly thought but would never say in front of Bill or his mother. She sipped her soup quietly and dreamed of someday having a child whom she'd raise differently than Bill had been raised.

Thank goodness the two-day trip had kept her mother-in-law behind. Shelly made certain of that by emphasizing the difficulties they might face, not being certain of the roads, having to stay at an unknown inn, and the possibility of bedbugs.

Shelly's plan to leave her mother-in-law at home had caused a bit of friction with Bill. "She lived alone in that house before I married you," Shelly said.

"But she was younger then. Now she's frail."

"Perhaps we should all move to Annapolis, then, where you can come home to us each evening. Every evening."

"And leave the gardens here? The thing she loves?"

Of course not, Shelly thought but didn't say. She didn't say a lot she wanted to.

Shelly waited to hear the growling of the autobus. Instead, only the soft voices of the other women interrupted the birdsong. Her friends wore big hats with feathers that drooped like yesterday's wash on the line. In the threesome that included Shelly near the corner of the library, conversation bubbled up as the younger women conversed about the "Hill of Difficulty" article Margaret Sangster had written in the latest issue of *Woman's Home Companion*. "To climb such a hill of living," the columnist wrote, "we cannot shirk the duty of standing on our own two feet while lending a hand to our neighbors and lifting a little ourselves, if we are to occupy the place God means us to, and do our part in service to the age in which we live." Shelly liked the article very much and was surprised the *Companion* had printed it, as they were generally a traditional magazine not entertaining ideas that might offend the men of a household.

On the other hand, "standing on your own two feet" could be considered quite radical, and to a number of women in the Maryland Horticulture Society, Baltimore chapter, it was. Shelly awaited the Letters section next month, as she was sure there'd be wisdom falling like timbers on the editors. Mothers, Shelly decided, were vigilant; at the very least Maryland mothers were.

"We're a smaller group than usual," Mavis noted that May morning as she looked around. Often twenty-five or thirty joined in the monthly gathering, many more when they had exhibits hoping to attract new members. Mavis was a matron with a wart on her chin that was difficult to ignore until one spent time with her and appreciated her intellect and goodwill enough to distract from the facial flaw.

"Their husbands might not have been as enthusiastic as ours," Beatrice noted.

"Or they lacked proper negotiating skills," Shelly said.

"My husband wasn't all that enamored with my going, but I guilted him into letting me."

"Guilted him?" Mavis turned to her friend. "What sort of word is that?"

"A very useful one," Shelly trilled. "Very useful. Oh, he knows what I'm doing when I ruffle his hair and tell him how sad I am that he's always leaving me during the week to work, and then on the weekends, he has this 'other woman' he devotes his time to."

"His mother." Mavis patted Shelly's gloved hand resting on an umbrella she might later need for shade.

"No, his lilacs. He's always out there in the garden, and even when I'm right beside him in the greenhouse, he speaks more to the cultivars than to me. I call them 'the other women,' and out of guilt, he lets me do things he otherwise might not or that his mother finds foolish. Like this trip. Especially this trip."

"I know a woman or two who secure fine jewelry out of their husbands' guilt." Beatrice was closer to Shelly's age and was without children too. The three of them formed a cluster at the horticultural events.

"We're standing on our own two feet," Mavis said, bringing them back to the article by Margaret Sangster. "Being here, doing what we feel is necessary for our survival."

"How does a woman actually do that?" Shelly'd been trying to strike out on her own as a wife, but it took enormous energy just to disagree with Minnie Snyder about a table serving. The interactions wore her down. If only she could have given Bill a child by now. She would have gained credibility with her mother-in-law and had a purpose in her life. "I sometimes feel lost in my efforts to stand on my own." Shelly sighed.

"As do we all." Mavis shaded her eyes with her hands, looking for the autobus.

Her companions quieted, allowing the noise of the engine of the approaching vehicle to fill the summer morning. Mavis fanned herself. Beatrice loosened the button at her neck.

"Margaret Sangster says, 'Pluck counts more than luck,'" Shelly said.

"Did you see where she advised one young woman to consider pet-stock breeding as a way to earn a living? Angora cats were mentioned." Beatrice had a slight lisp that caused Shelly to listen carefully whenever she spoke.

"Does the world need more cats?" Mavis asked. "I should think that to help one's neighbors while standing on one's own two feet would mean more than the nurturing of cats or thoroughbred dogs. I'd say a leader more like—"

"Mrs. Edward Gilchrist Low."

"Who?" Shelly furrowed her brow. The name was unfamiliar to her.

"Imagine, starting a school of your own like that." Beatrice shook her head in wonder, and the ostrich feather fluttered at her face.

"What school?" Shelly said.

"Oh, it's a landscape architecture school, for women."

"Truly?" Shelly turned away from the approaching bus to stare at her friend. "Where?"

"Massachusetts. Their graduates travel about and consult on the great estates as well as smaller gardens. I suspect at the Hampton estate we'll see evidence of the Lowthorpe School." Mavis seemed well informed. "Imagine bringing beauty into the lives of others like that."

"And getting to travel and work with interesting people. From all over the country. Even Europe," Beatrice mused.

"Yes, imagine." The autobus pulled up in front of their meeting site. The driver stepped out. Their club leader scuttled to the front of the group and explained what would happen next, asking people to be calm. Calm would be difficult for Shelly, for she'd just had an epiphany, her anxiety no longer related to transportation but rather pushing her toward a plan to stand on her own.

The three women ducked their heads and hats as they stepped up into the vehicle. Shelly's feet felt light at this new adventure as she made her way down the aisle, glad she didn't have to manage a bustle as well as her carpetbag.

A school for women interested in landscape architecture. Shelly had hoped to design a garden when she had her first child and after that for each milestone of the child's life: the day she started school, her first pony ride ribbon, her first grade of Superior, her first formal dance. It would be more than simply planting a tree or plant to honor someone; it would be a story of a life, told in flowers. A story of her child's life.

But none of those gardens would occur without the child, and it looked like that wasn't going to happen. She had lost two babies. She was barren.

The idea of designing gardens for others—consulting with a mother to create her stepping-stone landscapes in honor of her child's growing—might be how she'd create and wash away the fruitless part of her existence.

"Isn't this fun?" Beatrice settled into a seat.

"It surely is." Shelly selected a leather seat facing the aisle.

"I wonder what we'll take away from this trip," Mavis said. "I always try to bring something back to use in my garden."

"I've already found my wisdom," Shelly said. "Now I just have to make it happen." Make it happen, indeed.

TWENTY-SEVEN

PLANTING TRUST

Hulda, 1906

After the funeral, Dr. Alice told me that for a time we'd all have to be watched to be sure there were no early signs of that dreaded tuberculosis disease, since we'd all had time with Nell Irving before he went to the sanitarium. Some of us could be carriers and give it to others without our ever becoming sick ourselves. I thought that a double evil of a disease, making every one wary and watching one another every time someone sneezed over a hydrangea or magnolia bloom.

I was tired of grieving, tired of all it took to make sense of the vagaries of life. A terrible earthquake had struck San Francisco in April, and the churches in town had worked together to send bandages and medicine to that troubled community. I was grateful we had no relatives there, for there was distress enough right in our house. Lizzie's ache had returned with her sister's loss, and Delia, always quick to find a cheerful solution to a problem, couldn't find the route to calm. The Lewis River flooded, and I had a change of grief by directing Frank and Fritz to build log rafts.

"Rafts?" Frank washed at the sink. "For what?"

"We're going to pull the lilacs and put them on the rafts until the water goes down. Tie the rafts to the trees."

"Pull them up by the roots, Ma?" Fritz said. "Won't that kill them?"

"No. It'll stress them, but it will also save them. We'll have to replant."

I knew it meant much work, but physical labor was good for the heartache pushing against my ribs. The rafts were built, and they worked, my lilacs like fragile children huddling on a churning sea as the rafts bumped against the tree trunks. The water receded, and the sun came out, so that before long, even the daphne, a plant that abhors wet soil, perked up. But still, I could not convince Delia that she should come home, that her baby should be born closer to the doctor's office, not way out there on her farm. Frank brought a load of aged manure from the pasture on the Bottoms, and we mulched it in with the garden earth. We were replanting the lilacs when Ruth's father, Barney Reed, stopped by to pick up Ruth for the weekend.

"Fair amount of work you have to do then, eh?"

"We saved the lilacs, though, Papa." Ruth pointed to the log rafts now stacked beside the potting shed.

"God gives us challenges to shape our ways," he said.

"And he gives us new blooms each spring as a reminder He's always with us," I countered. While I agreed with him, I didn't want him suggesting that those challenges were any more than a flood in spring or a neighbor's horses running through the lilacs.

Barney nodded, but he chewed on his mustache, so I knew he had other thoughts. He adjusted his glasses.

"We should go, Papa. Mrs. Hulda has a lot of work to do." I heard the horse at Barney's buggy stomp its impatience and noticed Ruth's subtle urging of her father to leave.

"You've had a fair number of sad challenges in these past years since you've been messing with creation." Barney adjusted his glasses.

"All part of learning new things. Nothing troubling about that."

"Maybe. Or maybe you're being taught a lesson."

"About hybridizing? Oh yes, I'm learning a great deal about patience and persistence, keeping good records that my husband helps with and my girls. We've had a good time together, making this garden a place where people come now and again to be reminded of the refreshment creation brings. Not to mention the lessons of weeding before it gets out of hand or how each season requires new things of us."

"The Bible teaches that gardens are places for wrestling with temptation, Mrs. Klager."

"Oh, snakes are good things in a garden. They get after the insects and gophers."

I wished Ruth would leave, as I didn't want to argue with her father in front of her. I wasn't sure how long I could keep my happy chatter voice, especially when each evening I wrestled with whether my fervor for lilacs, for "messing with creation," might have brought on the pain my children suffered from.

"Mama will be waiting." Ruth touched her father's arm crossed over his chest.

"Suffering happens for a reason, Mrs. Klager. You best discover why it might be happening for you." Ruth tugged at his sleeve, and they left.

The man infuriated. I fairly burned my hoe up the rest of the day, chopping at crab grass, bending instead of squatting to pull weeds, making myself suffer, as though that would remove Barney's words and their echo of my own. It did trouble me that so powerful a God would let bad things happen. And I often did learn something when a tragedy struck. But did I have to suffer to learn the lesson?

"Will you be out here all night?" Frank stepped out onto the porch. "Lizzie put a plate back for you. She makes a good meat loaf."

"I wanted to finish this plot, get it ready for the annuals."

"No. You've got a bee under your bonnet. What is it?" He came beside me, touched my shoulder.

We could hear frogs croaking and cooing of doves settling in for the night.

"Oh, Frank, Barney Reed... He just said out loud what I've been wondering myself, and yet I can't believe that God would make Lizzie and Delia and their husbands' families too, and us, suffer just because I'm interested in lilacs and propagating and hybridizing. I can't believe that doing what I have a gift for cuts against God's grain. Do I care too much about the garden? Have I ignored my family? Is that why Delia won't come stay with us?"

He took the hoe and led me to the swing on the porch.

"I submit those are questions for the reverend, not for me. Why do those we love have to die while we go on living? Can't answer that, Huldie. It just seems to be what is. But I do know that your crisp apples keep reminding me that God gave you all the materials and the inclination and willingness to persist. Can't see that as divine defiance. It's a gift, and you'd be defying God if you ignored it. That's what I submit."

Could I have loved Frank more at that moment? I vowed to remember as much of our conversation as I could, especially when thoughts of uncertainty snuck in like snakes in the grass.

I renewed my efforts to convince Delia to come home and to appreciate more my shrubs and the joy they gave me. Lizzie and I made planting notes in my book that Frank rewrote in legible form. I checked the tin labels and compared them to what I observed or witnessed in the lilac nursery as I'd come to think of the rows and rows of plantings. Several of the shrubs were over four feet high, and I had hundreds of starts to pollinate.

In June, blooms and fragrance permeated the yard, the neighborhood, in fact. Emil and Tillie lived next-door with son Albert and their two girls, Elma and Hazel, and even Elma, only seven, said how nice it was to "smell pretties" every morning.

Then, two miracles: a double pale lilac, nearly cream, appeared. Lavender Pearl I named it, and if those plants and new seeds gave up that color again, I'd have my first unique variety. Then to my absolute delight, one of the deep purples I'd crossed with the Lemoine presented me a single bloom with six petals! Six!

"Frank, you've got to come here and see this!" I dragged him from the barn to look at that shrub, making a note of the label, my eyes seeking any others with six petals or even five.

"Imagine, Frank! Six petals!"

"Good work, Huldie." He patted my back. "Were you breeding this one for petals? I thought it was the color you went for."

"Color, yes, but increased petals, oh my, yes, that too. I'd love twelve petals one day." I wiped at my eyes. "Imagine," I said. "Crying over petals."

Frank smiled. "Twelve's a mighty big number."

"It's only twice as many as this one." I cradled the deep purple bloom in the palm of my hand, fingering the tiny petals, velvet gems; counting and recounting.

Giddy was too weak a word to describe how I felt.

"Look here, Frank. These are all the same color. A pale lavender. It's... I believe I've created a new cultivar."

Frank walked along that row, lifting the tags, staring, trying to see what I could. "I submit, you're right."

"I know! And now six petals on another. Oh, Frank, it's working; it truly is!"

"Your work is what's working." He pulled me to him. "All those cultivars started and tossed because they didn't meet your exacting standards." He shook his head. "Guess I'd better get those mole traps set so we don't lose these gems."

I danced a jig and went inside to call Delia to tell her. I stopped before I lifted the receiver. How could I share such an achievement when my daughter was so low? Yet weren't these moments of accomplishment intended to interrupt the trials we couldn't stave off or even understand? But some people took the joys of others and compared their own lack, making their melancholy deeper. It startled me that I didn't know Delia well enough to anticipate how she'd respond.

I finally decided to call Delia late that afternoon when the day's labors had tempered my enthusiasm a bit.

"I'm pleased for you, Mama. You've worked so hard." Her tone was as flat as a frying pan, and I wished I'd kept my tongue.

"Not sure how hard I've worked, but I've been persistent at least." I kept my voice cheery. "You'll like the color."

"You are that. Persistent, I mean."

"Which brings me to another reason I've called. Please, Delia, reconsider and come home."

"Everything's fine here, Mama," Delia said. "I help move the cows with Edmond in the morning so I get good exercise. I can make it to the phone, and Dr. Alice lives down here on the Bottoms, so she's only minutes away now. She has a car. We've gone riding a time or two, and she's come for dinner."

"But we don't have a car, so it'll take us longer to get there, to be with you."

Silence.

"Just think about it."

"I'll think. But Alice is good at what she does."

I knew God loved and cared for us, guided us through the storms, found us when we tried to hide. But I questioned too, took to my weeds with a vigor, swatting at my desire for certainty and to make things happen as I wanted them to. I could protect a flower, but I couldn't protect my children.

Alice Chapman was more than her doctor; she was a skilled friend, able to protect her better than her mother. Perhaps she didn't need her mother.

"She doesn't want to sell," Lizzie said over dinner one night. It was June, and the lilacs had faded. I'd carefully collected seeds from the deep purple with six petals to cultivate in my sun-porch nursery and had cultivars of my Lavender Pearl heeled in and growing in tubs to be planted. "She's hanging on to the farm as a way of keeping Nell Irving alive."

"I think Lizzie's right, Mama," Fritz said. "She cries when I come there, and we walk the fields. Selling those cows would be one more loss. She pets them like Nell Irving did, scratching behind their ears like they was big dogs."

"Were big dogs," Martha corrected as she passed the sliced ham to her father.

"Were big dogs. What'd I say?"

"Was."

"You knew what I meant," he said.

"The discipline of good grammar speaks to who you are, Fritz. When you apply for a job, you'll want to put your best foot forward to take a step up," Martha said. "So you must speak every day as though you have the highest command of the language."

Fritz sniffed.

"She says that to us in school too," Ruth said. "I think she means well."

Martha suppressed a grin.

Ruth didn't speak up all that often, and I saw her words as commiserating with Fritz. He did too and saluted her with two fingers above his forehead, then forked back into his ham. Nelia watched the interaction without a word. The child was so well behaved one could almost overlook her.

"As I was saying. Frank, I wonder what would happen if you talked with Edmond and suggested it might be time to sell the cows. Delia's due any day."

"It's a good herd," Frank said. "Makes her a good living if the prices stay up for cheese. Maybe time with our Delia helps Edmond miss his brother less, both young people, grieving."

I ignored my husband's wisdom and decided he'd need more attention before he'd be an ally. We finished eating, and I washed dishes with a vengeance, nearly scrubbing the green leaf edging from one of my mother's Haviland plates. I should save them for special meals, but what was the point of having lovely china if used only once a year at Christmas? "If Edmond didn't come out and milk those cows, she'd sell them. What's she going to do after the baby comes? Besides, is it acceptable that she has morning coffee and suppers and dessert with a hired man?"

Lizzie smiled. "I'm surprised at that coming from you, Mother. You've never paid attention to what people think."

"Maybe I should."

"Have you asked her to come live with us after the baby

is here?" Martha sat at the table, grading student papers. Ruth and Nelia were upstairs, reading, I hoped.

"Of course. But see how long it took Lizzie to return, and that was after I asked a dozen times."

"Delia isn't me," Lizzie said.

"Has she said something?" I turned to her. It was nearly four months since we'd buried Nell Irving and Delia had carried on alone.

Lizzie shook her head. "No. And while she might want to stay out there with her cows, and she does, if she thought it wasn't good for the baby, she'd be open to an alternative. Knowing she wouldn't be alone when the baby came... Maybe that would be enough to get her here."

"I've proposed that to her."

"But you've put it as though it would be good for her and for you. What about being good for the baby?"

She had a point. Frank and I went up to bed. I looked out the window. I loved summer when at nine o'clock in the evening, it was still light enough to see color and shape. Birds-of-paradise bloomed outside the window, their red beaks sentinels to the petunia beds beyond.

"Lizzie said she told her sister she wished she'd come home sooner after Fred's death. You'd think Delia would listen to Lizzie, if not her own mother."

"I agree. But her coming here would cause quite a rearranging of the household. She might want to save you from that misery."

"What misery?"

"Of having to tell Ruth and Nelia they need to go back to their families."

I stopped in my tracks. "Those girls need us. Ruth needs her confidence built up, and she needs piano lessons, and she needs to know she's important, and she needs exposure to a few other ways of seeing the world than the myopic view of her father. Besides, Martha's the best teacher ever, and those girls need the best teacher ever, not stuck upriver where Ruth's parents live. And Nelia, bless her, she's smart but doesn't know it, and she needs time for healing from a great loss I don't even know, and her father rarely talks to her and would have her living way up the Lewis River, and both of them are attending school and doing well because they're here in town, and—"

"You need them," Frank said.

I startled. *Do I?* "Yes, yes, I do, and not just for the work they do," I said. I needed them for the way they made me feel when I pointed out the intricacies of horticulture and gardening and linked it to life. I loved seeing their faces when I spoke an encouraging word or honored their incomparable souls. I couldn't imagine working in that garden alone, even though I disappeared there with people working by my side. I needed them to be excited and blessed and healed by the blooms as I was.

"I submit, Delia doesn't want to see you lose those girls. She knows how much they mean to you and how much you've meant to them."

I sat down on the side of the bed. "But Delia's our daughter. Of course she'd come first."

"Delia has a tender heart, Huldie. She might be thinking of those girls as much as her own child."

Frank was right, and it grieved me that I hadn't thought of it myself. "We could put all three girls in our bedroom and put Ruth and Nelia in the back room. It's almost big enough for a couple of cots."

"Three females in one room? One with a baby on the way? Hulda." Frank shook his head. He stripped down to his underdrawers and crawled into bed. The nights were warm, so only a flannel sheet covered us. I drifted my linen nightgown over my head, tugged out the long braid I slept with, and crawled in beside him. Frogs croaked near the birdbath set below the window.

"I can't put the girls out in the tack room with Fritz, for heaven's sake."

"No one's asking you to. You'll think of something." Frank yawned. He fell instantly asleep.

I lay awake, fiddling with my braid's end hairs. Frank's soft snores filled the room. The Thompson clock downstairs ticked loud enough for me to hear it giving rhythm to my prayers. There'd be a solution. I just had to trust.

TWENTY-EIGHT

LAUNCHING LIFE

Hulda, 1906

An odd series of short and long rings shrilled from the phone. It meant someone tried to reach as many people as possible. Delia's baby! I ran down the stairs and grabbed the receiver. "Alice Chapman's been injured bad," Jennie the phone operator said. "She was out in her garden and forgot she had a mole trap there, and it snapped her hand nearly off. Her husband's been called back from Kelso, but if you were hoping to see her at her office today, don't go. Nobody knew how to drive that car, so she tried to drive it with one hand. She's lost a lot of blood."

"What can we do?" someone on the line piped in.

"Who can go there and drive her to meet Dr. Chapman? Take them to the dock so she can get to Seattle and St. Joseph's?"

"I will," another voice said. It wasn't Delia, but I wondered if she was on the line.

A few other arrangements were made as the community rallied around their only doctor. A neighbor offered a prayer, and together we said, "Amen."

Poor Alice. Delia would have to come here now. We could deliver that baby. I'd had all mine at home without a doctor. My sisters had too.

Delia counted on Dr. Alice, though. They were friends. Delia might think Alice needed her and want to stay even closer.

A week later, Dr. Alice returned from the hospital, her hand removed, thus ending her surgical career.

"Alice and I buried her bag of medical tools behind her house," Delia told us. I was at the farm fixing soup she could eat the next few days. Her legs were swollen, and she could hardly bend over to fill her cat's dish she was so large with child. I poured milk that Edmond brought in. The cat lapped happily by the stove. Edmond remained, drinking a cup of coffee as he leaned against the dry sink. He seemed at home in Delia's kitchen.

"Why bury perfectly good medical instruments?" I petted the cat, now swishing against my legs.

"It's illegal to have doctor tools if you're not a doctor," Delia said.

"But her husband is. He could have used them."

Delia was quiet. "Maybe it was her way of putting that past behind her, burying what could never be again. I'm not sure. But she asked me, and I was pleased to help her. She'll be moving, both of them, to Kelso. I'll miss her."

"So our town will be looking for a new doctor," I said.

Delia nodded. I noticed a caring look Edmond gave to my daughter—and how his face turned the color of a geranium when he saw that I was watching him, watching her.

"I read a piece in *Woman's Home Companion*," Ruth said as we fixed breakfast. "Martha said it would be all right to read the magazine."

"I'm sure it is. That's a good periodical for young ladies as well as for older ones." I sliced bread, and Ruth toasted it, spearing the finished slice from the triangular-shaped tin set over the heat of the wood stove. She buttered each slice as she talked, her voice clear and firm. Quite a change from when she'd first come here.

"She says we need to step out on our own, be good neighbors. I've been thinking about that. Maybe…maybe it's time for me to return home. I could come in with my father a few days a week and still help with watering and such, but that would give you more room, at least this summer. Maybe Miss Delia would come home."

My heart ached with her words. "Were you listening at the door the other evening?" I shook my finger at her, but not sternly. "That's not polite, you know."

"No, oh no. Nelia and I have both talked about this. We're getting old enough. I'm fourteen, and Nelia is eleven already, and well, things have changed for you and Mr. Frank, Mrs. Hulda. That magazine article just made me think that I might be ready for a change too."

"I need your help, Ruth." My heart pounded. "And you need the money and the lessons."

"If we weren't here, though, Delia could have our room all to herself. She and her baby."

I scrambled the eggs, bought time. Finally, "That's kind of you, Ruth, to make this offer. I...I'll have to talk with Mr. Klager about this."

Ruth might be ready, but I wasn't sure Nelia had a place to go to that wouldn't send her back into that old sadness. And Delia didn't want to come anyway. I could end up alone.

The idea came to me while I planned a Fourth of July gathering in the garden. I suggested to my brother and his wife that Tillie could use Nelia's help with their toddler, and I could pay Ruth extra—as Frank approved—so she could pay them for room and board. I'd still have her help, she'd be saving still for schooling, and my adoptive family would be on the other side of the fence.

I also enlisted more "bucket boys" again. The seven- and eight-year-olds came after school and hauled buckets from the pump to the hundreds of plants, pouring a ladle of water on them, one by one.

"They get a nickel an afternoon," I told Frank. "And this way Delia won't think she has to be out there working the garden. She'll see we have plenty of help. Nelia and Ruth can keep them in line, Martha too."

"That could be full-time work, I submit. My dad used to say: 'one boy's a boy, two boys are half a boy, and three boys are no boy at all!'"

"Oh, Frank, they'll behave."

"In between splashing each other with water and flinging mud."

"All boys aren't you, Frank."

He laughed, and Delia moved back home.

On the Fourth of July, everyone came to celebrate. Nelia and Ruth had just finished moving their things to Emil and Tillie's, and later we planned to go to Woodland to hear Col. J. E. Stone do the annual oration to remind us all of what the occasion stood for. The Kalama lawyer didn't speak every year but often enough that we could predict the words he would say next. I promised Tom Chatterson, the undertaker, fried salmon eggs, his favorite, if he brought his banjo along and played. He did.

I'd planted a small flag garden that spring, knowing that

Delia's baby was due around the Fourth. Earlier in the day, I'd picked from those plantings and arranged bouquets of flowers composed of reds, including anthurium—my one exotic flower the catalog called Flamingo. I added carnations, roses, and tulips, and then I stuck into the cluster white roses, daisies, peonies, and a calla lily or two, finally ending up with blues to make the patriotic centerpieces. Hyacinth, veronica, and delphinium brought the sky to mind. I'd hoped for a hydrangea bloom, but none gave up the shade of blue I wanted. I stuck little flags on sticks that Nelia colored for me and Martha glued. They rose up out of the blooms at each of the outdoor tables. Flowers had a way of bringing celebration into an event. Martha told me once that *celebration* meant "to fill up," and that one had to do it over and over again. That's what we were doing.

Frank got the children to take turns grinding the handle on the ice cream machine. In the distance, we could hear the band in Woodland playing marching tunes. I was glad to be alive.

I looked across the lawn at the lilacs bearing mostly shiny green leaves. They stepped back for the Fourth of July bouquets to shine, plucked from the flag gardens.

Bobby—the third dog we'd given that name—sniffed and rolled in the tall grasses and then barked at the occasional automobile that puttered by. He was another collie mix. Cars slowed as people gazed at the flatiron garden or stringing abelia with its pink-and-white flowers.

Delia was as big as the water tower, and she sat next to Edmond. He belonged here too, was family. The Drs. Chapman arrived, and I wondered how Alice would find her way with her gift for healing so interrupted. Nelia's father sat to the side, drinking lemonade Nelia brought him; he looked content. Ruth's parents came too, which surprised me most of all. They even walked among the lilacs, with Ruth showing them the small tags, explaining what each meant, her mother smiling all the while. I avoided Barney, not wanting any theological discussion to ruin this day.

Frank brought me a glass of lemonade and watched the line of children he'd arranged as each turned the ice cream machine. "I submit you got what you wanted, Huldie, all the Kinder home with you, and a few more right close by." He tugged me to him.

"Is there any place as lovely as a garden?" I asked.

"So long as it's one of yours and you're in it, I think not."

I turned to peck him on his cheek when, from the corner of my eye, I spied Delia, her face twisted in discomfort. She whispered to Edmond, and the tall young man nearly knocked his chair over as he stood, spoke, and Delia pointed. He strode to Frank, saying, "Delia says"—he swallowed—"it might be time. Says it's been going on awhile. Says they're not far apart, the pains, and well…"

Well, why not? I thought as I gathered up my daughter, who put things off until the last moment, and signaled Bertha and Amelia and Tillie, and we headed to the house. I sent

Edmond to wait with Frank. *That's one smart child deciding to arrive today.* We helped Delia up the stairs to sit in the bed we'd arranged for this moment, the Drs. Chapman at her side. What better place to begin breathing air than surrounded by family and friends and the fragrance of flowers?

Irvina Guild entered the world on the Fourth of July, early evening, in a home her great-grandfather had built with his own hands. Her arrival came as a John Philip Sousa marching band *oompah-pahed* in the distance. Eventually, Delia asked us to leave, so she could rest. Dr. Chapman took the opportunity to show off his 1906 Harrison Model B touring car and thrill the men and children with a few turns around town, arriving back before dark and the fireworks started. Alice and Lizzie stepped up into the car too, and the Drs. Chapman found they had to stop by Mills Grocery, the first place in Woodland to sell petrol. Roy Mills came out to admire the car, but Lizzie told me later the proprietor looked more at her than the doctors' auto. It pleased me no end that she had noticed. A new birth reminded us all to let grieving step aside for the day at least. Maybe Lizzie, like a tulip opening slowly to the sun, was coming back to living.

Irvina was adorable from the beginning. I was torn at times between tending my plants and sitting for hours in the rocking chair, baby in my arms, allowing that small being to press her tiny fingers around just one of mine. Her lips were like rose petals, soft and pink and moist. When she opened her eyes and gazed at me, I thought that she could see into my soul and must be close to God, as close as all of us once were when first we left that womb.

TWENTY-NINE

GIVING AWAY

Hulda, 1907

The year or two that followed brought new delight and frustration. Our home sighed in fullness with my girls near, and I saw Ruth and Nelia daily. Lizzie began giving me piano lessons. I was not a good student, spending time in the garden rather than practicing, but it was something Lizzie said she liked doing. As only babies can, Irvina made us laugh as we watched her discover her world. Together we women mulched, planted, pollinated, watered, and evaluated blooms and stems and heady scents, mostly of lilacs. Frank and Fritz helped in between milking the cows at the Bottoms, where we still kept them pastured. When we all worked together in the garden, it was like worship. Each day I looked forward to the next bloom, the next subtle change in a cultivar, the next surprise. Each day was an affirmation of the goodness of life. I marveled as I watched my daughters renew hope and saw my plantings as the best way to tell them that life goes on; we get through each season, finding joy when we can and being grateful for the chance to seek it.

There were frustrations too. One spring I pulled up a dozen nearly-creamy-white lilacs that so disappointed. Maybe they were creamier than a few others, but the stems were weak and the fragrance paled and the blooms lasted about as long as my patience.

"Pull them up?" Frank had his elbows akimbo. "You sure?"

"*Ja*, I'm certain. Into that wheelbarrow they go."

I hated discarding plants nearly two feet high, but they had to go. They simply weren't moving toward the prime flower I desired.

Frank loaded them up and wheeled them just beyond the picket fence and left the wheelbarrow sitting there. He stepped into the barn and was gone for a time, while I mulched and wondered if the soil was the problem. In the distance I heard men working on the railroad that would border our four acres on the west. They built a dike nearly as high as the house and would lay the tracks along the top, hoping to foil the Columbia River when it flooded.

When Frank came out, he was carrying a sign. He held it up for me to read: Take a Lilac Home.

"Not that anyone will. They're discards for goodness' sake."

"A Hulda Klager lilac discard is a treasure to the masses," Frank quipped and stuck the sign in the wheelbarrow.

By nightfall, the lilacs had disappeared. I hadn't even been aware that so many people walked or rode or drove by. Frank had put a box out there, and when he brought the wheelbarrow back, he had three dimes too.

"I didn't get to see who took them, to ask them where they planned to plant them," I complained.

"You'll have more to rip up and give away." Frank flipped the coins in his palm. "Maybe there is a future in your lilacs."

His collecting the money bothered. I didn't want to sell them. It didn't seem right. "I prefer giving them away. But good ones, not discards. People should have the best to plant, and if it's a gift, it's even better."

Edmond Wilke continued to be a part of our lives. Delia contracted with him to run the farm, and while the work to be done was on those acres where cows needed milking and hay needed cutting and storing for winter, Edmond appeared often at our doorstep. He took supper with us. Irvina charmed him, as she did everyone, and he'd chat with Delia and more than once even held the baby, the child treated like a porcelain vase in his big hands. I ached when I watched that scene, thinking it should have been Nell Irving holding his child or Fred holding his and Lizzie's baby. As his brother had been, Edmond was tall, good-looking, with graceful fingers. He always tapped the baby's blanket at her heart whenever he handed the infant back to his mother or me. Then he and Frank would play a game of checkers together, while we women stitched or read and Delia went upstairs to nurse her child.

In the summer of 1907, after celebrating Irvina's first birthday, I wrote to Luther Burbank to tell him of my success with having achieved a six-petal lilac and my Lavender Pearl. I told him I'd begun the registration process with the lilac society. I knew he wasn't much interested in flowers, but I wanted him to know of the success and to thank him for his earlier encouragement. I also asked him about soil issues. The busy man wrote back, answered my questions, and added a note of congratulations on my "little flower experiment":

Passion can be an aphrodisiac, attracting hope and inspiration. The founder of Methodism once noted, "Catch on fire with enthusiasm and people will come for miles to watch you burn." I suspect that's why many come to my Santa Rosa ranch, just to watch me burn. Perhaps a few will come your way as well.

My steady increase of cultivar varieties did put me on fire, and I did think it possible people might come and see what I'd planted, not just neighbors driving by on a Sunday. So I took another bold step and wrote another letter.

My dear Miss Givens,

I do hope your column continues to give helpful advice to your many readers. I like answering your questions and appreciate your sending me copies of the pieces I helped contribute to also. Now I have a favor to ask of you that you might think quite bold. Would you ever consider writing a story about a place far from Sacramento? It may seem out of the ordinary, but I have recently developed a new lilac cultivar, one I call Lavender Pearl. I believe you will remember my writing to you about the Lemoine I imported from France and how I hoped to hybridize new varieties from them. I have also recently uncovered a plant with six petals, a rarity I intend to pursue hybridizing until I have twelve! I began my work breeding apples and daffodils, and my garden now attracts a number of visitors each spring curious about my work but also enjoying the beauty of the garden. My work is nothing compared to your Californian Mr. Burbank's efforts, but we have corresponded. I think what I'm doing here could have an appeal beyond my little community of Woodland, Washington. Thank you so much for considering the idea. I look forward to hearing from you.

Yours truly, Hulda Klager

I read the letter to Frank. "Am I being too prideful, asking a writer to feature a story about the garden?"

Frank shrugged. "People enjoy a good story. And what better than about a German woman who taught herself how to make a better lilac?"

"I wouldn't say better." I thought of Barney Reed and wondered how many like him might read such an article and then come down hard on me. "Different. The flowers are just different."

"I submit they are better. Better smells, better stems, better blooms. You've taken what was and using your God-given talents, you've made something better. No sin in that, Huldie. To deny what your talent allows, that would be the sin."

"Oh, Frank. What would I do without you?"

"Just fine, Huldie. You'd do just fine. Now post the letter. Who knows, maybe we'll get a few nickels from visitors coming our way after the article comes out."

"I'll keep giving the starts away, you know that, don't you, Frank?" He nodded. I snuggled up next to him. "You think she'll write it?"

"I submit she will. You're giving her a chance to feature a unique story about a smart woman. Besides, who wouldn't want the chance to leave California to come to Washington, if only for a day?" He grinned.

THIRTY

CORNELIA AND SHELLY

1907

Cornelia stepped off the train in Groton, Massachusetts, and found the air hot and humid, so unlike Sacramento this time of year. August could swelter in the Far West, that was certain, but there were always breezes from the Sacramento River, and never this sticky hot. Groton boasted rivers too. The entire town grew in a V between the Nashua and Squannacook, but the rivers didn't cool the train station. Cornelia's mother didn't want her to head east. CK gave his blessings, though he cautioned that making a living writing as a freelancer was difficult for men and would be twice as hard for a woman, even a good writer like Cornelia.

She'd longed to travel, to taste the foods of other places and do more than answer questions with her written words. She'd arranged for a neighborhood woman to ensure that her mother was looked after, and then Cornelia bought her ticket and accepted an invitation from Laura Louise Hetzer to write a story about the Lowthorpe School of Landscape Architecture for Women. Now, here she was. She turned to survey her surroundings, sat on a bench, and wrote while she waited.

Sunlight kisses Revere's bell.
Birdsong welcomes travelers' weary souls
Like new blooms, adventures launch.

Cornelia finished the haiku, changing the last line to begin with "Adventures," then putting it back. This new form of poetry focused her mind and captured feelings quickly. She stuffed the paper in her bag. Laura told Cornelia if she was late to start walking toward the First Parish Church on Main and Lowell, seeking the tall white steeple "whose bell was cast by the Paul Revere Foundry" and wait for her there. The stretch of her legs felt good after the long trip, but she was tired and hoped Laura wouldn't be too late. She hadn't walked far when a horse cab driving toward her slowed and a woman stuck her head out to the side and waved.

"Laura? Miss Hetzer?"

"Yes, it's me. I'm so sorry I'm late."

The cab stopped, and Cornelia fanned her face with her hand. "You're not dressed for our humidity." Laura looked at her attire. "But we'll soon take care of that. An embroidered muslin will be cool and comfortable. You did bring an embroidered muslin?"

"Yes, and a soft mull too."

"I told the director about the story you were writing for the *Sacramento Bee,* and she's very excited."

"Oh." Cornelia listened as the cab continued down the street, the horse *clop-clopping* along. "I don't know if the *Bee* will use it. I…left my job there. I'm going to be a freelancer, take my chances with selling stories to magazines and newspapers." Laura frowned. "Not to worry. My editor said he'd look at what I'd write, so you haven't misled your director. But it might appear in other journals or newspapers as well. I can sell it more than once in noncompeting markets. That'll advance your school's outreach even further."

"Yes, of course, you're right. We'll explain that. Meanwhile, you'll have the best time discovering our school and meeting the many students who come from long distances to take their training. I'm so pleased you've come."

They shared more about each other than they had in the letters, including Cornelia telling Laura how her contact with Mrs. Klager had worked out. "She writes well and right back," Cornelia said. "She even shared a bit about her lilac orchard and how one of her deep purple lilacs produced a bloom with six petals! Imagine that. She's registered another cultivar with the horticultural society, and it's been accepted. She calls it Lavender Pearl for the unique color."

"Quite unusual. That sort of thing intrigues me. But I

think Mr. Child will find it of interest as well. He does the surveying and engineering, and of course anything new in the larger shrubs will intrigue him. I've arranged for interviews with him and Gertrude Sanderson, the instructor for Drawing and Garden Design."

"And Mrs. Low?"

"Yes, of course. You must speak with our founder. But all of that is tomorrow. Today, we simply relax, and I'll take you on a walk through the grounds and greenhouses. It's quite impressive."

And so it was. The cab took them on a winding road lined with sycamore trees and elm, with underbrush of flowering shrubs and woodsy plants unfamiliar to Cornelia. She pulled out her notebook to sketch, writing a name beside it that Laura gave her. When they approached the school, Cornelia's jaw dropped. "It looks…palatial," she said. "Massive."

"Three stories, wraparound porch. Instructors sleep on the top floor where the dormers are. The students sleep there as well, and I rather like having camaraderie between student and instructor that isn't delineated by class. We're all lovers of plants and trees here. We can learn from each other; that's the school's philosophy. The plants teach different lessons to each of us. It would be tragic if I didn't get the lesson because I thought my student offered less than what I had to give."

"That's very egalitarian." Cornelia knew then the direction her article would take, about how plants and shrubs and natural things made equals of those who might otherwise never cross paths. This would not be just an article about an interesting landscape school for women.

"Gardening is a very democratic activity," she wrote in her journal that evening, "with no plant seen better than another, each having a place in the scheme of things and each generously allowing the other to shine at various times without the others becoming jealous." She looked forward to proving the thesis in her article and wondered if CK would still be interested in such a common woman's point of view.

Shelly's wrapper needed washing, so she took it to the laundry room along with other personal items. It was Monday morning, the day for her to fill the tubs and build the fire to heat the water. She liked it that students were assigned the time by reverse alphabet, and this term there were no people whose surnames began with letters after the *S* in Snyder. Well, Mrs. Thorpe, of course, but she lived off campus, as did most of the lecturers. Only the instructors stayed with students on the dormitory floor. Shelly liked the hard stirring of her clothes that let her put strong feelings into effort. Her favorite class was Gardening Out of Doors with Miss Hetzer, for the same reason. She got to shovel and dig and put her back into a task, which transferred the ache in her heart to a muscle ache in her arms and her legs.

Bill had not been happy when she'd returned from her

tour of the Lowthorpe School and had advised him of her plans to enroll. His mother had feigned a terrible illness the next day, and Bill stayed home that week from his classes in Annapolis to look after her, which both angered Shelly and hurt her since he would never cancel classes for her. She was angry because in between her mother-in-law's coughing— how had it come on so quickly?—the woman managed to put suggestions into her son's head about the frivolity of his wife. "She goes bicycle riding, wearing those bifurcated skirts!" *Cough, cough.* "I've seen her jumping up and down in the back garden, rolling one way and then another, one hundred times. 'Exercising' she calls it. Looks to me like one of those strange religions one reads about in that *National Geographic* magazine." *Cough, cough.* "And now she wants to go to school? At her age? For women? I suspect it's a cauldron of suffragettes. Don't you let her go, William. Don't you let that woman run your life into ruin!" *Cough, cough.* Her mother-in-law would recover as soon as Bill returned to his classes, but not before Shelly and Bill had a week of arguing.

"It's beyond discussion," Bill had told her, as he fixed mint tea for his mother. "No wife of mine is going to be gone to another state for months on end, to what, draw plants? There are plenty to draw right here in the garden, if that's your interest, though I must say it's a new interest. One of your fleeting interests, I suspect. Like the lyceum attendance."

"I attend horticulture meetings regularly."

"And see where that's gotten you."

"The few friends I have here, that's what it's gotten me." She'd stood tall and straight as he poured hot water through the tea caddy. It had been months since he'd made tea for her, even longer since they'd sat and just talked about what the future might hold for them. She changed the tone. "What's happened to us, Bill? I keep looking for yes in your face, and all I see is no."

Startled, Bill spilled the tea. She reached for a towel and held it to his hand, her fingers closing over his wrist, his palm. Once that touch would have brought currents of emotion through her and Bill as well. She pressed against his hand, urging the feeling to reappear, to reach him. He looked at her, really looked at her, and she felt his own sadness in the gaze, a sadness she longed to alter.

"Shelly, I—"

His mother coughed from her bedroom.

Bill pulled the towel from his hand, lifted the teapot, and carried it away from her. Carried everything away.

She'd packed her bags and left the next morning before anyone else was up. She opened the front door and heard a sound and turned. There stood her mother-in-law, looking chipper and in the bloom of health. She smiled, then coughed, pressing her hanky to her smirking lips as she waved a tepid good-bye.

That had been more than a year ago. At least Bill hadn't

refused to pay the statements the school sent, or she couldn't have remained. Perhaps it was better this way. She could take every course in each of the four subject divisions, which would require another year or so. But then what? She stirred the tub of her clothes. Cauldron of suffragettes. Her mother-in-law's charge still irritated. She'd found no suffragettes here, only natural beauty, living things needing nurture to survive. As the months passed, she found she liked the lack of stressful talk—there was no need to defend all the time.

She loved having her hands in soil, earth like face powder come together, patting around the roots, careful not to cover the crown, being wary of overwatering. These were things discussed at the horticultural meetings, but here, at the school, they were like a religion, each plant looked after with reverence.

With her sleeve, Shelly wiped her forehead of perspiration. She lifted the soaked wrapper and twisted it as free of moisture as she could before sinking it into the boiling rinse water. Her eye caught the dying rhododendron outside that had been discussed at length in the Gardening Out of Doors class. The rhododendron had been planted wrong, where it could not flourish. It had been exposed to the harsh cold, though of course rhodies thrived in mountain zones with heavy snow and intense cold. The consensus was, the plant was dying.

Laura Hetzer had used the occasion to discuss what

plants need—what all living things need, she admonished—and looked for ways they might work to restore it. "Though there are times when one must simply pull the plant up by the roots and toss it aside, as it is gone. Dead. Finished."

Is this my marriage? Shelly wondered.

But she found herself focused on restoring the rhodie as a necessary task. Her desire to repair had not lessened since she'd been here. She still wasn't sure she should go home in December, to see if she and Bill could replant the seeds of their relationship. Her mother-in-law's words—or was it her cough—and Bill's bowing to them made her think it wasn't possible. She had no way of mulching a marriage back into health by herself. She still hoped Lowthorpe might give her those tools.

In the classroom, Shelly took her seat, surprised when Mr. Dawson, the instructor, introduced Cornelia Givens "who will be interviewing some of you today, if you care to participate, as she is working on a story about our school and its students. She's from California."

Murmuring followed. Mr. Dawson coughed loudly to gain order. "Ladies, if you please. Are there volunteers?" Every hand except Shelly's went up.

"Could I ask you to suggest a few students?" the reporter said. She was a petite woman who wore her hair in that new fashion with a french twist. Her smallish hat—with one short feather—cocked jauntily to the side.

Mr. Dawson looked over his glasses. "Mrs. Snyder would be a fine interviewee. She's one of our few married students. And she has a special interest in rhododendrons." Mr. Dawson urged Shelly to raise her hand. For some reason, Shelly complied, her palm barely reaching her chin. "Now that you've properly met, perhaps you can find a time after the class to talk. Will that work?" Both women nodded, and Mr. Dawson assumed his instruction, while Miss Givens took notes.

Shelly didn't know how she felt about being singled out for an interview because she was married. She wasn't at all certain how long that status would remain.

Cornelia Givens sat across from Shelly at the end of a long table on the dining porch. Several other girls, including a few instructors, spoke quietly, eventually leaving just the two women alone. Clanks of dishes from the kitchen provided background, and when they couldn't hear those noises, there were birds chirping in the trees beyond the screened porch.

"This is such a lovely place," Cornelia began. "How did you first hear of the school?"

"I attended horticultural meetings in Baltimore where I live, and they planned a tour to visit the Hampton Gardens, a fabulous estate. While we were there, the head gardener spoke of Mr. Child as one of the primary landscape engineers in the country. It's a very old estate. And he said that Mr.

Child was a lecturer at the Lowthorpe School. I'd never heard of it before and thought it intriguing, all female students in an occupation usually reserved for men. Not unlike your own profession, Miss Givens."

"Please. Call me Cornelia."

"And I'm Shelly."

"It's true I have an interest in rhodies, but my favorite plant is a lilac," Shelly said.

"I like them too," Cornelia told her and mentioned Hulda Klager.

The two talked away the afternoon, walking through the grounds, then back to the screened porch for afternoon tea. When students entered the hall for the evening meal, Cornelia and Shelly looked up. "Is it that time already?" Shelly said.

"I'll be here for a year myself if I take this long with one interview." Cornelia started to return her notepad to her bag, then hesitated. "Is there one lesson you'll take away from this course, a lesson about life perhaps?"

"Egad, I'm no philosopher—not that I wouldn't like to study Plato and Aristotle." Shelly sat, thoughtful. "This past year I've found there are lessons in these plants—many lessons—testaments to faith and an acceptance that it's the root structure as much as anything that predicts the kind of plant you'll have."

Now that she'd said it, Shelly wondered if that was what was missing in her marriage: a solid foundation where sturdy roots sank deep into family and faith and that could weather the trials of living and, best of all, permit deep feelings to bloom year after year.

Cornelia finished the interviews and stayed an additional day just to wander around the campus, taking in scents and sights that spiced her writing. In the kitchen, she chatted with the cooks, inhaling the aroma of fresh spinach salad with a hot bacon dressing and asking (and receiving) the recipe for a fruit drink combining apples, grapes, lemon juice, and ginger ale. She visited greenhouses and tried her hand at designing a small garden plot, realizing as she did the enormous task involved in creating a garden that matched one's vision.

The school suggested that graduates would find work in designing and planting for small estates, village parks, and forwarding-thinking cities. "People will more likely move to a town with a welcoming flower garden beneath its city sign than a pile of weeds blown up against its center post," the school's founder told her. Flowers spoke as clearly as Cornelia's words did, maybe even more.

As a result of the interviews, Cornelia planned a side trip to Arnold Arboretum run by Harvard University, where it was said there was a special lilac garden. That might lead to a series of stories about great arboretums across the country. There did seem to be a growing interest in the natural world, what with President Roosevelt urging Congress to set aside protected areas of landscape for all to enjoy as parks. She'd made notes on the journey itself, hoping she might sell a few pieces to travel magazines. She'd learned so much in this brief trip, not the least of which was confidence. She was a good listener, and people liked being heard. That was worthy work, even if she never got a story published.

But if she didn't get the stories published, what would she live on? She couldn't survive on the beauty she saw.

"Cornelia, I'm so glad I caught you." It was Shelly, breathing hard, running down the hill as Cornelia headed for the cab. "I wanted to give you this. It's a lilac start, from a variety here. It does well in neutral soil and cold weather. I had permission to cut it and meant to give it to you when we said good-bye earlier." She handed it to Cornelia. "Keep it moist, and you'll be able to plant it when you get home to California. Or maybe give it to your lilac friend, Mrs. Klager."

"She's not really a friend."

"Would you ask her if she'll send me a cultivar of one of her new varieties?"

"She did say she likes to give them away. I'll write and ask her. Should she send it here?"

"No." Shelly handed Cornelia a piece of paper on which she'd written her address. "I'm going home at Christmas. And God willing, I'll bring my husband back here next spring to see if the rhodie made it. But something back home needs tending more."

THIRTY-ONE

On the Road of Healing

Hulda, 1908

The spring floods weren't bad in 1908, which was good since we had a wedding to plan for, that of Delia and Edmond. On June 16 they spoke their vows at the Presbyterian church, but we had the reception at the house. Rain showers threatened any garden time, and when it began to sprinkle, we moved inside, and I served from the cupboard filled with pastries and pies.

The couple would return to the farm where Edmond had added potatoes to cattle raising, so this marriage was bittersweet. But I set my sadness aside by naming another new cultivar after Irvina, a single purple flower the exact hue I wanted.

Nearly two years old, Irvina already put sentences together and loved the sounds of words her aunt Martha would feed her. "Colossal petunia, Gamma," she'd tell me as she waddled along as I weeded and hoed. "Substantial!" Irvina squealed as I moved the grass aside with my hoe.

"Now don't you be upset by a little snake. They eat mice and are good friends in the garden. But see these strings here? That's where we have traps set. Danger. So you must, must stay on these paths, all right?" I could've kept those traps closeted while she was small, but teaching a child limits was a necessary part of them becoming aware and responsible adults. I might not think that way if she ever hurt herself the way Alice Chapman had, but I couldn't protect everyone I loved from every harm. I had to accept that.

Delia assured me that she'd come by often and that Irvina could even spend an occasional night with us.

"I surely hope so." We all sat at the dining room table having dinner after church. Edmond and Delia radiated that newlywed glow. "She's the only grandchild we have. My girls just aren't propagating as quickly as I'd like."

I hated myself as soon as I said it, for Lizzie's face turned pale, and she excused herself from the table, rose, and ascended the stairs to her room without another word.

"Mama," Martha said.

"I know, I know. At times my mouth goes visiting from my brain."

"I'll go talk with her," Delia said.

"No, no, it's me. I'm the one who said it." I frumped my napkin next to my plate and stood. Frank winked his support, though I thought how quickly I'd turned a nice day into sour.

"Lizzie? It's your mother. May I come in?"

I heard crying, then a tentative "Yes" allowing me to enter. One of my wedding-ring quilts lay folded at the end of her bed, and a summer sun shone through the window. A breeze sighed the white curtains back and forth against the handblown glass. The wedding photograph of her and Delia standing before their former husbands sat framed on the small table between her and Martha's beds. I picked it up and stared at it.

"He was a handsome man, your husband," I said. "And a good man too." She nodded, wiped her eyes with her handkerchief. "He'd give me a tongue lashing for saying what I did downstairs. It was the most insensitive thing I could have ever said. I am so sorry."

"And you'd deserve such a lashing," Lizzie said, but she had an uplift to the corners of her mouth.

I winced. "Ja, I didn't think." I sat down beside her on the bed, hands in my lap. "I was being selfish, thinking of my own heart full of love for Irvina and missing them leaving to go on their own. I have room for other children...but it was thick-skinned of me, words I should have told my mouth not to spew."

"I know you didn't mean to hurt me, Mama. I know." She sighed. "I just miss him so. I'm happy for Delia and

Edmond, I truly am. I adore Irvina. Yet each time I see her, I'm reminded of what I don't have, what Fred and I wanted but will never be, and sometimes I wonder what I did to deserve that. Did I offend God? Is my punishment that Fred and I would have so little time together, and I'd have a life of teaching music with a broken heart?"

This was that moment when a mother wants more than anything to be wise and give something to her child that will feed her soul and heal it, but we are so impaired, we humans. I sent a prayer that I might think before I spoke. "God doesn't work that way." I picked at a thread in my apron. "At least I've never known Him to be a vindictive God, but rather one who is tender and loving. He would no more punish you by having Fred die than He's punishing Martha for not finding a hand to hold." Was that the proper comparison to make? "God gives us hope." I paused. "The way I have hope my lilacs will bloom and maybe even one day give me the cultivar I imagine with many petals on hardy stems. Remember where it says, 'I, even I, am He who comforts you'? That's what I think God's about. Sometimes there are troubles. And God is there with us."

"Then why don't I feel comforted? And when will this awful hurt ever end?"

It had been three years since Fred's death, and some had suggested to me, and to Lizzie too, that "it was time she moved on, got over it." But there was no one time that spoke to every heart. I hugged her to me, letting her sob into my shoulder. I remembered when she was four and broke her wrist falling when she climbed over a fence to chase a rabbit. The pain was great, but I knew with the bone set and a little laudanum, she'd soon be out racing and running. Heart and soul pain took so much longer to heal, required so much more faith that things would one day be better. I so wanted to give her that faith, and to assure her the pain wasn't a consequence of anything she'd done wrong—despite the words of Barney Reed. I just didn't know the words to say.

Martha opened the door, came to sit across from us on her bed. She stayed silent for a time, then said, "Shakespeare wrote that we should give sorrow words," her voice as soft and illuminating as the afternoon light. "'The grief that does not speak whispers to the o'er-fraught heart and bids it break.' I don't want your heart to break any further, Lizzie."

"Me either," Lizzie said.

Martha reached across to hold her sister's hands. "Maybe you can put how you feel into words, help another wife who grieves."

"You're the wordsmith, Martha." Lizzie blew her nose into her handkerchief.

"Maybe you could compose a piece of music," Delia said. She'd come up the stairs and stood in the open doorway. "Maybe that would be a way of honoring Fred."

"That's a splendid idea," I said, rushing in too quickly. "I mean, a song for Fred. That's a lovely thought. I think through flowers, lilacs, roses. You…you're the musician. Martha's got words, and Delia has sewing and baking to give to others."

"And Fritz has the river," Martha said. "We each received something different to help us through our sorrows."

"And our celebrations too," Delia added.

"I will compose a piece, for him and for me." Lizzie lifted her chin.

"Music cleanses the soul of the pain of daily living," I added. "That's an old German saying my grandmother used to tell me."

"I thought it was that music washed away the 'dirt' of daily living," Martha said.

"We can adapt," I told her.

"Adapt. Yes." Lizzie straightened her shoulders, wiped her dark brown eyes and smiled. She'd make it. That's what mattered.

THIRTY-TWO

THE POWER OF PASSION

Hulda, 1908

Fritz took a job on the river working for a dredging company. I confess to a disappointment in that. I knew he was intrigued by the river's personality—wild and raucous one river mile and then a flotsam holder meandering about the lazy bends the next. But I could see what dredging did to a river and how it changed the beds and banks.

"Ma," Fritz told me when I complained. "It's progress." He shoveled pickled beets into his mouth, then wiped his face with his napkin. "No different than the railroad. That banked-up area that borders us now acts as a dike, and with the tracks, it certainly has changed things."

"Yes. The trains rumble our beds at night. I'm hoping that dike will keep the river out of here when it rises, that's the only reason I sold them the right of way. Well, that and the farmers and shopkeepers need the transport for business."

"Maybe it will keep the Columbia out in June floods, but the Lewis on the other side, that's always the problem with winter runoff. When they build a dike there, then you'll be nice and safe between two high earth walls." Fritz pointed his fork at me.

"Will they do that, you think, build a dike there along the Lewis?" I sat beside my son. "How would it get paid for?"

"Farmers will tax themselves, I submit. We've talked about it at the creamery meetings."

"A tax for a dike I can see, Frank, but I don't see any value in the government paying to bring those dredges up the river farther. Every time they do, and those steamships too, the water pounds against the banks and breaks them down. We'll be sitting on top of the river before we know it. Or right next to the dike, if what you say is true and they build one. Not sure I like that."

"Don't complain to us," Frank said. "Complain to the government."

"Maybe I will."

"Good thinking, Dad." Fritz and Frank exchanged pleased looks for having put me off in another direction than at them.

My son was a handsome boy, and he had a fair number of girls twittering at him after church on Sunday, but he was like a fly at the honey pot, not wanting to settle too close for fear of getting caught. That was good. It was bad enough he worked away from home when we had plenty for him to do on this place. I looked at his hair and realized he hadn't asked me to cut it before church, yet it looked good. Fine, actually.

"Who cut your hair?" Martha and Lizzie both looked at their brother, just noticing too, I suspect.

"Joe Picard. He's got two chairs at his new tonsorial parlor."

"Pretty good job, I guess." I felt sadness that my baby boy had chosen someone other than his mother to look after his cutting like that.

"Progress, Ma. Just like steamships going up the river."

That night I composed the letter that the men in my life sniffed about me doing. I wrote to both the government and the newspaper editor at the *Woodland Echo* about the damage of wakes, whether from steamships or dredges, and how farmers were affected. I'd never heard back from Cornelia about my request for her to write an article about the lilacs, so I'm not sure why I thought a letter about dredging would persuade anyone to do anything, but I could at least try. Luther Burbank seemed to think my words were full of enthusiasm. I wrote and rewrote until late into the night, burning more kerosene than I should have. But the light of day is for propagating plants, while ideas often bloom in the dead of night. "Sow your seed in the morning and do not be idle in the evening," Ecclesiastes advises.

Certainty makes one say things firmly. The county road

was at risk of being undercut by the banks washing away every time a steamboat docked. I fully expected that before long, during spring flooding, the river would come over the banks and take out the road, and then the county would have to buy new land for a new road, whether the farmers wanted to sell their land or not!

I finished with, "Some will say, let those who own the land fix the banks; and others will say, let the county take the matter in hand and fix it; but I say, let the steamboat company and the government fix our banks; they should be the ones to do it."

I signed my name, Hulda Klager. Not Mrs. Frank Klager, but with my own name. I also didn't change the "I" to "we" in the letter, which a good wife ought to, but I was willing to own my opinion and not stand in the shadow of Frank's. The truth is, I didn't expect the *Echo* to publish it but felt better for having put the words on paper. Maybe that's why Barney Reed felt compelled to tell me what he thought now and then; it just felt better even if it didn't change anything.

That summer I pulled weeds, snipped suckers, replanted cultivars, made notes in my book, and watched steamboats dock daily. Sometimes I stood as they approached and scowled as the wake pushed into land, lapping at the black earth, tumbling chunks, exposing roots that before long would have no dirt beneath them and the shrubs would sink into the river. If we had a big flood, those banks would crumble like week-old cookies.

I'd given up hope of having my words read by others, but then one morning Delia called and said I should open up the *Echo*. "They published your letter, Mama."

"Did they?" I felt a flush of satisfaction. "I wonder what the neighbors will say."

"Oh, Mama, you did it so the neighbors would say something!"

She was right, of course. But I suggested that it was "a way of giving voice to lots of people's concerns. If we farmers agree to tax ourselves to build a dike, then why shouldn't the steamboat companies do likewise to fix the banks?"

"Won't Fritz be put out that you've chastised his employer?" Delia said.

"Fritz and your father urged me to write it."

"I hope he doesn't get upset with you, Mama."

"Oh, he'll survive," I said with just a twinge of regret. "We Klagers do."

THIRTY-THREE

TRANSFORMING

Hulda, 1908

Roy Mills of Mills Grocery and General Merchandise began showing up at our porch on his "way to the docks" he told us, but he had to drive a distance, so his suggestion that we were somehow on his "way" lacked the ring of truth. At first, he just chatted with Frank or me about the weather, the road conditions and how they might affect the new Model T introduced by Henry Ford. He was a tall, good-looking man, maybe in his early thirties. Clear thinking from what I could tell, with a good head for business. He spoke Chinook, he told us, and conversed with the few Chinook Indians left in the region who bought things at his store. He spoke with dignity about them, not demeaning the way some of our neighbors tended to toward that race.

Once, Roy asked if I'd consider selling him some of my cultivars for resale at his store.

"Why, she gives half of her stock away," Frank told him. "She'd undercut your sales."

"Just thought I'd ask." Roy took a second cookie from a plate Lizzie offered him. "If you ever do decide to wholesale them, I hope you'll keep my store in mind."

"Oh, I will. I'd want my neighbors to have first crack at them."

"Any real money in plants comes from catalog sales, I submit. Cooley's is a big distributor, near Salem."

"We'll go to them, then, when the time comes. After we give a fair number to Roy here."

Later we all sat on the porch, Lizzie, Fritz, and Martha included, and laughed about sending Lizzie off to Seattle to play piano at the new nickelodeon opened there. "You could play for hours and get to see free movies," Roy teased.

"I hear there are more than eight thousand open across the country," Fritz said. "You could travel on your music."

"Yes, and all I'd have to do is find another job so I could afford to live in Seattle." Lizzie fanned herself as yellow jackets buzzed in the flatiron plot. "No, I'm a Woodland girl with excursions to big cities and mountains." She told Roy then of her climb up Mount St. Helens. "Maybe when Woodland gets a nickelodeon, I'll see about playing. Until then, I'm happy to have my students, even if my mother is the worst one."

"Do you ever compose?" Roy asked.

Lizzie looked startled. "I...occasionally put some notes down on paper." She blushed. I'd heard her working on a piece I thought might have Fred in mind.

"You seem a natural for that." Roy stared at her.

"Do I?"

Then we were no longer all of us on that porch. Lizzie and Roy had drifted into each other's eyes and gone to a far-away place. I looked at Frank; he smiled, shook his head as though to warn me not to speak a word, and all was silent. Only the panting of Bobby on the porch broke the reverie of a summer dusk.

Until Fritz coughed and said he wondered what lands the president planned to include in the West for conservation purposes, a subject so far from the composition of the heart that Frank and I looked at him, speechless. Sometimes I wondered about my children and their strange timing. Surely they didn't get that from Frank and me.

A new doctor came to town that summer, Dr. Carl Hoffman. He was young, tall, tireless from what I heard. He owned a car too and stayed at the same boarding house as Roy Mills did, the only one in town. Dr. Hoffman stopped by to speak with Frank about cars—or so he said—but I noticed he also accepted lemonade offers from Lizzie and remained on the porch long after the cookies were gone. She could do worse than Dr. Hoffman, I thought. But I liked that Roy Mills too.

Ruth graduated from high school the following spring and earned a chance to study music in Baltimore of all places, at the Peabody Institute. I confess I found as much pleasure listening to her practice as playing on my own. Music floating through the open windows, while I pruned and seeded, was soothing to me. I'd miss that music, as well as anticipating Ruth's arrival home from school, lifting a bucket as soon as she greeted Tillie, changed her clothes, then crossed the field and fence to our garden, Nelia close behind her. Her contributions to the success of my growing garden were many, and I had already worried out loud to Frank about how I'd get all those lilacs and the mushrooming additional bulbs and shrubs watered every week without her.

"We'll manage. Add more bucket boys."

I asked Ruth if she'd like to hold her graduation party at our house. She hesitated. "Emil and Tillie offered. I—"

"Well, of course, that's fine. We can help them."

"It's just that my father..."

"Yes. I know. He thinks my garden is a den of iniquity."

"Oh, not that strong, Mrs. Hulda. He's mellowed, seeing as how I haven't asked to go to school in the sciences or anything."

"Nothing wrong with science." I puffed up my shoulders. "Perfectly compatible with faith, always has been." I didn't want Ruth to feel torn, so I changed the subject and asked what we could bring to Emil and Tillie's.

On the day of the party, I looked from Emil's backyard

across the fence to the lilac orchard to see the sun glint against the windows of the sun-porch nursery. I took the view in, as though new to me, and found it pleasant.

"You're responsible for the scholarship," Ruth told me as she came to sit beside us on dining room chairs brought outside for the occasion.

"Not in the least." I patted her knee. "You earned that honor yourself. You and Lizzie. She was the one who made all the connections. You have a gift for music, the raw seed that can be improved upon."

"But if you hadn't allowed me to live with you…if you hadn't paid for my piano lessons, I might never—"

"Yes, you would have. You have a strong heart, Ruth, and a giving one. I'll never forget your willingness to move so that Delia could come home. Even without those piano lessons, you'd have endured, kept going. I know that."

"I wouldn't have had any school recesses, though." Her eyes twinkled, and her wide face that I'd once considered homely was firm and filled with light, suggesting good health on her ample bones. We had that in common, Ruth and I, though she had enviable copper hair, straight and thick, while mine was frizzy and brown as dead moss.

"You'll do whatever is necessary," I assured her. "Persistence and prayer, that's the motto for a good life."

"You've taught me how to do that, Mrs. Hulda. You know how I enjoy seeing the shapes of things, rectangles and flatirons and circles and whatnot? Well, you've shaped my life. I'll be forever grateful."

I was humbled speechless.

As Ruth tended to her parents and spoke to other guests, Frank and I balanced teacups on our laps. Was it wrong to claim a part in giving that girl her good start, or at least for having nurtured her God-given gift of music? I didn't think so. I smiled to myself. Her father was always wary that what I did with my apples and roses and lilacs affronted God. But Ruth's music wasn't unlike that process. Born with a gift, the piano lessons focused that talent, and the Peabody Institute would do even more refining until the richness of original intention rang out across a concert hall to bless us all.

"You'll come to Baltimore when I graduate, won't you?" Ruth had come back over as we prepared to leave the party.

"All the way to Baltimore? Oh, I don't know. That would be quite a trip."

"It would be." Her voice thickened with the sadness of reality.

"We'll think about it," Frank said. "If not for your graduation, well, maybe some other time. You keep us posted about when you're playing, and I submit, one day we'll be there in the audience applauding."

"Will we?" I asked Frank after she'd left us. "Would we really go to Baltimore to hear her? The only trip we took far away was to Chicago for the fair. Course I've hopped from

Germany and Papa took us back and forth to Wisconsin, but I was too little to remember much of that."

"Why not? We just have to plan for it. Maybe sell a cow or two."

"Nineteen twelve. That's when she finishes at the Peabody. We could target that year."

"Yes, we could," Frank said, and his confidence kept away the sadness that Ruth's leaving brought. "Stop in Chicago and visit my family, too." It was a journey to look forward to.

"I want to give you something," I told Ruth as the afternoon shadows deepened and birds flittered in the cedar trees. "You worked hard and long last year, and we've had more successes thanks to you." We'd tended a big vegetable garden and canned and pickled until we saw jars of beets in our sleep.

We walked back across the fence and stood in my garden as I handed Ruth a box, the setting sun bringing out the auburn base of Ruth's hair. "You can plant it wherever you wish, but I want you to know that it's yours, given in gratitude for your generosity these many years. It's a brand new variety."

The starts were taken from the set of my Magical Three Lemoine. "I've called it Dark Dense Truss, Ruth."

"Is this the one I admired last spring?" Ruth asked. "I wasn't asking for—"

"I know. But yes, it's the one you liked." The root ball was wrapped loosely with damp rags.

Ruth tenderly touched the stem. "I…I'm honored. Thank you."

"You'll have to report back to me, because one or both of them might just come up with extra petals. They'll look much better when they're planted."

"Oh, it's fine, wonderful, Mrs. Hulda. I was just thinking of where I'd plant it, you know, where I can watch it and take care of it."

"I've thought of that. I think you should plant it where it will mean something special to you. Woodland has enough rain and sunshine that they'll survive almost anywhere here, and I hear they do well in Baltimore too."

She stared, thoughtful. "I'm going to take it home and plant it outside the kitchen window, where my mother can see it every day. A new variety. That's special."

I winced. Ruth's father might not like that. I said as much.

"But this is my gift to give my mother," Ruth said. "Papa won't say anything against generosity, Mrs. Hulda. That's a very Christian thing."

"Of course he won't, dear."

And to Barney Reed's credit, he didn't.

The next morning I told Frank, "I want Ruth to have another variety. One to plant in Baltimore."

"Not sure how that'll work." Frank sipped his coffee. "She's going to be living in a dormitory."

"They must have gardens there. And lawns around the school buildings. Surely she can find a place."

"Patience, Huldie. Send it to her when she's had a chance to get settled before she has to worry over a plant."

I knew he was right, but somehow the waiting annoyed. I was becoming impatient in my old age of forty-six. But I listened to him as a good wife should.

❧

Our lives went onward with me continuing to work on my lilacs. We kept the bucket boys, changing as they grew older or tired.

"You tell the same stories you told us, Mama," Martha said. "They've heard about grandma's geese and their red flannel suits a dozen times."

"I just repeat to remind them to be resourceful, that there is always a way through a hard time."

"Boys aren't interested in getting out of trouble. They like getting into trouble," my wise daughter told me.

So I expended my training on lilacs. A lilac from the President Grévy gave me a treat when it produced a deep blue the color of Irvina's eyes. I selected that one and pollinated it with another blue and trusted providence to bring me a surprise some years forward. A single white produced a double bloom one year, and that, too, required cheering and a letter to Mr. Burbank who did not respond. He traveled a great deal, lecturing, and I supposed he had so many letters, answering mine just took up too much time.

"I'm sorry if I've disturbed you, Mrs. Klager." I didn't recognize the voice nor did I recognize the young, smartly dressed woman who stood on my doorstep. "I'm Cornelia Givens, formerly of the *Sacramento Bee*."

Slender as a tulip stem, the young woman's face shone brightly, and I welcomed her inside the house.

"What are you doing here? When I hadn't heard from you, I thought—"

"I must apologize for not letting you know." She took a deep breath as she sat on the horsehair couch I directed her to. I offered her lemonade, which she accepted, took a deep swallow and then said, "I quit my job and decided to test my ability to write for magazines and other papers, become a freelance reporter. It took longer to get established than I thought it would."

"A freelance reporter. Good for you."

"I'm writing feature articles now. Maybe one day I'll work on a novel or a book of poetry, but for now I'm having the best time talking with people. I'm learning so many new things. Anyway, I'm here because I think writing about your garden is a wonderful idea. And I have a magazine interested."

"Do you?"

Her enthusiasm washed away that little annoyance I felt at her not writing the article when I'd first suggested it. "I can see from the front of your yard that you've been given a golden spade to make miracles out of dirt." She stood, looking out the window. "Transforming, that's what this is. How many plants would you say you have here? Would you grant me a tour?" She turned to face me.

"I guess by now I have six hundred or more, not counting the lilacs, and there are several hundred of them."

"Oh, that's just the sort of thing readers like. I know I can sell this. I had a long story printed in the *Atlantic* about the Lowthorpe School of Landscape Architecture for Women back east, and I visited a number of arboretums, interviewed the landscape architects and chief gardeners. I love it, even if I still can't grow a pansy on my own." She laughed. "I'm sorry I didn't get back to you. I felt strongly that I needed to take advantage of my time back east before returning west and finally getting to see your gorgeous garden."

"That's fine, just fine," I said. I showed her around my garden then, and she made notes, even sketched a few plants and the house and barn. She cooed at the lilacs, talked to the rhododendrons, asked questions.

Cornelia especially liked the iron-shaped garden with its daisies and petunias and pansies and the statue of a young girl that was a fountain overflowing with water. "I love the way you've laid it out with the color rising like a sea wave, light to dark, smaller plants to taller ones with the lilac bushes beyond, peeking around the side of the potting house. It's quite...soothing to the eye, Mrs. Klager. The fountain, it's lovely too. It speaks of abundance and generosity, as the water flows over the girl's basket."

"Thank you for that. I change things nearly every year, much to Mr. Klager's consternation, but I like seeing new things and how they'll complement each other or not. And the fountain says to you exactly what I hoped it would."

We wandered the paths, and she asked about Nelia's direction of the bucket boys. She wrote down what they were paid. The long rows of lilacs caused her to gasp. "So many."

"If I get one good plant out of four hundred, I'm doing well. So I have to plant a lot of cultivars, hoping they'll produce the innovation I'm looking for."

"It's so much work," Cornelia said as we neared the end of the tour and I showed her my nursery efforts in the glassed-in porch. "You and Frank do this all by yourselves? And run a dairy too?"

"Our children help, of course. And I've had hired help, young girls attending the new high school. My bucket boys show up regularly. It is a big production."

"Does it, I mean, can you…make a living doing this? If you don't mind my asking."

"I wouldn't recommend it as a profession," I said. "But I have a good husband and a productive herd of cows. The price of cheese has held, and our farm is paid off." I felt a little uncomfortable telling her this business about money. It wasn't the sort of conversation one had with a sister, let alone a near stranger. But I didn't want someone jumping into a garden arena without full knowledge that they'd be in the poorhouse for a long time, unless they had other means to keep their gardens flourishing. "I don't do this to make a living. Bringing flowers to others has been a gift I never imagined I'd be allowed to give. It was a hobby for a long time, a challenge, started when I wanted to have a larger, crisper apple that was easier to peel." I took her to the apple orchard and showed her, explaining that in the spring, I had any number of blossoms from different sorts of apples grafted onto one tree.

"It's so...impressive," she said.

A bumblebee lobbed up from orange poppy blooms and flew off.

"Not the work of it, but the result," I agreed. "God knew that we'd need beauty and fragrance to help us through the difficult days, so He gave us flowers and let us learn on our own how their cycle of living and dying is like a garden's rhythm, giving us hope each spring."

Cornelia nodded, then looked at her lapel watch.

"Will you spend the night in Woodland?"

"I have a room at the boarding house."

"You're welcome here. It'll save you money. A freelance writer has to pay attention to that." I wagged my finger at her. "And wouldn't you like to see the garden in the early morning?"

"I would at that, but I hate to impose. Besides I want to review my notes and put them in some order so I can ask better questions in the morning. But thank you. You're very generous with your garden and your time."

I wondered if she'd run into Dr. Hoffman or Roy Mills.

Cornelia came back in the morning and had a few questions for Frank. She had a bit of advice for us too before she left. "If my article is published, there'll be visitors coming here. I'll mention that the time to come is what, between mid-April and early May? That's when they'd see lilacs blooming, correct?"

"I submit that's so."

"Then my suggestion is that you have scads of lemonade made up you can sell for a penny to help compensate for the inconvenience of visitors."

"Not inconvenient. We'd love it, wouldn't we, Frank?"

"Maybe I'll put a box out, with one of my signs: Give a Klager Life. Donate Here."

"Oh, Frank." I punched his shoulder.

"I'd also suggest you think about places for people to park their vehicles," Cornelia said.

"Ach, no. Not that many people are interested in lilacs."

"You'd be surprised. Keep in mind this article will reach thousands of readers, and good writing is meant to move people to action. I hope they'll move along the rivers and the roads and come here, to Woodland, just as I did."

I took her enthusiasm as a young woman's enthusiasm for her work. I never dreamed that she'd be right.

THIRTY-FOUR

MOVING ON

Hulda, 1908–1909

Nelia instructed the bucket brigade like a nurse giving directions to orderlies. I said as much, and she laughed. "I plan to be a nurse one day. I'm going to school at the new Swedish Hospital in Seattle."

"I've never heard of the place." Nelia had just popped a blood blister on one of the boys' hands, wrapped it, and sent him off to nurse it while he urged his bucket brothers onward.

"They're raising funds now, and by the time I graduate, they'll have a program where I can work and go to school too."

"Nursing. A wonderful profession."

"I'll have to get over being squeamish."

"You handled that blister just fine."

She shrugged.

"I miss Ruth," I told her.

"Am I not doing enough?" Nelia looked alarmed.

"No, no, you're a wonderful worker. I just loved teaching the two of you. I wonder how she's doing in Baltimore."

"She's like my sister." I nodded agreement. "And you're like my mother," she said.

"Am I? That pleases me." It did, more than I could say. I swallowed, hoping I wouldn't push this bud of conversation too fast. "You've talked little about your mother."

"I don't remember much of her. Even Jasmine seems miles away."

I stopped pouring beer into my snail and slug pots and listened.

"She's buried up the Lewis River," Nelia continued. "On the Runyan Property where we stayed."

"You've had a lot of losses in your young life."

"The work here was good healing, Mrs. K." For the first time, I saw the girl with tears in her eyes. She'd taken tragedy and loss and been a good steward of it.

The next morning when she came over from Emil's, I told her I had a gift for her. "I was going to wait until you left for school, as I did with Ruth, but I decided you needed this now. Its name is Chrystle. It's a new variety. White, but still not the perfect cream I'm seeking. It does have petal edges that are crisp like they've been cut with very sharp scissors, and the lilac society agrees it's a unique plant."

"It's beautiful." She held the cultivar as though it were a newborn, then put it in one of the galvanized buckets. "I'll take the best care of it."

"I have no doubt." I stroked her dark curls. "It's who you are."

Roy Mills came for Christmas dinner where our house abounded with happy conversation. Irvina was the delight of the day as she opened her presents, giggling.

Frank bantered with Roy about business, how logging brought new people and new customers to the store, whether hop farmers were doing well this season. They spoke of vehicles, weather, men things.

Then in January, Frank announced his intention to buy a Model T Ford.

"Now?" I asked.

"I need an auto in time for Lizzie's wedding."

"What?" Lizzie and Roy were downstairs sitting in the living room, while we were upstairs preparing for bed. A January wind howled against the house. "How…? When…?" Why hadn't Lizzie said something? Oh, I knew Roy was interested. He often came from Swartz's boarding house carrying a lantern in the night to make the half-mile trek. Once, a wag had painted Roy's lantern red, which did not please him one bit. But that he planned to marry Lizzie, and she might say yes, well, I wasn't ready for that. No one had mentioned that!

"Man did the right thing coming to me to ask for my daughter's hand," Frank said. "I had to keep his confidence. Lizzie'll tell you everything, I'm sure, as soon as the man leaves. Barely has enough privacy to court the woman with Martha and Fritz and us hovering about."

"Proper chaperoning is all." I punched the feather pillow.

I listened to the low murmuring downstairs, wishing I could make out sounds coming up the stairwell, but I couldn't. Finally, I heard the door close and Lizzie make a phone call, then she sauntered up the stairs.

"Mama, are you awake?" Lizzie knocked at the door.

"You couldn't keep her down if she was dead," Frank said.

"Come in, come in." I sat up. "You have news?"

"Roy asked me to marry him. We set a date in March. Will that be all right? I know it isn't very far away, but things get busy for him at the store after that, and I know they do here too with your garden."

"Lizzie. Don't worry about our garden. You set the date any time you wish, and tell us what you'd like for flowers. We'll push them in the sun porch to have good blooms."

"Crocus, Mama. I'd like blue crocus, just a small bouquet for Martha and Delia and me to carry."

"Your sisters already know?"

Martha stuck her head around the corner. "Don't be upset just because we all knew that tonight was the night, Mama. We weren't sure you could keep the bubbling in your smile from letting Roy know that everyone knew."

"I can keep a secret," I huffed.

Lizzie hugged me. "I know you can. But Martha's right. You wear your emotions on your face, and I didn't want Roy to have second thoughts about maybe being swooped and smothered by this family of ours. We don't do much lightly, you know."

"Living abundantly, that's what we're charged with," I said. I was tickled for Lizzie and Roy Mills. I told Frank as much after everything settled down, with Lizzie and Martha together going to the tack room to inform Fritz.

"You're pure, Huldie. One of a kind," Frank told me. "You have not one wit of guile inside of you. You wouldn't have been able to stop yourself from greeting Roy differently, just knowing he'd soon be family. It's how you are, and I wouldn't change it for the world. But Lizzie, well, she wanted this to be her night, and I submit, a man can get chilled feet even when he's looking forward to warm socks to put them into."

"I guess," I said.

"You've a compassionate heart. And the best thing about you is that you don't carry hurt around for long. You turn it into something good, maybe even a deeper caring than what you might have before the hurt."

"When did you get so wise?" I buttoned up the top button on his long underwear. The wood heat from the kitchen didn't rise all that much to the second floor, and it was cold outside.

"Been living with you all these years. Some of your wisdom has to rub off eventually." He pulled up the crazy quilt with its velvets and wool pieces stitched together. I snuggled up next to him in my flannel gown, the comfort of ages resting in his sleeping sighs. I put my cold feet against him, and he let me.

I didn't fall asleep right away. Instead, I thanked God for a fine husband, a grand family. I thanked Him that my children were friends to one another and that He had given two of them another person to love and grow old with. I prayed they would grow old together, as Frank and I were, and that the loss of my sons-in-law so soon after their marriages would not repeat itself in my daughters' lives. And then I thanked Him for being there with us through it all, keeping the promise that we do not ever walk in darkness without light to reveal the next steps.

I hoped Roy and Lizzie would consider living with us after they married, just as Frank and I had lived with my parents for several years. I'd made comments about how nice it would be to have another grandchild born in this room, but Lizzie had remained quiet. I should have prayed for patience. Instead, I prayed that Martha would find a suitor to her liking and Fritz would settle down too. We could add on to the house, if need be. I would move the lilacs to make room.

⁂

Not much was in bloom on March 9, 1909, when Lizzie and Roy Mills spoke their vows. (It was two days after Luther Burbank's birthday.) But we did indeed have crocuses and just a few daffodils budding out. The lilacs with their heart-shaped glossy leaves and buds looked ready, but they hadn't popped, that spring being cooler than normal and rain having poured twenty-eight days of the last thirty-two. Lizzie chose a small wedding with just family and a few of Roy's friends, including Dr. Hoffman. No music students, no neighbors other than family, of course.

We listened to the vows and drove back to the farm, all of us. I remembered Martha telling me at the girls' first weddings how those ancient gods hated it when mortals looked too happy without their help. She called it hubris. Silly, I know, but every now and then, Barney Reed's chattering about my work made me wonder if what I did in my garden changing lilacs really did offend God, and if so, would He find a way to punish my hubris yet again.

As we neared the farm, I decided such unhealthy thoughts

should be set aside, not pondered on a daughter's wedding day. Instead, I vowed to speak of them with the reverend, soon.

My sisters had left the church earlier and had already set out dishes of food. Martha quickly joined as Nelia dashed around, pouring coffee for the men. I watched my daughter with her new husband, smiling, open as a lily, and I was so grateful. Then Lizzie sat down at the piano, adding something special to the reception at our house.

"This is a composition I've been working on for a while. I want to play it for my new husband." Roy's faced turned a lovely shade of red—the very color I wish I could get a lilac to give me. "I call it 'Take His Hand.'" I recognized a few sections as portions she'd worked on, but I had never heard it all put together. We all applauded when she finished. Roy bent down and whispered in her ear, and she laughed, a sound as free and open as a brook. Irvina scurried up beside her and began one-finger pounding.

"Your next student," Edmond said before Delia whisked her daughter away to laughter.

When Lizzie and I were alone upstairs, as she changed from her wedding dress to a traveling frock, I asked her if it was Fred's song she'd played.

"It started out to be for him, but as time went on, I realized that music speaks to the living not the dead. Fred would have wanted me to sing for the living. So the song is about taking the hand of a true love and going as far as you're allowed, and then having the courage to believe you can take another when the time is right."

"That's beautiful," I said. It was.

Later that day, we waved good-bye as the couple drove off in their new Model T Ford. They planned a honeymoon trip to California, where Roy "promised" Lizzie it wouldn't be raining.

"I hate to see them go," I told Frank as we stood on the porch, and I chewed on the side of my finger. I hadn't done that for years.

"They need time alone." Frank took my hand in his and held it, then moved me to lean against him, his arms around me.

"Oh, I know. Of course they need that. I just mean they're leaving us." I sighed. "I wish they'd consider staying on here. I put out enough hints. I guess Roy wants to surprise Lizzie when they get back as to where they're going to make their home. They certainly can't move into the boarding house!"

"They could. But they won't." I turned to look at him. He had that little grin, and he wiggled his nose at me.

"What do you know that I don't?" I pulled away from him, poked him in his ribs. "Tell me."

"They're coming here to live, Huldie. At least for a while. Lizzie wanted me to wait to tell you until after they'd gone so you'd have something to look forward to."

"I always have something to look forward to." I laughed, then added, "I'm a gardener."

Lizzie came downstairs one morning in June to tell me that she thought she might be with child.

"Lizzie!" I said. "That's wonderful. When?"

"At Christmas time, if we've calculated right."

I counted on my fingers. I shouldn't have, but a December birth was right in line with an early March wedding. Every mother is relieved about such details as that.

"Oh, that's so good. Best to get right on it and have that family. It'll be like when you Kinder were young and we all lived with my parents. I'll sew her christening dress. Make a quilt too." My cup was full.

"You don't know that it'll be a 'she,'" Lizzie said, adding, "We'll have the baby here, Mama."

"Well, I should hope," I said.

"But we'll be moving into our own house soon."

"You will?"

"You know I'll come by every day. I've got my rhododendron hybrids to keep track of."

I felt as deflated as an old feather pillow. But I didn't resist. At least she'd told me, hadn't kept it a secret so everyone else before me knew. "You've already told your sister and father, I suppose." I bit at the side of my finger.

"You're the second. I only told Roy this morning."

"Fritz can move back into the house, this way. I'm sure he'll like that. I never felt good about his being out there alone in the tack room."

"Don't get your hopes up, Mama. He's got quite a parlor out there, and no one bothers him. He might not like sharing snores with you and Papa and Martha again."

"We don't always get everything we want," I said, though I didn't really believe that.

A blizzard roared on December 9 when William Mills entered the world. The next morning, a rare snowfall carpeted the ground, covering the garden but leaving ornamental rocks and urns exposed. I pulled on my boots and coat and let Frank sleep. All our cows were dry, so he didn't have to make the two-mile trek to the Bottoms twice a day now. Instead, he read and looked at garden catalogs with me. I would have liked to stay in bed myself, snuggled up next to him, but the fire was out, and that baby would need a good warm stove.

I pulled my gloves on and went to the woodshed to let the cats and Bobby out. I loaded my arms with wood and told Bobby to bring the kindling. Nelia and Fritz had been working with that dog to do tricks, and he'd picked up "kindling," carrying a couple of the thinner pieces of fir in his mouth while I trudged through the powdery snow toward the house.

Kittens mewed and purred and followed me up the back steps with dainty feet not accustomed to snow. I stamped my feet on the back porch and dropped the logs in the wood box, took the kindling from Bobby's mouth, and shooed him inside with the cats rolling back and forth, tails up, mouths open looking for their goodies. "In a minute. Let's have a little patience."

Before stepping inside, I turned to look out at my lilacs. Snow powdered the south side of the branches, making a picture of black etched against white. They could look so dead in winter, those shrubs. But spring would come. That was the promise, that spring would always come and with it new life.

I heard William crying in his mother's arms and then the silence of a baby fed, a new family making their way. Frank stood in the kitchen. "I'll start the fire."

My heart could fill no more.

THIRTY-FIVE

GENEROSITY

Hulda, 1910–1911

March 31, 1910

Dear Mrs. Klager,

Thank you for your encouragement about my freelance efforts and for keeping me informed of your own. I trust you and Frank and your children are well, as am I. Your suggestion that we visit Luther Burbank's farm in California is most intriguing. We will keep each other interested until we find the proper time and date that might find Mr. Burbank at his experimental station and not traveling the country giving lectures. Have you ever thought of giving lectures? I think you are a natural in telling stories.

The reason I'm writing today is to enclose a pre-publication article about your garden. It will appear in the *Oregonian* the second week of April. The editor said it was so interesting that he might even take the train to Woodland to see your remarkable garden. I hope that's so. I did want you to know that you might wish to get those lemons squeezed for the lemonade.

I have also offered a chance to see your fine gardens to a friend of mine whom I met at the Lowthorpe School. We have corresponded since then, and she has an interest in lilacs. She plans a visit to the West, and I have promised her we will drive to your garden. I hope that is agreeable and that I have not overstepped the bounds of decency by inviting her before I secured your agreement. The date of her visit is uncertain, but I am hopeful it may occur before all the blooms are gone. She's also wishing to return with one of your cultivars.

A Mother's Day celebration is being planned in Sacramento this year, following the events in West Virginia and Philadelphia two years ago. Isn't it grand that lilacs bloom in time for such a noteworthy occasion? Perhaps when Mr. Klager makes up his donation sign, he might add "take a start home for your mother."

Please reply back to me if my visit with my friend will intrude. Otherwise I will plan to see you in person within the next two months.

Yours with admiration,

Cornelia Givens

Post Script: The lilac start you gave me is doing well! It has blooms this year, and I look forward to seeing how many petals it might have!

"I can't believe it," I told Frank. "Look at what Cornelia wrote in this article: 'It's always lilac time in the Lilac Lady's garden.' That's just not true. They only bloom at certain times. She knew that. Why would she say that?"

"Huldie. She's being poetic. You're always doing something related to lilacs; that's all it means. It's a fine compliment; that's what it is."

"Oh. I just don't want people to think they'll always see lilacs in bloom if they come visit." They'd see dozens of other varieties of plants in bloom, in season, so I hoped it wouldn't be a waste of people's time—if they came. A part of me couldn't imagine people driving a distance to my gardens, not with the price of petrol. The train was more convenient, and those steamboats, but the idea of people taking a day out of their lives to walk among flowers was both amazing and gratifying. Perhaps people did realize how hopeful and healing flowers could be. And I did so want to share what we'd done.

The article was published just as Cornelia said it would be. They gave it the headline "Where Lilacs Still Bloom." On the Saturday following the article, in mid-April, people began to come. A trickle on Saturday, people saying they'd read the story and especially liked the idea that I'd propagated my own varieties, nearly ten now, and that I'd done this work without benefit of botany studies or degrees. But Luther Burbank didn't have a scientific background either, I reminded them, not that I wouldn't have loved to attend a school or two. I wouldn't have wasted so many plants, I told people. It's good to build on the work of others.

"I had a family willing to support my efforts too," I spoke to a crowd. "This is not one woman's garden by any means."

On Sunday afternoon, more people arrived from Kelso and Kalama, almost neighbors they were, but none had ever come to my garden before. By the second weekend in May, a day called Mother's Day, more than twenty cars parked along the road, and I showed them the lilac plantings, pointed out the three surviving Lemoine that had started it all (Cornelia had written of them), and lifted several of Frank's tin labels. A few people's eyes glazed over as I gave them more detail than they wanted. I sent them to lemonade on the porch where Lizzie and Delia had been conscripted to serve. Nelia cut blooms for bouquets that she sold for two cents apiece. I told her she could keep the money.

A couple from Massachusetts, visiting their daughter in Vancouver, thought it would be a nice outing for them to come here on the steamer. They likened my garden to Arnold Arboretum. "They've dozens of plants, hydrangeas and azaleas, holly, and lilacs, just like you have."

"Oh, surely not. I've only a few acres here."

"But you've created an Eden with what you have," the man said. "Would you consider allowing us a start? We love lilacs, especially new varieties, and it looks like you have what, four or five?"

"Ten. So far. But I have so many others I want to develop. A red, for one. Wouldn't a deep red be astonishing to see? And smell?"

They nodded, and as we were standing by my newest cultivar creation, I took my pruning knife and cut him a start. "I call this one My Favorite."

"I love the magenta color," the woman gushed. "Double flowers too. Thank you so much!"

"We'll be sure to label it 'Klager My Favorite' so people will know where it came from."

"Could I have a start of your purple?" A woman about my age asked, her voice soft as chamois. I was back on the porch and took my seat in the rocker. I'd been standing and talking most of the afternoon, and my ankles were starting to swell. "My mother planted one beside her dooryard back in Minnesota, and when I smell this"—she inhaled the bloom, closing her eyes—"I am brought right back there to that place. And to her."

"Certainly. Frank?"

He pulled his pocketknife from his vest pocket—we hadn't even had time to change our clothes after church before people began to arrive—and walked with the woman to the lilacs. She pointed at the one she admired, and he snipped a length with bloom. When they came back to the porch, she said, "Will fifteen cents be enough?"

"Fifteen cents?" Frank looked at me. "Ah, I submit, whatever you deem fair."

"Oh no. I'm happy that you want them. I love hearing how lilacs remind you of your mother."

"Leave whatever you'd like in that box there," Frank said. "If you've a mind to." I frowned at him.

She started a flood. Others came forward with requests for various snips, and I began to wonder if we shouldn't have cut them ahead of time or had suckers in water and labeled so people could take whichever one they wanted.

The lilacs were generous that year, and I loved seeing the faces of people and hearing where they planned to plant them. It was a wonderful day, even though Cornelia and her friend never appeared.

At twilight, everyone left. We sat, stunned. I put my feet up. "There must have been two hundred people here, just today."

Frank rattled the donation box and began counting. He looked up. "Huldie, I do believe we have nearly ten dollars in this box."

"Ten dollars? From sales?" That bothered me, it did.

"And donations," Nelia said. "I saw people putting coins in who weren't carrying out any starts. In the line at the privy, people talked to each other like they were old friends, all the while asking where they came from and sharing stories of their lilacs. They were happy to be here. Maybe they put coins in to show that."

"Next year we'll put a second box out, then," Frank said. "Right beside the hollyhock that winds over the privy. It'll help pay for moving it to make room for more of your lilacs."

"Oh, I don't think this will happen again. It was Cornelia's article that brought people."

"People talk," Fritz said. "And what better to talk about than having a fine outing just outside of Portland and down the road from Seattle where you can see as many lilacs blooming as at some famous arboretum back east."

The following weeks, more people arrived, and while the lilacs were finished blooming, there were other things to see, and people didn't seem too upset as they asked about my work. They told me they'd be back next year.

The other arrival of the summer was Clara Wilke in August, the first child of Delia and Edmond, a new sister for Irvina, born at our home with Dr. Hoffman presiding. The Wilke family didn't stay long with us after Clara's birth before heading back to their farm, but I was pleased by their presence while it lasted. That's what a flower teaches one, to enjoy the moment while you can.

People did talk, and in 1911 Cornelia wrote another article that was published in a national gardening magazine, and our yard filled up with interested people from as far away as

San Francisco and Denver. I wore my apron and walked the grounds with them, happy to share stories of my desire for a deep red lilac. I still worked on that creamy white, and I hadn't given up on the twelve petals either, but one has to keep finding new things to work toward.

Cornelia visited that summer, along with her friend Mrs. Shelly Snyder from Baltimore. Mr. Snyder came too. They stayed at the Hobb Hotel at the corner of Davidson and Third the two days they were here, but mostly they were in the garden, or on the porch with Frank and me and Martha and Fritz, when he was home.

The Snyders were an interesting pair, she with her short skirts, though her ankles were covered, and he with his tightly buttoned suit coat. It was linen, but the weather felt sultry those days in May when they walked my garden. I'd have thought he might have relaxed a bit, but he didn't. Both had botanical interests, but Mr. Snyder questioned me about my techniques of grafting, then gathering the seeds and growing them under glass. He wanted me to explain what would trigger my pulling out the plant and tossing it. "A terrible color. When I wanted red and got some putrid form of it. Those had to go."

She asked questions about the garden design and layout and the shape of the plantings. I chuckled when she asked about the shapes. "You remind me of my young friend Ruth Reed," I said. "She was always commenting on the shapes of things. I think that's why she liked my flatiron garden best."

"It is the first thing you see when you come into the yard, except for the trees," Mrs. Snyder said.

"I hate to iron, myself, but I do it. I figure a garden of the iron shape suggests that woman's work can be made fun."

"Especially if you can get a daughter to do it," Martha said, but she smiled.

"I wanted to make gardens for occasions in our child's life." Mrs. Snyder let her fingers linger on an azalea. "A first birthday, maybe in a pony shape, if she took up riding. Something with a fishing pond if we'd had a boy."

I started to ask her about her children, but Mr. Snyder interrupted. "Do you sell your starts?"

"She won't let me," Frank said. "We've two catalog companies wanting cultivars they'd finish and sell."

"Why wouldn't you offer them through catalogs?" Cornelia asked.

"I like seeing people come here. I do all the work. Why shouldn't I have the pleasure of seeing firsthand who receives them?"

I told them about My Favorite and how it and three others had been the true beginning of my lilac breeding. They listened with great interest, but when I asked about their garden, they exchanged looks, and something kept me from asking after their children. He coughed, and she looked down, and then she said they'd been having a discussion about what to do with the garden and not having great results.

"It's a great deal of work," Mrs. Snyder said, "as you know."

I didn't think the issue was the work. "It is. But good work. I have help. My high-school girls and the bucket boys. Why, you have one of my garden graduates right there in Baltimore. Ruth Reed attends the Peabody music conservatory."

"Perhaps she could use summer work," Mr. Snyder said.

"She just might. She's hard-working."

"How is she with…elderly people?" Mrs. Snyder asked.

"Oh, for heaven's sake, the two of you aren't old at all!" I said.

"Not us, but my husband's mother. She's getting on in years and…has quite a bit of say about the garden."

"If she's an opinionated and stubborn woman, well, know that Ruth comes with past experiences for having worked with me. She'd do just fine."

I gave them Ruth's address. Baltimore is a big city, and she might live miles away from the Snyder estate. Still, I imagined Ruth and the delicate but vibrant Mrs. Snyder walking in a garden together, talking about the shapes they could make and fill with blooms.

THIRTY-SIX

LIFE LIKE A RIVER

Hulda, 1912

They say that life is like a river or the garden, both images to remind us all of seasons, cycles, the rise and fall of living.

Nelia ran from the postal box to the backyard. With Lizzie and Delia and their families on their own, she'd come home to us. She squealed now, "I've been accepted!" I stood with my hoe, pushed my hat back. "Swedish Hospital says they'll take me!"

"Did you doubt?"

Nelia stepped around matted grasses still wet from the spring floods to hand over the letter. She'd graduate in just a few weeks and be gone from this place that had nurtured her through the years. The garden had weathered the spring Lewis River flood, but it had taken lots of hard work, digging and potting dozens of plants that I didn't think could make it otherwise. Now, with drier soil, she'd soon be working side by side with us. But first, we'd have to celebrate.

"Congratulations, Nelia," Martha said. "We all knew this would happen."

"Did you? I wasn't certain."

Fritz laughed. "I've never known you not to be certain. You're like Ma, here, in that."

Nelia grinned. "A nurse," I said. "We'll have a nurse in the family."

Fritz frowned at that, and I took it as a subtle statement that he didn't consider Nelia as a part of the Klager family.

"I guess all that nursing at school has paid off," Martha said.

"Nursing at school?" Nelia looked surprised.

"All the times we teachers call on you when there's a cut or sprained ankle and the child is crying and distressed. I call that nursing, and we always think of you."

"I guess it is. When I get to go with them to Dr. Hoffman's office, that feels like real nursing. Sometimes I even get to hand him needles and thread, for sewing stitches. I think I could even do it myself."

One of the tabby cats swished his tail against Nelia's legs, then plopped down next to Bobby.

"You'll be leaving us," I said. "But we'll get good work out of you before you go. Now scat. Get those clothes changed and head back out here. We have a dozen things to do before the next Lilac Day."

It was what they'd started to call the spring event when people came to Woodland to see the blooms close to Mother's Day. This year, 1912, there was no article by Miss Givens, but people would come anyway. *Woman's Home Companion* had run a short piece last year about the garden. But because the article had pictures included, I thought we might have ourselves a crowd.

Nelia skipped back upstairs. Both Martha and Tillie, who had once worked for Dr. Hoffman as a nurse, had written letters for Nelia, and so had Dr. Hoffman himself. All of Woodland in a way had played a part in the success of Nelia's future. In Ruth's too. That girl would graduate from the Peabody Institute, and Frank and I planned a trip to Baltimore. Martha would go with us while Fritz stayed and watched the farm, looked after Bobby, the cats, and the cows.

Cornelia planned to join us and visit Snyder gardens and a few others back east. I wished Nelia could come, but she'd be off to Seattle, anxious to get her scholarship details into place. After supper, Martha complained a little of a headache and said, "I believe I'll go upstairs and lie down." That's what she said, just like that. She held her head, and I asked if she wanted a hot water bottle or something, and she said no, that she just needed to rest.

In the morning, she was late coming down to breakfast, and I shouted up the stairs. I hadn't heard any stirring from her room, and Nelia was already dressed and off to take her acceptance letter to show her father.

"Ja," I said. "He'll be happy as a tailor with a new batch of cloth."

I did wonder if Nelia's father might object to having her go so far away, but then I'd recalled a similar pondering about Ruth's father letting her move to Baltimore and how that worry had been wasted; he'd been pleased she could pursue her music interests.

Nelia left, and I called up again and said to Martha, "Don't piddle around now, come have breakfast, and we can talk awhile before we face those flowers." I turned a few pages of a catalog, looking at the exotic ornamentals calling to me for next year, when I heard the clock chime and realized Martha had still not come downstairs.

"What's with you?" I walked up the stairs. She wasn't usually a hard sleeper, though with her twenty-six, we didn't talk much about her sleeping habits. I knocked on her door, and when there was no cheerful, "Come in," I pushed it open.

"Martha," I said. She lay with her face turned away on the bed, and I touched her shoulder gently. "Do you still have a headache?"

Her body felt cool. And still. Deathly still. I shook her, but there was no movement.

"Mein Gott im Himmel," I said. "My God in heaven, keep her safe," I whispered, then loudly went to the window and shouted for Frank. "Frank! Come, at once! It's Martha!" My voice broke speaking her name, and I felt the tears well up.

Martha's body lay before us in an open casket. Frank sat bowed over on a low chair, his hands clasped between his knees, their grip broken only when he reached to wipe his eyes with his forearm. Delia shushed Irvina, who asked, "Why won't Auntie Martha get up?"

"I'm so sorry for your loss," people said as they spoke to us in hushed tones. Such simple words, meant to be kind, sympathetic, and yet they couldn't begin to breach the pain. Martha's death sliced through me like a pruning knife: sharp, leaving a clean cut open and exposed to all the elements. What was the word Nelia used? *Incarn,* the growing of new flesh over a wound. It would take a very long time for that to happen. New words, that was Martha's talent, teaching us words.

"Let's go outside. Take a short walk," Nelia said. Martha had been in the parlor for more than a day now, first taken from her bedroom to the undertaker, then returned in the casket.

"No, no. I have to stay with Martha. I have to. If I'd gone up to check on her, maybe I could have saved her. Called Dr. Hoffman. I might have."

"No, you couldn't have," Nelia said. "Dr. Hoffman said it was likely an aneurism or maybe a brain tumor, but nothing he could have done anything about, or you either."

"She worked too hard in the garden. I worked her too

hard. She said she had a headache. I should have told her to lie down sooner." No last good-byes like Lizzie had with her Fred. More like Delia's not being able to tell Nell Irving her last thoughts nor his to her. He left this earth without his knowing how much he was loved. Martha wouldn't know that either.

"Mama." Delia covered my hand with her own. "You have to believe that her death wasn't anyone's fault. No one's. Seeking blame, even blaming yourself, robs you of strength you need. To carry on. To do what Martha would want you to do."

"What's that? Worry over my lilacs? What are lilacs compared to a daughter?" I so hoped Martha knew that, but had I ever told her? Were these bad things happening to my children because I wasn't a listening mother, learning from the tragedies befalling us?

Dr. Hoffman patted my shoulder. I looked up at him and spoke aloud my questions. "No," he said. "No. Bad things happen, and we learn from them, but they do not happen so that we will learn. God is a good God. Martha's death is not a consequence of anything you did or did not do. It's what is."

Yet I looked for something or someone to blame, though I knew it would keep me grieving her life with guilt rather than remembering it with gratitude.

Nelia said, "Remember, you told me that Martha said we should give our sorrow words."

"I...I can't find the words."

"Scripture, Mama," Lizzie said. "We'll find comfort there." Lizzie picked up the family Bible and read passages from Isaiah and Jeremiah about God as comforter and the planner of our lives, "plans for good." I said the phrases over and over in my mind. *Plans not to harm but to give a future and a hope.* Martha's students and their families came and sat for a time. Lizzie played softly on the piano. It seemed to me that the music comforted Lizzie as words couldn't. I lost track of time, and then Lizzie brought in rose of Sharon. "It's a healing balm, Mama. You said so yourself."

"Look what blooms on this April day," said Nelia. "Martha liked this flower, didn't she? Would you like me to put it next to the casket?"

"No, I'll put the flowers in her hands. It's how I wish to remember her."

Nelia walked with me to the casket, where Fritz stood. I pulled the flowers one at a time from the vase and nestled them into Martha's still hands, then patted them as my lips trembled. I gasped getting my breath. Frank slipped in between Fritz and me and took me in his arms. We held each other, lost together, parents outliving their child. The deepest of hurts.

THIRTY-SEVEN

REPLANTING

Hulda, 1912–1915

We did not go to Baltimore. Instead, we sent a letter to the Snyders telling them of Martha's passing and that we must stay here. I had looked forward to visiting the conservatories of the East, walking through Arnold Arboretum at Harvard and a new site Cornelia had been invited to in Locust Valley, New York, called Munnysunk. Munnysunk was a private tree arboretum bought by a man with wealth, it was said, but who felt empty. Until he began to plant and protect rare trees, and that had filled him up. I loved trees almost as much as lilacs and other ornamentals, but mostly I liked the idea of meeting someone who cared deeply about plants and wasn't puffed up about himself. Certainly a man who named his farm Munnysunk would have a sense of humor. But it would have to wait. We weren't entitled to joy with Martha's death.

"I wish you'd go with me." Cornelia had taken the train from Sacramento as soon as she got my letter telling her of Martha's death. "It would cheer you. We could go after the lilacs stop blooming; there'd still be plenty to see."

"No. Lilacs in bloom are what we wanted to see, and now that's gone. They're gone. Or almost. But you should go. Hear Ruth play, and tell her we are so sorry to have missed it. I'm so pleased she made contact with the Snyders. She gave them a start from the lilac we sent her off with, so now they have more than one Klager variety in their garden."

Cornelia nodded. "I believe Ruth has been of help to them. Or at least to Bill's mother."

We spoke of these things while I showed Cornelia around the garden, pointing out new bushes, brighter colors, and shaded hues that I liked and would crossbreed for. She told me that the Snyders were thinking of selling and moving to Massachusetts. Mr. Snyder had been offered a teaching position at Harvard, and Shelly thought she could find purpose in volunteering at Arnold Arboretum, which the university maintained and used for study. In between the conversations about families and life, we'd stop and discuss a bloom, or I'd tell her a story about the plant or its planting. Martha's name often came into it, and when it did, I ached inside, a weight like rocks settling on my heart and threatening to crush. Sometimes it was hard for me to breathe, I missed her so. The previous sons-in-law had been close to that age at their deaths too. I feared for Fritz, for Ruth, for Nelia, my nieces and nephews, and wondered why Frank and I had been left to live past our youth.

"So unless you come now, you won't get to see the Snyder garden," Cornelia said.

"What? I'm sorry. My mind wanders of late."

"If the Snyders move, you'll miss their estate. What about next year? Should we try for a Luther Burbank visit? I could check his schedule. That wouldn't be such a long trip."

I shook my head. I had no interest in leaving my garden except to put blooms on Martha's grave.

Bobby number three died not long after Martha's passing, and I wondered if maybe he wasn't running through the clouds of heaven with her, both young and vibrant and full of life. I grieved that dog and Martha all over again. We didn't yet have another "Bobby" in our lives, which was good because in 1913, the river flooded with a vengeance. When the rains came, we bundled up the cats in a big box and along with ourselves, carried them to Bertha and Carl's house on Martin's Bluff. We went back daily to pull plants, put them in tubs, and set them up on the porch, hoping the water wouldn't reach them. It rose slowly, but that meant it would probably go down slow too.

Water didn't rise to the porch level, but it was still a

devastation. I wasn't sure I had the gumption to start again, hauling out dead grass, mud-caked leaves, my boots squishing for weeks in the drenched soil.

Fritz had a camera, and he took a photograph from the barn looking toward the house. We have it now for the stereo-opticon, and I can look at that even all these years later and just feel sick inside for all the work that had been washed away. A lake surrounded the house deep enough—and standing in water long enough—that the trees reflected in the water. Frank moved all the cows up to Bertha and Carl's when the rain poured nearly sideways. We knew the Lewis River, and maybe the Columbia too, would rise. I didn't feel safe having the bucket boys helping us pull plants while the water rose, and Nelia was in Seattle, and I didn't have a new high-school girl yet; so we did the work ourselves with help from Edmond and Roy, Fritz and the girls. When we'd done what we could, we moved over to help Emil and Tillie and their family.

I missed Ruth. She was such a hard worker. Ruth taught in Baltimore, and in her last letter, she said she was being courted by a young man who was a cellist. "Mama says we'll be poor for life as wandering musicians," Ruth wrote. "She doesn't understand that as classical performers, we won't be wandering, but she's probably right about the poverty."

As the water receded, it was already May, and Frank and I looked at each other, and he said out loud, "Are you up to this, Huldie? Ready to begin again?"

"What else could we do?"

"Rest. Sell the cows. Visit the Rose Festival in Portland come June instead of trying to remake the garden for Lilac Day."

"There won't be any of that this year. The river took those days."

But I couldn't imagine not gardening, even with the work that lay ahead. "How would the grandkids know about working and waiting if it isn't by weeding and hoeing with their grandfolks?"

"I don't know. But I submit you'd find a way to teach 'em."

"I'll stick with lilacs." I pulled on my boots. "Though I am glad you let it be a choice, something those rivers never give us."

The garden and being on this farm was the way I kept Martha alive in my heart. Since her death, I'd been working on a lilac to memorialize her. It would be a creamy white with a yellow center. With a sigh, I waded through the water toward the house. I had things to check on in my sun porch. "You've lived through another flood," I told myself, pulling my boots from my shoes. I checked the tubs. It's what we do.

❦

"I've got a good strong back," George Lawson said. Nelia's father was at our picket-fence gate. "My daughter wrote, asked that I see if you needed anything."

"Oh, we're doing all right." Frank shook his hand. "Good of Nelia to mention it, though."

"Your lilacs, did they make it?"

"Most of them," I said. He stood with hat in hand and was probably not as strong as my wiry husband, though working with bolts of cloth and the leather work he'd expanded into required muscle strength too. Still, he didn't look well, with a pasty sort of color to his skin. His paunch drifted over his belt buckle like overrisen bread dough on the counter's edge. He might have a heart attack and die trying to help us. Business might have been off for him, what with Mills Grocery and General Merchandise carrying more readymade clothing. Autos were putting horses out of work, so people didn't need new harnesses or other leather tack either. "The lilacs didn't like the transportation from ground to bucket or raft, but they wouldn't have liked the swimming they'd been doing either if we hadn't pulled them. Some of the older ones"—I pointed toward two long rows west of the woodshed where the cats slept—"weathered it without being put into buckets. Old, deep roots does it, I suspect."

"My wife, she used to like lilacs." His voice caught, and he cleared it. "When last they bloomed in Mississippi, she was just twenty-five years old. Nelia will be that age before long."

I didn't know what to say. Nelia told me he never spoke about his wife; had few words for his daughter too. Ducks flying overhead quacked their intended landing. They didn't have to fly as far with water still standing in pools in parts of the yard. The birds rescued us from words.

"How is Nelia's lilac doing?" I asked then.

"She has one?"

"Planted on Jasmine's grave. Years back I gave it to her."

His eyes dropped. He chewed on his lip. "I…I haven't been out to Jasmine's grave. Buried her in the back forest, being she was a Negro and we were new here. I didn't want attention drawn to trying to find an acceptable place to bury her. Back up in the trees. Don't know how the lilacs fair in conditions like that."

"I can go with you and check, if you want," I said. "They can handle shade but prefer the sun."

"No, no, I'll do that. For Nelia. And let you know. But if I can help with the restoring…"

"We accept." I glanced at Frank to see if he'd object. He didn't. I think he saw too that here was a man who needed to do things for others.

"Whenever you have time," Frank said.

Our next big Lilac Day we held in 1915, and it was the biggest and best of them all. One Sunday I had a banker, an undertaker, a chief of police, and a Japanese artist step out of a single car. All those men loved lilacs! But at last we women were getting a little recognition for our horticulture interests too. After all, here they came to my garden. And Lowthorpe School graduated women in landscape and horticultural work, and they had to know about plants to receive their diplomas. Maybe Cornelia would keep advancing the professional role of women in hybridizing and not just show us as beings who like only the blooms.

A few men visiting acted like they were dragged by wives. Yet here stood four men who felt big enough, I guess, to show up without the crutch of a woman at their side. They all talked easily about varieties and didn't just take in the aroma but studied the blooms, commenting on how "this one's dark red on the outside and lighter on the inside. I've never seen that before." Or, "Look at how the petals incurve and then come out with handsome buds. Exquisite." Thus from the artist whose name I had trouble remembering. Ja-sue-o is what his colleagues called him.

"My Favorite," I said.

"I can see why," the banker said.

"No, I've named it My Favorite. It's one of my unique varieties." They each asked for starts. They'd driven from Seattle and Lynnwood and surrounding areas and had read about the garden from a piece of Cornelia's that was rerun in the *Seattle Times*.

"There is much interest in lilacs in the Seattle area," the artist told me. He painted flowers, he said, and lush gardens too. He was soft spoken and walked through the garden with his hands clasped behind his back.

"I looked for your varieties in Cooley's catalog," the

banker said. "Didn't find any there. How come? Don't you have several unique cultivars?"

"About fourteen now." We sat on the porch, drinking lemonade. Frank rejoined us, letting Delia give the current cluster of visitors their tours. Lizzie would have come, but her youngest son, Roland, born the previous July, had the croup, and with the cool breeze, she'd decided to stay home. Delia would give the update on Lizzie's rhododendrons and their showy blossoms. Even Fritz led a group of young women along the paths. He knew as much about the lilacs as the rest of us. Peals of laughter bubbled up from his charges like steam from a teapot. He was having too much fun, I thought. I wasn't sure if he was the best tour guide. Might have to change that for next year.

Cranes warbled in the distance, and I missed not being able to see those lanky gray birds with the railroad grade so high, but as Frank often said, that was progress. What I was seeing with Fritz was progress too, but I wasn't sure I liked it.

"You really ought to think about letting a couple of the nurseries distribute them." The banker's determined voice brought me back to the moment.

"I like meeting the people who get my starts."

"True enough," the banker said. He had a big mustache and an even bigger belly. Corpulent, Martha would say if she were here. "But others are deprived of the beauty you've designed. Think of how many more might enjoy the fruit of your labor. Hundreds may come here, but thousands would buy from the catalog."

"I've been trying to get her to do that for years," Frank said.

"Think of it as...diversifying. You have this operation, your garden right here where people come, leave you donations as I see it, and you get the pleasure of seeing who will take one of your little pets home."

My face felt warm. I did think of the flowers as my pets, loved them like I loved each Bobby and my cats.

"You have your goal for that operation."

"Bigger blooms, hardier stalks, richer color, and finer fragrance." I repeated the phrase often enough on my garden tours.

"Exactly. Then you have your outreach division, where you sell starts to nurseries, and they develop them a few years and market them as shrubs to an even wider range of enthusiasts. They might never meet you, but they'd likely be pleased to tell their friends they had a Klager lilac."

"One day, when you traveled to Seattle or back east, you could walk into a garden and see your lilac there, planted by someone else but that your hands had a part in." This was the chief of police speaking now.

"This could be a very anomalous time for you," the artist said, bowing slightly each time he spoke.

I wondered what Martha would have said about the word

anomalous. That did mean exceptional, and in my plant world meant something out of the order of things, just what I was always looking for, hoping the next anomaly would take me closer to my longed for twelve petals.

The undertaker hadn't said much of anything, but he nodded now and rose to collect a few more specimens from the tubs where we'd cut starts before Lilac Day began. He returned and said, "You've given me an idea, George." He nodded to the banker. "I think I'll start these and give one to each family at the time of our service to them, as a sort of memorial to their loved one. My work"—he turned to me— "it's filled with stories told when people are grief stricken and weakened by loss. They let me into their lives in the most intimate ways, dressing and caring for their loved one, some-thing that used to be done at home." I thought of Martha and how we'd bathed her body and dressed her, choosing the right dress, weeping as I gently brushed her cheeks, prayed over her, all acts of reverence honoring her life. "So giving them a plant that they could put in the ground as a remem-brance, I think that would be a good thing, and a reverent thing to do. I do love the cut flowers," he said. "But these will last past the present misery."

After they left I told Frank, "I think it is time to talk to a couple of nursery people. Cooley's catalog is in Portland. You could sell the cows that way and not have to work so hard."

"Those cows are my pets," Frank said. "But it would be

good to think ahead, getting ourselves a nest egg so we could hire help. What with the war in Europe, if we get into it, Fritz might have to go."

"Oh no. I don't like thinking of that."

"Don't, then. Think of all those people who'll find your lilacs in the catalog. Get the names of your varieties registered, Huldie. Then we'll take a drive to Cooley's and see what they say."

We rocked away the evening, quietly together, thinking. It was more the undertaker's view of things than the banker's that had me considering selling my pets, allowing others to nurture them and list them for sale. I wanted people to experience the fruit of my labor, and I guess it was selfish of me in a way to keep them to myself, only letting them go when I could see to whom they went. Lilacs didn't really belong to anyone, even if they had a registered name with Klager preceding each one. They were gifts meant to grow in gardens all around the country—however they got into the new caretaker's hand.

"We'd better talk with Roy too," I said to Frank as I fixed our supper. "I promised him first dibs to sell them at his store. We ought to keep it in the family as much as we can."

THIRTY-EIGHT

CORNELIA

1922

Cornelia held it in her hand as though it was a child she'd given birth to. Well, she had. She'd had all the labor pains of researching, writing, getting permissions, illustrating several plates herself, locating other artists for the additional ones, finding a publisher, then having the war change everything. She had to locate a second publisher, then a third (the second having gone out of business), until finally, in 1922, everything came together, and she had the book of her heart. The publisher had used one of Laura Hetzer's sketches, which gave Cornelia great joy. Cornelia had also located a fine artist, Yasuo Kuniyoshi, at the Art Students League of New York. He'd once lived in Seattle, and of all the artists whose work she looked at in the league's files, his were the best for her baby, her book.

American Arboretums: The Stories of America's Beloved

Botanical Laboratories. By Cornelia Givens. She didn't really like the subtitle, or at least the word *laboratories,* but that is what distinguished an arboretum from any other garden. It was a place to study scientifically and educate others, as well as care for unique clusters of plantings in perpetuity, from tall trees to the tiniest violet.

She called out to George Bath, her husband. They'd been married two years, and he'd supported her journey to finish this tome from the very beginning, even suggesting that she maintain her maiden name on the cover, since the work had been done while she was single, supporting herself and her mother until her mother's death three years previous. She and George met while Cornelia volunteered at a hospital in New York City, where so many were being treated for the flu that swept away thousands. George Bath was a physician, and while Cornelia was no nurse, she was a faithful volunteer who comforted both families and patients, writing letters for them, reading poems she wrote.

"The Tireless Miss Givens" George called her. She reminded him that he was as tireless as she. He'd invited her for coffee; she accepted. They shared stories, a touch, a tender kiss, and before long he'd proposed. She accepted, surprised beyond words to be marrying at forty-two.

George held the book, his pleasure in his wife's accomplishments evidenced by the wide grin on his handsome face.

"It's a beauty." He kissed her nose. "And so are you."

Cornelia had continued to write articles. When she felt she had gained proficiency, she chose arboretums as subjects, hoping the book would urge more people to make spaces for education and beauty for the rest of the world to experience. *For the rest of the world,* she thought. That would make a good title for a book about gardens.

The only hesitation she'd had was knowing that if she wrote about specific arboretums in America, she could not include Hulda Klager's lilac garden, and yet it was that woman and her garden that had pointed her in this direction. The possibility of leaving her out was so distressing to Cornelia that she'd taken the train back from New York for a Lilac Day in 1920. She had other business in Portland but drove up to Woodland just to talk with Hulda.

"It looks like Horace Liveright is going to publish my first book," Cornelia told her. They were in the shed, wearing large aprons as Hulda repotted one last geranium. It would sit on the porch steps blooming red along with a flower for each step already set there. "They usually publish classics, so this is a departure."

"Ja, that's good. You've worked so hard on that. Hand me that pot there, would you? *Danke.*"

"I have, it's true." Cornelia handed her the clay pot. "And I think it will open the eyes of people to know how many arboretums there are in this country and how, despite income tax and wars—"

"Isn't that increased tax something?" Hulda stopped, gloved hands holding another geranium. "I can't imagine what Congress was thinking to pass that revenue act."

"It will help the local conservation agencies do their work and the new National Park Service," Cornelia said. "And it will fund new laws meant to assist widows with children. Families aren't always able to take care of each other on their own."

Hulda sighed. "I suppose you're right. Let's go in and sit a spell, ja?" Cornelia thought she might be slowing down but wasn't sure how old Hulda was. She sounded more German than previously, age nurturing words of her youth. They walked inside as Hulda continued to talk. "We farmers taxed ourselves, to begin levee construction along the east bank of the Lewis. They've already got plans for a Planter's Day in June, when we won't have to wait to plant until the river recedes. Guess we have to think of those taxes as bounty counting. If we didn't have money, we couldn't pay the taxes; so God's been good."

Cornelia was pleased that they were the kind of friends who could disagree about a thing but still respect each other and enjoy their conversations. "You were saying, before I had to speak my piece." Hulda took Haviland china cups out.

"I only hope that the book will remind people of the importance of science and education, about botany and horticulture. I want people to see how those who can are putting their wealth into these laboratories of greenery, despite taxes and earthquakes and disease."

"We're very proud of you, Cornelia, very proud."

"There is something I need to tell you, though." Cornelia stared at her cup. "It's one of the reasons I came to see you."

Hulda turned to look at her. "I thought it was because you missed my charming disposition." She grinned. "Didn't you come to tell me stories about your new husband?"

"After supper we can talk about him," Cornelia said. "He is worthy of the time. No, I came because my book is about arboretums."

"So you told me."

"As a result, I'm not able to highlight your garden in this book."

"Oh, that's fine." Hulda continued to lift tea leaves from a tin pot. "Mine is just a flower garden, nothing scientific about it at all."

Cornelia detected no disappointment, no feigned acceptance. Hulda really didn't mind.

"Don't diminish your work, Hulda. It is both scientific and educational. Just not at the scale that I cover in my book. Arboretums are usually created by wealthy donors or through endowments to universities given by passionate people, like you, passionate about plants. But they're large, acres and acres, and the recipients have the ability to maintain them. You do it all yourselves here, and that's so admirable and worthy of recording and sharing too. I've felt so torn about not including Hulda Klager's lilacs."

Hulda turned to her. "You've given far more than we deserve. Lilac Day has become Lilac Days, and we had dozens of cars here last May, because of you. Even the city plans events now around lilac blooming time. I doubt there would have been such wide interest in my flowers without your articles and people visiting to see my newest cultivars."

"How many are you up to?"

"Over one hundred. Imagine." Hulda poured hot water from the stove reservoir through the tea leaves, the scent of mint rising with refreshment. "But you worry nothing about having to leave our garden out of your book. I hope it does real well for you." Hulda set the steaming tea in front of Cornelia. "You have one of my varieties in your New York garden, don't you?" Cornelia nodded. "I'll send another back with you. In honor of your book's publishing. You just keep them alive, and give a few starts away now and again; that's all the thanks I need."

Cornelia rose and hugged the older woman. "Thank you." She felt the smoothness of Hulda's cheek and the pervasive scent of lilac that defined Hulda Klager.

That evening they did speak of Cornelia's husband, and Cornelia told her of their brief courtship and still-romantic life together. "Out of that terrible epidemic, love bloomed," Cornelia said.

"My Frank has a romantic streak in him too. Every now and then he puts dahlias in a vase and sets it in the privy."

Cornelia laughed. "The two of you. You have quite a time together."

"That we do. Or as Frank would say, 'I submit,' we do."

"I lost my sister and her husband, the same day in 1917," Hulda said, getting serious. "Right after we survived the flood of '17. I often wondered if it was early flu, but the doctors said it was gangrene. They each must have had a terrible infection. Don't know where they got it. Maybe cleaning up after the flood, getting cuts and ignoring them. Amelia wasn't one to go to a doctor. She brought me the Harwood book all those years ago that got me out of bed." Hulda sighed. "I guess it's good they didn't have to suffer along without each other, both dying on the same day like that." She sat quiet for a time before adding, "I miss her. There's something awful about losing a sister, no matter what the age."

Cornelia thought of her own sister. She'd lost touch, something she needed to remedy.

Frank finished reading his newspaper and joined them briefly in the parlor, talking about cheese and milk prices, catching up on Cornelia's life. Cornelia thought his color was off, his face as pale as a mushroom. But he bantered and opined as usual. He said his good night, and Fritz asked if Cornelia might like an escort back to the hotel. Cornelia accepted, and the two of them chatted like old friends as he walked with her. Hulda's love of plants had brought them together, and her generosity of knowledge and time had melded Cornelia into this fabric of family. Cornelia wished the same for the rest of the world. *For the Rest of the World.* That's exactly what a garden was, and Hulda's was the finest.

Thirty-Nine

Lilac Starts

Hulda, 1922–1930

The years passed like a good story, swiftly, full of momentum and change, characters coming in to warm us, set us straight, drifting in and out of our lives but knowing they were part of the story line, hoping it wouldn't end but taking us there anyway.

Irvina blossomed, Clara close behind. Lizzie's boys had already discovered their love of flowers, and they liked playing sword fights, while I tried to keep them from trampling my heather or holly. "You stop that now," I had to tell them more than once. "Don't you get into my plantings!" They'd simmer down, and then before I knew it, they'd be chasing and laughing. So long as they didn't wreck my pets, I might let them race around for a minute or two, then send them to the field or the barn or into the house. Still, I liked having them around. Children bring vigor to a soul, and I needed that to tend the ever-growing acreage.

The railroad interrupted conversations as it rolled through, sometimes rattling the china in the cabinet and once knocking the Lifebuoy soap off the side of the tub. I chipped a tooth crunching down on a piece of popped corn, wishing I'd added sugar and milk the way the Indians used to eat it. My girls wanted me to go to the dentist, but so long as I could still chew, I didn't see the bother.

My brother still lived next-door, and their Elma, now twenty-four, worked for Dr. Hoffman in his office, but she came by on a weekend to work with me in the garden. Amelia and Solomon's children were pretty well grown when their parents died, but it was still a shock, and I found myself visiting with them in Vancouver, bringing them fresh bouquets of blooms to help the grieving.

Cornelia Givens Bath came to visit a couple of years back, wearing a skirt just below her knees. In public! I was surprised but said not a word. She's from New York now, and they do things differently there. We hear from Ruth occasionally. She's married and already has two active boys, settled down in Baltimore. She's giving lessons, and her husband teaches at the Peabody Institute. She always reports on her lilacs and says she's given away dozens of starts and occasionally visits the Snyder garden to check on theirs, even though the couple doesn't live there anymore.

Fritz has been teaching our new Bobby tricks. He dances and twirls and puts his head on his paws like he's praying.

Silly thing, but Fritz likes working with him, and the shepherd in the dog needs to keep busy, or he'll herd the chickens and geese whether they want to be herded or not. Frank's got him working with the cows down on the Bottoms during the day, but that dog doesn't seem to need rest and will chase the cats in the evening, if we don't give him things to do.

"I wish I had some of his energy," Frank told me. We listened to crickets chirping in the early April twilight as we walked through the gardens, a soft misting rain covering us, collecting on Frank's hat like silver sequins. I checked the lilac buds, hoping they'd be in bloom by Planter's Day. The levee didn't hold in 1920 when it was built; but it did last year, the first year without water covering the fields. I looked forward to Planter's Day this year. "I think they'll bloom," I told Frank. "But you can't push them. Just have to be patient."

He nodded. "So you've told me now these many years."

He looked tired, I thought, and I mentioned that. "Might be time to sell those cows. You are nearly seventy, you know."

"I know. But if I didn't have those cows to milk, you'd put me to work right here. Who knows how many beds you'd have me dig for that next generation of lilacs you have in mind." He grinned.

"Just lilacs. I still want that twelve-petal double white."

"I submit, you'll get it," he said, then stopped.

"What is it?"

He turned to me with the strangest look on his face, started to speak. His face was as pale as a piano key. He grabbed at his throat and sank to the ground.

"Frank! Frank, what's wrong?" My heart pounded, my breath short. Already my hands felt clammy, as though they knew what I couldn't say. "Frank!" I shook him. Wet grass stuck to his face where he'd fallen. I picked it off. "Fritz! Fritz! It's your father. Come! Call Dr. Hoffman! Oh, Frank, oh no, not now, not now." I knelt beside him and cradled his still body in my arms until all the warmth of him had gone, leaving me cold and alone.

I moved through the following days and weeks without direction. Nelia came down from Seattle where she worked at Swedish Hospital and stayed a few days. The girls stopped by every day to see that I ate something, not that I cared to. I'd spent many a day alone while Frank was working with the cows and whatnot, but now the time unaided felt unfinished, as though I'd started repotting a flower and stopped halfway through, not sure why I would want to go on. I hadn't realized how much a part of my day Frank was, even when he wasn't here. All the things I wanted to share with him at twilight were made brighter by anticipating my telling him, more comforting from his hearing it. I kept wondering where he was.

Now I couldn't seem to notice anything worthy of remembering to tell him. Or anyone.

Elma said she'd stay with me, if I'd like, and at first I thought I would, but then I hoped I'd have a "moment" more with Frank and that it couldn't happen if people were here. After Martha died, I had a strange visiting in the night that was likely a dream, but it put my mind at ease as she came before me and told me not to worry over her, that she was fine and that we'd meet again one day. I think the Lord just gave me that dream to console, and I didn't want to miss the chance that I might have that same comfort with my Frank. Elma insisted, and I let her, grateful family didn't think of me as a burden.

We were just weeks away from Lilac Days, but I had no interest. Fritz said we should sell the cows, and I bawled like a baby when we did. They were Frank's pets, and he'd raised a good herd of Holsteins. Fritz was able to get a single buyer, and that was good; the herd didn't have to be broken up. "Pa would be happy. He really was going to sell them anyway. Someday."

"We saved him from the pain of it, I guess." I wiped my eyes when the buyer came in a truck to pick them up. They were going to Tillamook. Frank wouldn't like that, what with all his years as secretary for the creamery cooperative and Woodland's being in competition with Tillamook. But the price was good, and they'd have good homes there. Frank would like knowing we got a fair price.

One morning a month or so after Frank's death, I rose early and dressed and began digging up lilacs. I thought of it in the night, during those hours when I'd wake in the dark and know that something was amiss. I'd turn to find Frank but seize only sorrow instead. What was the use of continuing on with Frank not here to share it? I had hours of regret, wishing I'd spent them with him instead of with my nose and magnifying glass staring at a pistil to see if it had been pollinated by a bee yet or if I could do it myself. Frank never complained about my time in the garden. I knew I couldn't have done all I'd done without him. So I began ripping up plants. I shoveled and dug and dumped them in the wheelbarrow, sweat dripping from my forehead, forcing away tears. My shoulders ached as I moved to the next row, the cooing of doves in the magnolia and monkey puzzle tree serenading my destruction. *Frenzied* would be the word that Martha would use. I was frenzied.

"What are you doing? Mama, stop it!"

Fritz stood beside me. The sun was just coming up, and he wore his striped pajamas, bare feet in this May morning cool. "Stop it, Mama. Pa wouldn't want this."

"I can't have them. I don't deserve them."

"Yes, you do. Pa was so proud of you, illuminating all his friends about your good work. Why we'd sit around in the barn with our beers, and he'd tell Solomon and Emil and Carl and all the uncles and friends what a genius you are and how he fully expected one day you'd concoct a totally new plant, not just a new variety, like Luther Burbank did."

"I never wanted to do that," I said.

"He knew what you wanted, and he admired you for it. He was a smart man, Mama, you know that. He respected you. He understood the need for a mind and body to be engaged in complicated work. What could you possibly say to him when you meet him again that would explain what you've just done? It would kill him to see this."

"Do you know what you just said?"

"What?"

"That it would kill him. He's gone, Fritz. He's dead. And maybe I did already kill him, making him work those cows until he was an old man, having him dig up lilacs to float during floods, replanting, digging, digging, digging, planting, planting, planting." I held my head with my hands.

"Being busy kept him alive, Mama. Dr. Hoffman said it was his heart. Could have happened anytime. He loved the cows, you love the lilacs, and you both loved each other."

I heard what my son said, that my husband admired my work, respected me.

"He wanted you to do what mattered to you, and he knew you wanted lilacs with 'bigger blooms, hardier stalks, richer color, and finer fragrance.' He could quote you in that and often did." Fritz had taken my shovel and held it. "You can't destroy what you've done, what the two of you did together. You can't."

My shoulders sank. It would be a cloudless day, blue sky

over the lilacs. He took me back inside and poured me tea. "You warm up. I'll get dressed, and then we'll go back out there and plant those lilacs. Again."

Spent, I nodded. But I was grateful too. I'd felt my chest ache as I dug up those plants, worse than when I'd dug the grave for all those Bobby dogs or our many cats. Frank would want me to go on with the lilacs. Fritz was right about that. I wasn't sure I had the energy to do it.

But what else could I do? I didn't want to become a busy-body to my children or their children. I didn't want to simply sit here and sink away into self-pity. I could only quilt so much before my eyes needed a rest, and I could only can and give away so much produce. And while I spent many vigorous hours dreaming of buying bulbs and seeds and starts from catalogs, I didn't have Fort Knox as my financial backer, so I'd have to be frugal from now on. No milk or cheese money coming in. Once I'd used up the sale of the cows, I'd have to rely on the small catalog sales of my starts and the generosity of visitors. Our latest Bobby came trotting in and curled at my feet. "We're going to keep the garden going. Fritz says we should." The dog's tail wagged. "And Frank would want it too, I submit."

I watched a hummingbird flutter near the columbine lining the shady path. Those flowers spoke of faith and fidelity, and now, Frank. Oh, how I missed that man, especially his loving touch to my face just before he kissed me. But he would want me to go on, touching others in my way.

After we replanted the shrubs I'd pulled out, I told Fritz he'd have to drive me to the schoolhouse.

"What for?"

"I'm going to see if there aren't some young girls who might like to live in town in exchange for doing garden work."

And so I did, having high-school girls to nurture for the next many years, each one a reminder that Frank would have wanted me to keep going.

Delia and Edmond surprised us all by telling us they expected a baby in 1924. Delia was forty-one when Fred Wilke was born, a full fourteen years after Clara. Like all the other grandchildren, Fred was born in this house too.

"Oh, Mama, I've forgotten how to do things! I can't even remember how to fold the diapers."

"Fold them different for boys than girls, anyway," I told her and showed her how to put more cloth in the front.

"I wish Papa was here to meet him," she said, holding Fred in her arms.

"I do too." Not an occasion passed that I didn't remember Frank and how he would have loved it.

In 1927, the *American Magazine* wrote a one-page article about my garden. It was written by someone other than

Cornelia, but she'd apparently been the impetus for this writer's visit. He said he'd read a haiku dedication to me in Cornelia Givens' book on arboretums. "She gave enough information to whet my appetite," he said when he called asking if he could interview me and see the garden. Interview me. We'd have a conversation while we walked the paths; that's all we'd really do, but I was secretly pleased for the attention. I'd seen Cornelia's kind words to me in her *Arboretums* book but didn't think anyone else would notice. I didn't know the dedication poem was named haiku either.

The magazine article came out in July, so it missed being a buildup for Lilac Days, but Frank would have liked it. I told the writer that Frank was my greatest supporter. And he was.

The following year there were two articles: one in *Better Homes and Gardens* and yet another on May 2, 1928, in the *Lewis River News*. The latter article appeared just in time for my Lilac Days and helped promote Planter's Day, following in June. They were covering the news, and we had made it!

> In the afternoon, a count showed four hundred cars
> parked at Hulda Klager's Lilac Garden in one hour,
> the road being lined for a quarter of a mile. It is
> estimated that at least twenty-five hundred people
> were there for the day, coming from points all the way
> from Seattle. In addition there were several hundred
> cars during the week to avoid the rush.

I chuckled with the last line. "Maybe they avoided the rush," I told Marjorie, one of my high-school girls, "but we sure didn't." I read the newspaper with our electric lights, something we'd added this past year. I thought about lighting up the garden at night, the way the exposition did in Portland all those years before, but it wasn't cheap, and besides, it kept the stars from glittering overhead. One should never mess with a view of the heavens.

Over one hundred of my individual varieties were in bloom that year, and we had delegations from cities come who wanted to each choose a variety and name it for their towns. I thought that lovely. City of Kelso, City of Kalama, City of Olympia, City of Gresham, so many more. The article went on to say it had been twenty-five years since I'd read that book about Luther Burbank. Mr. Burbank married again in 1916 and died only ten short years later, and I never got to meet him. But look what had happened in that time. The article listed some of the cultivars I'd developed and named: Mrs. Klager's Choice, Mrs. Lizzie Mills, Clara, Irvina, R. W. Mills, Fritz. I realized they hadn't mentioned Delia or Martha. I wrote a letter to the editor correcting that. I didn't want my children to feel slighted in any way, thinking I'd neglected to name a cultivar for each one.

The weather had been cool, so I fully expected more to bloom the following week, and with all those people having come so far, I imagined they might have missed the best flowering.

But another several hundred more didn't! The privy was in use all day, and I told Fritz that before next year we'd have to construct another, though I wasn't certain if this could really continue, this attention to flowers, my flowers, by strangers.

But it did. By 1930, more city delegations came forward requesting lilacs be named for their constituents and planted at the local courthouse or next to the bridge leading into the city. Someone from the Scott Arboretum at Swarthmore College in Pennsylvania came that year and took a Klager lilac east.

But then things began to change. Oh, the Northern Pacific kept rolling along, bringing with it free riders who'd wave from open freight doors as they rambled on by. I wondered where they were headed and if they'd find when they got there what they'd been looking for.

Fewer visitors trekked the grounds in the 1930s, what with the economy as it was. I started noticing more hobos along the railroad too and decided to put out boiled eggs and bread for them.

"Mama," Lizzie complained when she came by one day and I was getting ready to take a plate of egg sandwiches out to the men. I'd listen to their stories, and they'd listen to mine. "Please don't serve them on the Haviland china!"

"And why not? They deserve as good as any of us. Just circumstances placed them there, bankers and businessmen making poor decisions all the way in New York and the stock market crashing."

"Still. They'll tell everyone else, and you'll be deluged with people."

"So long as the chickens lay and I can bake bread, I'll have something to give them. Besides, they tell me they like stopping here, sniffing the breeze and seeing the greenery and color. Brightens their day. Why, a few even ask for work before they eat, and I always have things for them to do. They make good bucket boys. A couple even asked for starts, though I don't know what they'll do with them."

"They could be dangerous, and Fritz isn't here during the day."

"That's possible. But Nelia's father comes by often and shows them what to do, and he sets any on their way he thinks might not be savory souls. Most are, though, so my shared lunch is well compensated for."

When Bertha's husband, Carl, died, we hosted a huge funeral and I brought the flowers. Carl and Frank had come to Woodland together, best friends they were. His passing alerted me to what would change as years went by. Somehow we'd have to keep their memories alive. For me, the best way to do that was to develop another variety and know that particular one was birthed the year Carl died or the year that Amelia and Solomon died or the year that Fred Wilke was born, so long after his sister. Lilacs were something living to go on after them. It became my new purpose, to weave some-one's story inside every new cultivar.

I was up to a hundred and fifty varieties now. Still, I had no double white with twelve petals to claim. When that happened, I'd probably quit.

FORTY

RUTH

1933

R uth tried to keep the anxiety from overwhelming her. They had so little money now; prices were high. John's music lessons had dropped off but for a few of the wealthier families. Ruth gave free lessons to a few of the more promising students who had no money and who spent most of their nonmusic time killing sparrows for meat. Both of her sons lived with them, had to. She'd even turned the backyard into a vegetable garden—digging up all except her lilacs.

"You surely do pamper those flowers," John Jr. said as she clipped and trimmed, gathered suckers she put in water and would later give away. He'd had to drop out of college—both boys had to—finding odd jobs enough to keep them from the soup lines. Ruth was grateful that she had them under her roof, knew where they were and what trouble they weren't getting into, because their mother was right there, watching.

But she worried over them too. What mother didn't feel that sons at home meant she'd failed to properly launch them.

"Yes, I pamper my lilacs. They remind me of the woman who kept them blooming and how she dug them up when high water came and floated them on rafts tied to trees so they weren't ruined by standing river water. She taught me about persevering and trusting that providence would provide. I've needed those lessons. I hope I've passed them on to you too."

John was silent, had always been a bit of a sullen boy, and yet until now, he'd had privileges not known to her or his father growing up. She hoped she hadn't spoiled them during the good times. Charles loved the dirt, but John didn't, which was odd for a boy, Ruth thought. He especially didn't like coming upon slugs—well, who did? At least his fastidiousness kept him cleaner than Charles so she had fewer loads of laundry to do each week.

Maybe she should have told them about working for families in their gardens or taking care of elderly people in order to make ends meet. She hadn't talked much about her own life, living apart from her parents for most of it, staying with the Klagers through her school years. She'd wanted better for them than what she'd had. But now that everyone struggled, she realized that what she'd had with the Klagers should be celebrated. They should be honored for their kindness, their diligence, the day-to-day commitment to their family, their farm. Especially Mrs. Hulda who persevered to bring all those varieties to share, self-taught, carrying on even without her Frank beside her.

Ruth imagined what the garden must look like now. A couple of the magazine articles she'd read included photographs. While the iron-shaped garden still adorned the front yard, she also saw how many more plants bloomed, how many different colors of lilacs dotted the greenery. Yellow, pink, magenta, red, purples of various shades. It was stunning. And soothing. She tried to recognize whether her starts were in the photograph, but the pictures were too small.

"Do you remember my telling you about the Klagers?" she asked her son.

"Yeah. Some of it. Mostly about the flowers."

"I suppose I pamper the lilacs because it takes me back to them," she said. "She developed these varieties herself. The lilacs represent survival. And that's what we're about now, surviving until better times come through."

And when they do, Ruth thought, *I'm going to go visit Mrs. Hulda.* She owed it to the woman to tell her face to face how much she'd meant to her, how many lessons she'd taken from the lilacs in her life.

When John came home that day from teaching at the university, new for him since the beginning of the decade, he was upbeat. "There's talk about a Federal Music Project," he said. "Maybe years out, but they'll pay small salaries to musicians, and we'll give concerts, for very small fees. There'll be projects for writers too, perhaps. And artists."

"That would be…inventive," Ruth said.

"People don't have much money to spare, but the arts feed the spirit, Ruthie, they do."

"Like gardens."

She stood with her back to the window, watching her husband. It was good to see him looking forward. He caught her smile, spread his arms, an invitation, like the opening of a tulip. She stepped into his embrace, warm and safe in this garden of love.

FORTY-ONE

OVERWHELMING

Hulda, 1933

The first storm came on December 5. I'd never seen such rain in all my years. I couldn't even see the barn for the density of the water. Thunder and lightning didn't happen often here, but that day, we had both, along with the downpour, a word that seems miniscule to what we endured. Bobby hid under the table, and even though I usually didn't let the dog and cats stay in the house, that night I did. I didn't go to bed, stayed up in my rocker listening instead for the siren that might announce a breach in the levee or something else gone wrong at one of the dams built on the Lewis these past years. I dozed in the rocking chair, stoking the fire when I awoke. I could hear Fritz snoring upstairs. My high-school helper Marjorie had gone home. Her parents lived up on the bluffs. I never heard a siren, and in the morning I thought, well, all those dams have been worth it, taxes and all.

By the evening of the second day, the rain let up, and then we had days of the usual rains, soft, misty ones that allow walking without umbrellas. A few sunbreaks in between. I had puddles of standing water in the yard, but any pooling near the roots of my plants I channeled with my shovel, draining them away from the lilacs especially. I was glad we lived close enough to town to walk for a few groceries we might need, because the roads would be slick snakes of mud. The main paved road south toward Portland, it was said, had water over it in places. I checked my new rain gauge. Two and one half inches in the past day. The weather warmed up too, above freezing, so at least we didn't have snow. Of course that meant snow would be melting in the high country, sending the melt to the Lewis and Columbia Rivers. Nothing to do about it, but I thought maybe we should dig up lilacs, just in case.

I heard on the radio that the coast had been wrecked with seventy-mile-an-hour winds along with all that rain. I was glad there was a hundred miles between us and the onset of that storm, so it had a few hours to wear itself out. Aberdeen and Hoquiam, coastal cities, had two to six feet of water standing, or so they reported. I looked at the wall trying to imagine water that high coming into my house.

The rivers crested on December 10. Kelso, north of us, reported major flooding, and we learned a railroad bridge collapsed. I looked at the railroad grade next to the house and didn't see seepage, but it was saturated from all the rain just as the levee along the Lewis was. If we got dry weather, we'd be all right. That's what Fritz told me, and I agreed.

On the seventeenth, we had another storm, pouring rain into every crack and corner. I noticed a leak in the kitchen and set a pot to catch it. Rainwater is good for plants, but I didn't like collecting it inside my house. Heavy rain continued for days, and when it lessened, we waited in the misty rain for word about when they thought the rivers would crest again.

On December 22, a dam at the headwaters of the Lewis broke, and all that rain and snowmelt headed toward Merwin Dam on the Lewis River. Sirens told us to evacuate, and we learned that they were going to open the gates at the Merwin Dam, hoping to let water through, controlled; but then something happened, and they couldn't get the gates closed, or the water couldn't be controlled, and all that water and debris and logs and trees just kept coming our way. The Lewis River ran ten feet above what it had ever run before, and it was heading toward Woodland.

There is nothing so alarming to a farmer or a homeowner or businessman as seeing water rising, pouring, flattening out around all you've worked for all your life. The rushing river demolished dikes 11 and 5. By then, Fritz and Bobby, the chickens and the cats and I were at Bertha's, up on Martin's Bluff. It was a good thing, because Woodland—and our farm—was underwater. We could see portions of our village, rooftops mostly, from the grade at Martin's Bluff. The bottoms of barns that hadn't floated away were left to the imagination. Many of the roofs had rocks on top hoping to keep them secured, with second-story windows peeking out like eyes under hats. The islands on the Columbia were gone. I looked across that river and could see that the town of St. Helens was underwater too.

We spent Christmas with my sister, high but not dry as the rain continued in its usual drip, soaking every bit of dirt there was and worrying mud slides into being. Finally, the weather cooled, keeping snow in the high country, and we waited for the rivers to recede.

I made Fritz take me out in the boat to survey the damage, bundled up with a scarf on my head. For the first time, I was glad Frank wasn't here to see it. The house still stood but with water well into the first floor, halfway up my sun porch. I couldn't tell if the plants in there had made it or not. They likely floated off the shelves. Trees survived. Even the barn stood and the windmill tower too. My farm hadn't floated away or been smothered by slides or taken out by log jams racing on the river making new channels. It had to, I suppose. We would have to make new channels too.

Our county had more than twenty inches of rain that December, twice what we might usually get, and most of that fell during those two storms.

"Do we begin again?" I asked as Fritz rowed us around the woodshed. I touched the tops of lilac bushes, which was all I could see of them, the ones we couldn't get onto rafts. How long they could endure in the standing water I wasn't sure. "Do we begin again?" I asked again, realizing it was a prayer. Did it really matter, having lilacs bloom for Planter's Day?

People said later that if we had to have such a devastating flood, that we were lucky it came in December of 1933, because in November, Congress had created the CWA, Civil Works Administration. It was meant just to get the country through that winter until new programs could be brought in to help the folks most damaged by the downturn, the Depression, as they were calling it, by putting millions of needy people to work. Oh, there was politics about what was right, people arguing, complaining about paying taxes on land that was washed into the river and taken out to sea.

Whole bunches of men that December filled sandbags, patrolled dikes, and helped evacuate people during the flooding, some even served food at soup kitchens. It was worthy work for any man, and in January more than one hundred people formed the Cowlitz County Flood Committee to start repairs, seeking approval from the CWA, then enacting what they got money to do. Later we'd learn that more money was expended to recover from the flood in Cowlitz County than any other county in the state, even though the rest of the state had been hit hard too. We got "coordinated," Fritz said, and he worked the dike repairs. We'd never have begun our recovery so soon if the flood had occurred the year before. Of course, timing can be everything, and at least for flood recovery and the beginning work to restore my garden, we were on the right hand of time.

But time stole other things from me those years. My brother, Emil, passed the year after the flood. His wife, Tillie, had died not long after Frank, so my brother and I had continued on as neighbors, looking after each other, being beloved and helped by each other's children.

At the farm, we began again, shoveling mud, planting. Because so much was ruined, it seemed proper to make changes, look at new ways of landscaping, think about drainage differently so we might recover better if we had another breach in the dikes. Future thinking is good, and I kept reading about horticulture and engineering too. No Lilac Days that year, even though I had my girls and Elma, Emil's daughter and her husband living next-door to help. Hobos came by and worked a day or two for eggs and bread, and we had a vegetable garden that year so I did my usual canning.

Those government programs brought surprises to our country too, with men from other places seeking work, and we'd had good "coordinating" using those precious federal funds. I met Ruth's oldest boy, John, that way. He'd come from Baltimore to live with his grandparents, hoping to find work in the West when there were mostly soup lines in the eastern cities. Nice boy, who made it a point to tell me he'd smelled lilacs all his life, and he guessed they'd begun right here in this garden. He worked the soil around lilac roots, as his mother had directed. "She taught us a few lessons she said came from you," he told me. They must have been about being generous and helpful, because he was, or ones about being persevering and willing to make changes.

I guess his younger brother had his problems. John didn't go into detail, but every family had one or two stories of hope gone to drink and degradation, and I'd come to see that even with the best of upraising, circumstances and choice can take a soul down.

My dear Delia died in January. Not unlike Martha, Edmond told us. "She just went in her sleep."

Not that I thought losing another child would be less painful than the first, but I had hoped. It wasn't so. Even grown and on her own for years, a grandmother herself, didn't change the painfulness of my having lived long enough to bring a soul to earth, nurture it, watch it grow, and lay it to rest. I'd watched her pass through painful losses and singular joys and now had to live with knowing when that phone rang, it wouldn't be Delia calling me. I'd have no news of how her day had gone, couldn't ask if her roses bloomed yet or had she found a new recipe for pickling cucumbers. I wouldn't see her at church, never hear her voice lift above the sandhill cranes, nor stare with me as we watched their wings span wide, circling upward as they left the fields beside the Lewis River. Of such mundane things are lives made and woven richer—and so missed when they have passed.

At least I could go to sleep at night savoring memories of my daughter and be grateful she'd allowed her children to be so much a part of my life: Irvina comforting me after Frank died, Clara walking beside me in the lilacs till she was old enough to marry and move to Oregon. Those girls stayed in touch, writing notes and remembering their grandma or coming across the field to bring me rhubarb fresh picked and stay to talk a bit about when we thought the lilacs would be blooming. That's how my Delia would live on.

I thought of pioneer families who told of traveling across the plains and losing not just one but two, three, four children, buried and covered with wagon tracks to keep the coyotes out, no other markings for their graves. I thanked God I knew where Delia rested. We'd saved her named lilac and replanted it. Edmond helped, and later I thought that his broad shoulders and handsome looks reminded me of that screen actor John Wayne, the first "singing cowboy" who graced Woodland's movie house in 1933. Delia and Edmond had taken me to that movie. I'd never forget seeing Delia's face, hearing her laughter. I'd remember the feel of her cheek when I pressed mine to hers before they closed the casket and I said my final good-byes.

Before we left those dirty thirties (as I thought of them), Edmond, Delia's husband, had succumbed in 1936, and the next year my Bertha left us. We grieved them both, knowing that with each passing, ours came closer too. That walk alone to parts unknown moved closer, and I often woke in the morning with a start, my heart pounding, feeling fearful of what lay ahead. But then I'd remind myself that I was not moving toward places unknown. Aging made me think there's no sense waiting for a time free of trial and temptation; living looked like this. One had to grab abundance when one could, smelling lilacs when they bloomed and thanking God and dancing a little jig when a double white gave me ten petals on a hardy stalk.

"I'm close," I told Frank as I inhaled the fragrance, gently thumbed the petals between my fingers. I was overwhelmed by the goodness. "Maybe ten is all I'll see before I die." But while I was here, I'd keep working for twelve.

FORTY-TWO

SHELLY AND BILL

1940–1941

They were part of the Emerald Necklace now, the system of parks and waterways and transportation corridors that marked the parks and ponds between the colonial Boston Parkway and Arnold Arboretum. Shelly could not believe the thrill these landscapes gave her. She remembered the lectures at the Lowthorpe School given by Mr. Dawson of the Olmsted Brothers firm. He taught them how to "fool the eye," from the French *trompe l'oeil*. What looked like a natural place of woody trees and gentle ponds was actually designed by men who moved soil for sewage and drainage, visualized where conifers and cedars, rhododendrons and pears, and cherries and crab apples would surprise the eye. Visitors rode their carriages through the greenery or walked the lazy paths meant to slow the world down from its hectic pace and breathe in air purified by plants. A place of health and beauty, that's what these linked parks of Boston were, and feats of engineering.

Bill worked with the herbarium collections and was happier than he'd ever been. Shelly had worried that she'd taken him from his beloved Baltimore and Annapolis, and yes, from his mother too, but she felt certain that if they had not made this change, she would have gone on alone. Did a wife have the right to say "This is what I need" if it appeared to be at the expense of what her husband required? She wasn't certain. She only knew that as she prayed for guidance, how to keep her marriage and her spirit from sinking into despair, that this idea of moving him, urging him on to different climes could bring them the resolution she sought and that he needed as well.

His mother had resisted and finally said that she would not go and that Bill must choose between his mother and his wife. Shelly felt no exuberance as they packed crates of personal things. Minnie Snyder forbid the removal of furniture or anything other than personal effects. But Bill stood firm when it came to plantings and the labeled starts. Those flowers would move with them. Beautiful lilacs with blooms of exquisite yellow.

She could see the pain in her husband's eyes as they arranged to leave. They'd secured the assistance of the woman they'd hired some years earlier to help in the garden and serve Minnie Snyder. Ruth was competent, patient, and loved lilacs, which endeared her to Bill and Shelly, if not to Minnie. But Ruth didn't let the woman's demeanor disrupt her care, and they were grateful that she could overlook the sometimes insensitive statements the elderly woman made. But Shelly was hopeful, oh, so hopeful, that her husband would experience the joy she imagined in these many parks once they moved to Boston.

"Fool the eye." That's what her lecturer said was part of the design of landscapes, to make the eye think all was natural, when in fact it had been planned this way, organized with thoughtfulness. She remembered that visit to Hulda Klager's lilac garden. The woman had an eye for design. Her walkways curved just so, then straightened past the lilac plantings. Birdbaths and water fountains offered glimpses of finches and warblers and red-shafted flickers who used the trees as cover, then zipped to dip in water. Colors blended so subtly one didn't realize how the woman planned ahead, planted with an eye to the future.

Today, as Shelly trimmed the lilacs, she noted the scientific name and common name of a magenta lilac labeled Klager My Favorite at the very top of the curving walk. How could she ever decide what to name them, and which would truly be her favorite?

John Wister had come through the arboretum in 1941, surveying lilacs across the country. He'd graduated years before from Harvard and gone on to design and lead a Philadelphia arboretum for many years. It was good an avid horticulturist took the time to catalog all the lilacs in the United States. They were a part of the history of a nation and ought not to be forgotten.

Bill joined her for lunch, and in the evening they worked in their own garden, miniscule by comparison to the one they'd left behind in Baltimore. They'd had no children, so Shelly's idea of arranging for a planting to honor all those childlike firsts never came to be. Instead, she had developed her interest in bonsai, seeing the natural characteristics of a plant and training it and trimming it in such a way that it was a smaller version of something larger but equally magnificent. She had found her passion through a practice she learned was hundreds of years old and brought from isolated China to ancient Japan and from there eventually to the Lewis and Clark Exposition in Portland. Shelly hadn't seen them there, but Laura Hetzer had, and thus had begun Shelly's journey, a desire to create within nature and enhance a landscape like their small garden with the bigness of imagination that bonsai nurtured.

She'd even tried her hand at bonsai lilacs. It offered quite the satisfaction, though she'd slowed down with her knuckles swollen with age now. But amazingly, Bill enjoyed working with bonsai beside Shelly. She watched her husband, slightly bent now, walk toward her. He waved a greeting, a smile fresh upon his aging face. He looked happy to see her, distinct among the plants. What wife could ask for more?

FORTY-THREE

ACHIEVEMENT

Hulda, 1943–1947

During the Second World War, people started coming back to visit the garden. A whole new town had built up along the Columbia River called Vanport City, because it lay between Vancouver and Portland. Built on the flood plain, the city fast-housed workers needed to build ships. Fritz said thirty-five thousand people lived there close to Portland, the town springing up within weeks. On a Saturday or Sunday, many of those working in the shipyard—women too—took a break, and in May I'd find ready visitors at my picket fence. A few hours in the garden, a blanket spread at the grassy areas, watching and listening, gave rest to those worried about husbands and sons and grandsons in faraway places, took their minds from building things used to carry men to war.

Our lives kicked along like the can the children played with down the street. I passed the twentieth year following

Frank's death, stunned that I could have gone on a minute, let alone all that time without him. The flowers were my ballast, that and faith that I'd be with Frank again and have so much to tell him when I was. I looked forward to it. Will Rogers used to say, "If you live life right, death is a joke as far as fear is concerned." I had no fear of it; but neither did I wish to hasten its arrival.

Cornelia wrote me to say that a few of my lilacs were "listed in John Wister's *Lilacs for America,* a tome much bigger than mine." She wrote, "I checked, and there are fifty-one Klager varieties named."

I called her on the phone when I got the letter, even though I didn't much like spending that kind of money for long distance, but her words astounded me. "He included my lilacs, that many?"

"All the city-named ones are there, Klager Dark Red, Klager Dark Purple, Miriam Cooley—that's the wife of the nurseryman, isn't it?" I told her yes, and she continued. "Will Rogers and my personal favorite name you gave: Klager Large Dark Double Very Fine. No question of what that one looks like or how you felt about it." She laughed. "Wister traveled extensively all across the country in 1941, surveyed classifiers from all the arboretums for the Arthur Hoyt Scott Horticultural Foundation. The book just came out this year."

My lilacs, in a book with hundreds of others, but recognized individually. It was 1943, and you could have pushed me over with a lilac bloom, I was so surprised and humbled.

I missed Frank especially when, one day in 1947, I was invited to the Oregon State Federation of Garden Clubs to receive an award. I was eighty-three years old and getting honored for doing something I'd loved to do my whole life. It bothered me a little that it was Oregon giving me the award and not my beloved Washington where I'd done my plant breeding. Martha might have said that wish for different kept me from the consequences of hubris. I'd have been too proud if Washington had honored me. Lizzie drove me to Portland for the luncheon, and it was time with her as much as the award that got me ready, checking my new shorter haircut in the mirror, then covering it with my hat, after all. I wasn't in love with the pads that broadened my already ample shoulders, but Lizzie had bought the coat for me, and I needed to wear it as the May day promised cool.

"For Distinguished Achievement in Horticulture," the plaque read. I know my face burned with all the things they said about me and my work, especially knowing that I hadn't done it by myself. "This is the first such an award we've given to a living horticulturist," the president noted, the feather in her hat bobbing toward me as I sat in front looking out at people.

"Glad you didn't wait," I said, and everyone laughed.

Still, as they read the names of some of my now nearly two hundred cultivar varieties, I remembered my papa's words about honoring a gift given. Horticulture. Imagine, me, a simple German immigrant with an eighth-grade education learning horticulture, letting the complexity of an apple or a lilac define my life and trusting that there was nothing new under the sun; we mortals are all drawn to simply unfold secrets, reading flowers like a book.

Before adjourning, there were pictures, and then Lizzie asked for help to haul in a galvanized tub of starts we'd brought with us, and all the members took home a lilac from the Klager Garden.

"Ich freue mich wie ein Schneekoenig," I told Lizzie as the women selected their starts.

"What does that mean, Mama?" she asked.

"I am as happy as a snow king." My father used to say that.

❧

The Oregon federation's citation hung in the sun porch, so when I was frustrated with a failed start with a cloudy color or wimpy stem, I could be reminded of achievement, that word Martha would have told me meant "success by exertion, skill, practice, and perseverance."

I didn't do much hybridizing anymore. Mostly it was producing plants for commercial sale on Lilac Days that took our time. Just keeping the garden ready for Planter's Day took the rest of my effort.

Nelia drove up from Seattle the May I turned eighty-four, she and her friend, Benson, which was how she introduced him. She teased me when I said I'd had a few "friends" come my way too, through the years. "A jeweler from Portland bought several lilac starts, then came back, even when the lilacs stopped blooming," I told her.

"A vibrant woman like you is attractive," she told me. "You could marry again."

"Oh, piddle," I said.

"No, really. Didn't that writer who cataloged lilacs marry late? To a woman who was also a horticulturist. I know I read that somewhere."

"John Wister was seventy-three." He called matrimony "the fatal plunge," which I didn't think spoke hopefully of his union. "I think Fritz might have driven my jeweler off," I told them. "But that was fair play, I submit, since I'd driven off a few of his female interests too." Nelia laughed, and so did her companion, a nice-looking man in his late forties, ten years younger than Fritz. "I had to check them all out, you know, make sure they were blooms worthy of keeping and not just young women chasing after a man close to fifty, but still looking tall and willing. I could see their good points but noticed a few flaws too. Of course, I had to let him know about them." Nelia smiled. Benson nodded his head. He was a handsome man and Nelia not too old to marry. I told them that, and she blushed. I'd gotten blunter in my old age, though Lizzie said I'd always been so.

"We're both too busy for that."

"Speak for yourself," he said as he flicked lint from his pant cuff and adjusted his hat resting on his knee.

"Fritz has been faithful to you and this garden."

"I submit, he has. I couldn't have gone on after Frank died and couldn't have recovered from that devastating flood of '33 either, not without Fritz."

I'd had a good life. Nelia reminded me of that.

It got better.

On a May morning in my eighty-fourth year, I came out to check my lilacs. The bushes with a blend I'd worked toward, a purple and white together, looked good and healthy and had opened up with the warm weather. I checked my City of Vancouver bloom. They looked good too, and lo and behold, there among the double whites was one with twelve petals. *Twelve!* I counted again. "Twelve," I told Bobby. "Twelve petals on a double white." I teared up then. That happened more easily as I grew older. "Oh, Frank, we did it, we actually did it."

The fragrance was heavenly, as glorious as I'd imagined, but I could hardly contain my delight at the dozen petals curling at the edges, clustering, each keeping the other into the perfect bloom.

I called out to Fritz, didn't want to cut the bloom just yet, wanted him to see it and the others on the bush, each with twelve too. I'd chosen right, hybridizing for the petal growth, crossbreeding plants that tended toward producing more than they ever had before. "Fritz!" I shouted again, and he came out of the house, still chewing on a piece of toast.

"What is it, Mama? Did you find a lilac that just has to be moved?" He coughed, something he did a lot of lately. He smiled, though, and as he stood beside me, he said, "What's up?"

"This is what's up." I showed him the bloom. "Twelve. God's given us twelve petals. Can you believe that?"

He brushed his toast-crumb hands on his pants, then held the bloom in his palm, his finger counting every petal. "Yup, it's twelve. Congratulations. You better go tell Lizzie. She'll be pleased for you as I am." He coughed again, seemed short of breath.

"Are you all right?"

He brushed away my concern, nodded again toward the lilac, distracting, now that I remember. He smiled.

"This belongs to all of us," I said. "And all those who'll come by and get a start."

I collected seeds from that lilac, and in the fall I planned to cut the suckers from the plant. I'd give a start to Lizzie and Roy and send packets of them to Cornelia, telling her they'd give up twelve petals and made sure that Nelia and

Ruth and all the grandchildren got some too. I'd tell them it was my crowning achievement. With that goal met, I wasn't sure what I'd work toward now. I considered sending a seed packet to Luther Burbank's widow. Why not? Even if he didn't spend time on ornamentals, his wife might. Who couldn't love a lilac with a dozen petals?

But I never got any of those packets sent off. Life intervened.

FORTY-FOUR

SPLENDID SPACE OF GRACE

Hulda, 1948

In the foothills of Mount St. Helen's, the snow was still many feet deep in May of 1948. Our Lilac Days had brought any number of new people to my garden, and I'd enlisted the grandkids and nieces and nephews and others to help out, serving lemonade and giving tours. The blooms were magnificent, perhaps the best I'd ever seen. There was a fair amount of attention paid to my double creamy white with twelve petals, and I worked on getting that same number in other varieties too. That's what I told folks. "There's always more to do."

Several people celebrated Mother's Day by bringing the family to the gardens. Now that the war was over, Vanport, that city between Portland and Vancouver, housed veterans going back to school on the GI Bill. That was a good thing the government did, helping people further their education.

We'd be lost in this world without minds staying bright and new ideas getting acted upon by those who study. The flowers offered a rest for others, even though it was a crazy busy day for all of us.

Not long after Lilac Days, it warmed up still more. It reached eighty degrees, which was unheard of in Woodland for that time of year. I knew it meant that all that snow would melt and melt fast. I was grateful we had the dikes, as it wouldn't be long before the rivers rose with snowmelt.

On May 25 I had Fritz drive me up on the bluff, and we could see how that river was roiling and rising its way south. The radio announcer said the Willamette River flowing north through Oregon was rising too. If both of those rivers crested at the same time, Portland or portions of it would be flooded, giving our Lewis nowhere to flow. If the Columbia kept coming up beside Woodland, it would put pressure on the dikes. So far, it appeared that they'd hold.

But on May 30, a railroad dike near Vanport broke, letting floodwaters pour through that city in minutes. We heard about it on the radio.

"I wonder if we should think about moving lilacs," I told Fritz. "Our dikes could break too."

"Tragic as it is, the breach at Vanport might keep the water from backing up and pressuring our levees."

I'd never known Fritz to be a wishful thinker, and I could see for myself that the dikes were leaking. The Lewis ran full and had nowhere to rage with the Columbia bloated with melt.

I thought maybe I'd move my starts in the sun porch up to my bedroom, just to be safe, and maybe pull lilacs and put them on the rafts and secure them to the trees. Fritz agreed, but before we could get started, the siren blew, and we got a call. "Tomorrow they'll try a forced breach, hoping to keep the floodwaters out of town, but the dikes are going to go," we were told. "Get to high ground."

I grabbed a few cultivars, my purse. Fritz grabbed plants too, and we pushed the cats into a pillowcase where they wouldn't see what might be fearsome, and we could haul them with us. Fritz pushed the chickens into the haymow in the barn, put Bobby and the cats in the car. I looked around. Too late to move things upstairs. These were only "things." It was the outside that I'd take with me if I could, all the tight plantings of lilies and peonies and lilacs and roses and rhododendrons and magnolias and poppies and on and on.

I stepped outside to Fritz's calls and gave a nod to them all. Maybe we'd survive another flood; maybe the planned break would save us from a deluge. Maybe not.

We stood on Goose Hill looking west toward Woodland on May 31 when the river took the dikes. There'd been talk about blowing the dike with dynamite in an effort to "control" the damage, but the dike burst before they could decide. Hubris, I thought to myself. I'd thought the sound would be louder. But it was muffled by the screams and gasps of those watching as the wall of water surged in like ocean waves, rolling barns and houses like small tops, bobbing people's lives and livelihoods beneath the muddy water. We couldn't see our home, but there was no need to. Everything we could see was flooded. No dikes nor land formation rise between the Lewis River and the Columbia to stop the water now. My garden bloomed between those rivers, and I knew it would be gone.

Lives were lost in Vanport, but not in Woodland. As expected, my garden was submerged beneath the dirty river water for six weeks. Lizzie and Roy's home wrestled with water in the basement, but the mild weather meant they didn't need their furnace on and could wait until the water went down. Fritz and I stayed with them, which was good. Fritz didn't look so well. Seemed to have a hard time breathing, but he walked across the street to see Roland's new baby, his great-nephew. Roland had married that pretty Betty Carlson a while back, a former princess of Planter's Day fame. Just the effort of crossing the street tired Fritz.

"You'd better go see Doc Hoffman." He looked pale, too.

"I'm fine, Ma. I don't like doctors any more than you do. Besides, he'll be busy with flood victims needing tending."

"Ach," I said, annoyed at him. My children could be so stubborn. I didn't know where they got that from.

People talked for weeks about whether they should have blown the dike, and if they'd gotten that decision made sooner whether it might have helped, but it was senseless talk. Looking back to visit blame and accusation is wasted time, even if you could win the lawsuit. Such time spent finding fault was better spent pressing the goal: learn how to manage living between two rivers that flood every now and then, even with man-made dams and levees and dikes.

They began letting a few people at a time step into row-boats to visit their houses—if they still stood—and get essential things out they thought they needed. Or maybe to give relief to those who'd taken us flood victims in. Even herds of cows were turned out into growing fields because there was nowhere for them to graze, the Bottoms just water now.

Fritz didn't feel well enough to row me out there, but I wanted to go, so Roy and my grandson took me, Bobby panting in the bow.

It was a moving lake we rowed upon, worse than the flood of '33. Debris, branches, leaves, parts of other people's buildings jammed up against the barn, the woodshed, the house. A whole passel of logs washed from the mill yard floated, and Roy said, "We'll have to get a bunch of guys to push those back, or they'll jam against the house and move it from the foundation."

We rowed right over the tops of my lilacs, the leaves and branches whispering along the bottom of the boat. Petals floated in the water, silent tears, drifting. I looked for places where I knew shrubs were supposed to be, where my oldest lilacs were planted, and couldn't see anything as we rowed over those areas. Cranes called beyond the railroad dike still seeping water. The smells of rot rose up in what had once been a palace of sweet aromas. Roy rowed up to the porch, and from the boat he pulled open the door to the house. Water stood in the hall and partway up the steps to the bedrooms. Since we'd raised the house three feet and three feet stood in the hall, overall we had over six feet of water everywhere the eye could see.

"I think this is as far as you should go, Grandma," Roland said. "Just looking is enough, isn't it?"

"I'm not going to piddle around with all your effort and not go up there," I told them. I wiggled my way out of the boat, and Roy helped me steady my foot on the step covered with water. The cool of it washed against my rubber boots. I walked up out of it to the second floor. I'd taken a few starts up there before Fritz said we had to go, but mostly, it being May and everything being planted for Lilac Days, there were no lilac starts. I looked around that room, sat on the bed surrounded by musty smells and damp clamming up from downstairs. Bobby bounded up the steps behind me.

"Leave me here for a bit," I yelled down to Roy. "Check

out the barn and the chickens." We'd brought along corn for them.

I heard him slosh away and just sat on the bed. The water would eventually recede. There'd be mud to clean up, and I hoped the house hadn't been pushed off kilter by the water. We'd have a roof over our heads, which was more than many had. Twenty-thousand lost their homes in Vanport; sixteen lost their lives there.

But what of the garden? Did I have the strength to once again renew it? And with what? The lilac bushes were under-water—many plantings would have been washed away by the impact of the river, ripped up by waves or the logs that jammed and clustered. Only the tallest, oldest trees looked like they'd made it. I had three hundred plants chucked into my garden design for Lilac Days. There wasn't a one that would survive standing in water for weeks. I looked out the window where my Magical Three Lemoine should have been. "Oh Frank," I said. That's when the tears began.

It was after the Fourth of July before the water receded and the mud dried enough that we could walk around the house, see what we could see.

Not a plant in sight. Not a one. Every cultivar of lilac, gone. Even the few we'd pulled and laid on rafts tied to the tree were gone along with the rafts. The monkey puzzle tree made it, a couple of magnolias that were big and sturdy. The ginkgo tree. But otherwise, the land was barren as Abraham's wife before her miracle birth. It would take a miracle to redo this garden, and I did not have it in me. Inside the house, in the sun porch, my cultivars and all the seed packets were washed away too.

But Fritz, bless his heart, he said we should at least try to clean up the area, maybe plant a few petunias, get dahlia and tulip bulbs. "Write to Nelia. She might…have bulbs to spare," he said. My boy's breath was labored. He couldn't do the work, and while I could do some, I was old. Those were the facts that worked against our reclaiming this garden. Fritz had seen the doctor, but he told me it was just "aging" and not for me to worry, not that I'd stop. A mother hovers. I didn't want to outlive yet another child.

"I can do all things through Him who strengthens me," I told Lizzie, quoting Scripture. "But let's just clean the house."

And so we began with volunteers not committed to critical rebuilding of the dikes and shoveling mud elsewhere. Nelia's dad, the Reeds, my grandkids and their friends, Roy and Lizzie, my nieces and nephews still in the area. We cleaned the house out, and the work was hard. I couldn't see how Fritz could continue. There was no way I could replant now. "There's a time to begin and a time to quit," I told him. "That may not be a proverb, but it ought to be. I can live in the house, and that's good enough. Forget the garden."

"You'll die without your garden, Mama," he told me.

And then on July 28, Fritz did.

His heart failed, Dr. Hoffman said. The man had retired the previous year, but he came when I called him to tend to my son. Like Martha and Delia, Fritz went in his sleep. I wondered what it meant that I outlived all but one of my children. Had I drawn all their strength, sapped them all and Frank's too?

We buried Fritz in the Independent Order of Odd Fellows cemetery where everyone in Woodland ended up. Lizzie invited me to stay with her and Roy permanently. "Let the garden be now. It's too much," she said. We sat in her living room—that's what they called the parlor now.

She was right. I used my hoe to balance in the yard, my cane everywhere else.

"You're rebuilding too," I said. "Roy's store's got water in the basement still, and there's work to do at your house. You don't have time for looking after me. Besides, I sleep best in my own bed. Mold I can live with, at least a little of it. And putting my hands in dirt, that's healing, Lizzie. You know that. I'll just have a few pansies and such in pots on the porch." She nodded. "I remember once Martha telling me about some word called *therapy*, what people were saying was a way to move toward healing without herbs and medicines and such. It's a word that means a service, attending. 'I wait upon,' Martha said. So I wait upon the Lord to lead me back into service, back into 'attending' as He wants. Maybe just a few plants on my sun porch. Not the garden, no, I agree. But I need to go home."

"Will you let us convert the parlor into a bedroom, so at least you won't be going up and down the stairs? And put in indoor plumbing, so you can avoid the privy?" Lizzie said.

"Well, all right."

"And you can't be alone here. Irvina said she'd come, she and her Mac."

"Or I could get another high-school girl to help. Either way, the garden is done. The rivers have won."

"I didn't know it was a competition, Mama," Lizzie said.

"I only meant that the rivers have been my adversary since I first began; the rivers and rabbits and coyotes and moles and whatnot, all wanting part of my garden." I shook my head. "And for what have I struggled against them? To grow a few lilacs."

"You're older; you could have a heart attack too, you know."

"I deserve it," I said.

"Mama!"

I smiled at her when she shook her finger at me. "I have to have a little time to remember all that Fritz and I did on that place after the last flood."

I needed to honor him with my memories, my son who had stayed faithful to me and even at the end had been the lift in my spirit that said we could start again. Maybe he'd understand that flowers on the porch could be enough.

The first starts arrived by mail. Cornelia sent them, all packed with roots covered with dirt and kept moist by a piece of tarp wrapped around them. "For your garden," she wrote. "I heard you lost your lilacs."

Well, that was sweet. I set them in a tub on the porch. A few days later Nelia drove up with Benson, and she had several starts taken from Jasmine's grave, she said. Her father had kept them living. And he'd gotten a few cultivars of other varieties I'd given him for helping out, and she brought starts of those too. Nelia helped the high-school girl and me put water in tubs. I didn't need girls now for garden help, but it was still nice to share a conversation with someone over breakfast, wish sweet dreams when we turned off the lights at night.

"We could just plant them," Nelia said.

"Oh, no, they'd be lonesome out there. Let's just leave them here." I sat in the rocker, not sure what to do.

Then cultivars from the garden club in Oregon arrived. I guess they checked with the mayor who told them the garden had been wiped out. City lilacs, as I think of them, showed up too, some as full bushes dug up and brought by truck from Kelso and Kalama, Gresham, and Silverton. Then Ruth wrote and sent starts from her Chrystle graduation lilac and others I'd sent her through the years. My grandchildren all brought a start from their gifted plants. Then the Snyder family called long distance to say they'd heard about the flood and wanted to send starts from the lilac planted at Arnold Arboretum bearing my name. Shelly said she'd contacted Lowthorpe School, and they had Klagers there and would send seeds next year.

"Lizzie!" I said into the phone that worked again. "You need to come over here. It's… You won't believe… Something miraculous is happening."

The banker, the chief of police, that Japanese artist now living in New York, the son of the jeweler who had passed on too, they all sent cultivars of different varieties and then came others, trickling in, from people who'd visited. Treasures appeared, from children whose parents said they had Klager lilacs in their backyard picked up as discards one sunny afternoon outside our gate. Dozens and dozens of lilacs arrived, so many the postman said he'd have to find a special room to hold them when the mail truck delivered them too late in the day.

My porch overflowed.

Lizzie's eyes gazed across all the starts that my new high-school girl had put into galvanized buckets sitting like lily pads in the pool of what had once been my garden. But there were bulbs too and seeds and still more lilacs I could yet work with a new variety. It might take a few years, but I thought I might even get the twelve petal double creamy white again. It would just take time.

The three Lemoine that started my adventure so long ago were gone, but the offspring, the next generations, were coming back to me as gifts! My Favorite, Martha's creamy white with the yellow center, so many more! I had no hope that I'd get all 254 varieties back, but the numbers didn't matter. It was the circle of service coming full, all of those starts "attended" through the years in yards by generations of people I neither knew nor met.

"We have to plant them," I said. "I don't know how we'll keep them up, but we have to."

Lizzie nodded. "It is amazing, just amazing." She had tears in her eyes.

"We might be ready for Lilac Days by 1950," I told her.

"Nineteen fifty?" Lizzie said. "That's only two years away."

"We'll tell everyone of how the lilacs were restored by people giving them back. I am so humbled, so humbled." I was crying too. "I will remain here where I belong. I will devote the rest of my life in rebuilding the garden. I have faith!" I said.

My daughter and grandchildren would help. I'd begin with the flatiron-shaped patch at the front by the porch: the symbol of beauty and work, what a garden is all about as it gives to its gardener, as it gives to the rest of the world.

EPILOGUE

Hulda, 1950

L etter for you, Grandma." Irvina picked the envelope from my latest Bobby's mouth, where he'd learned to carry it, saving me a few steps. The child went back to ironing my sheets, well, hers too. There are standards to keep, after all, though of late I wished she'd quit piddling with work and just sit a spell with me.

I looked at the postmark on the envelope. August 21, 1950. "It's from Santa Rosa, California. I don't know anyone down that way."

We'd had our grand opening of the Lilac Days earlier that spring with several thousand people coming by, marveling at the recovery. We showed photographs of what it had looked like after the flood. Every building in town posted pictures, their tenants knowing it's important to remember both the hard times and how we came through them. The tour guides told stories of people returning lilac varieties, asking each group if anyone might have a start they'd gotten years previous, and if so, might we have a snip of it. It was a grand day, and all of Woodland could feel pride in what they'd done helping restore the community to its quiet splendor, lilac fragrance wafting over Horseshoe Lake and all the town proper. On the tours I led with my cane, I always reminded them that "life is worthwhile when it holds some beauty. It needn't be flowers. It can be helping other people—that's beautiful."

I held the letter. It was a fat packet. A return address didn't include the sender's name. I slipped my old yellowed nail along the glue, and it flipped open. Inside was a paper packet with seeds. And a letter.

> In my continuing effort to catalog my late husband's notes and affairs, I often come upon correspondence I've overlooked. Enclosed is a letter and packets of seeds sent to me by Fritz Klager in 1948 from a double creamy white lilac with twelve petals that he said you hybridized. That's quite an accomplishment, and while I was tempted to keep and plant these—there is a small lilac grove that Mr. Burbank planted many years ago; it was one of the ornamentals he liked—I decided it would be better to keep his lilacs as they

were when he died and return these seeds to you,
knowing that one can never have enough seeds to
replant.

Sincerely yours,

Elizabeth Burbank

The Washington State Federation of Garden Clubs held their
annual meeting of 1958 in Seattle, and I was to receive their
prestigious award. Lizzie couldn't drive me this time; she
passed on in 1956. I'd outlived all my children and my brothers and sisters too. I did wonder now and then about Barney
Reed suggesting I wasn't doing the Lord's work in my garden
and if the price I paid was burying so many of those I loved.
But my father's words came to me with greater force, and I
found no sin in pursuing what I loved and embellishing
beauty and giving the results away. Suffering, I decided, happened, and so did good things, and the issue of God's power
was not so much in questioning why He didn't stop floods or
death but in all the rest of the time when He showed us how
to be hospitable, generous, and loving.

I took special pleasure in receiving the Washington State
Horticultural Award. They let me tell stories of a few lilac
varieties, the highs and lows of gardening they related to. I
made them laugh, which I always like to hear, then answered questions about the restoration after the flood and

was careful not to go on too long the way we old women who love to talk about our gardens can. I wished my Frank was here to see the award. I said as much, and then tears pressed against my eyes when the federation president said it was astounding that I developed all those varieties from just three surviving Lemoine.

Astounding, yes; and a miracle when a young mother with faith felt worthy enough to keep lilacs blooming.

Author's Note

Hulda's story continued on past 1958. For two more years, she worked in her garden. After Fritz's death, she invited her granddaughter Irvina and her husband, Mac Van Eaton, to live with her and take care of her, and upon her death she would give them the farm. These younger relatives happily did so. Not long after Irvina's death at the age of fifty-one, Mac remarried. He and his new wife, Edith, remained caring for Hulda until she died in 1960, two months before her ninety-seventh birthday. Hulda's later years included care from family but especially three generous women: Elma, her beloved niece; Irvina, her granddaughter; and following Irvina's death, Edith, her grandson-in-law's second wife.

For some time after Hulda's death, Mac and Edith stayed on in the house until their age and health required that they reluctantly sell. The gardens became overgrown. No one came for Lilac Days anymore without the hope of seeing Hulda's strong frame beside her beloved flatiron garden. A developer moved into the old farmhouse where all of Hulda's grandchildren were born, but he had no interest in the garden. Fewer people remembered her amazing gifts; her life and her work faded into history. Then came the rumor that the land was to become apartments, and the house and garden would be gone forever.

Ruth Wendt, in her delightful book *Those Wonderful, Annoying, Industrious, Ambitious, Busy, Stubborn, Determined, Caring, Clever, Talented, Gracious, Intelligent, Focused Women: The Story of the Hulda Klager Lilac Society,* chronicles how a group of dedicated women, including Alice Wallace Schiewe, granddaughter of Hulda's sister, Bertha; descendant Betty Mills; Ruth Lane; Irene Stuller; Crystal Schultz; and Daisy Grotvik—all Woodland Garden Club women—put their heads together and worked tirelessly to reclaim the Klager property and help establish the Hulda Klager Lilac Gardens. Using all those adjectives in the title of Ruth Wendt's book, the women saved the gardens and began the restoration to what is seen today, bringing to mind John Wesley's words about passion and people coming to watch one burn. These women also spearheaded the National Historic Site designation for the gardens, a task completed in 1975. The gardens have welcomed hundreds of thousands of visitors ever since.

For many years, people visited and purchased starts, as they had in Hulda's later years. These funds and volunteers allowed the garden to be maintained. But with twenty-five thousand visitors a year, finding a way to keep up with the demand for starts gave way to new science and tissue-culturing methods. This new practice allows many more starts to be available for sale each spring to the bus-tour visitors from all over the region and individuals who come from around the world to see this splendid space of grace.

Thousands of hours of volunteer time prepares annual Lilac Days that honor the Lilac Lady of Woodland, as Hulda became known. Blooms begin in mid-April and end around Mother's Day in May. Today, scouts and teens and retired service groups join the friends of the society and the board and volunteers participating in caring for the garden. The scouts are especially busy on Woodland's "Make a Difference Day" and are reminiscent of Hulda's bucket boys hired to water the more than one thousand plants within the garden. Hulda's home is open for viewing during those first two weeks of the lilac season, and the gift shop offers garden-related items for sale along with lilacs, including bonsai varieties.

Hulda's amazing ability to develop over two hundred fifty varieties of lilac from crossbreeding her Magical Three of the surviving Lemoine is considered remarkable. Her lilacs are part of collections at Arnold Arboretum at Harvard, Swarthmore College in Pennsylvania, and the Havemeyer estate near New York City, among others. Her connection with Luther Burbank is based on fact. More of Mr. Burbank's life and his influence on horticulture at the time can be found in an exceptional book by Jane S. Smith, *The Garden of Invention: Luther Burbank and the Business of Breeding Plants*. Hulda did begin her work with apple hybridizing, moved to daffodils, dahlias, and tulips, and then to lilacs. From the list of variety names, one can speculate about prominent people Hulda corresponded with, such as Will Rogers, as well as many plants named for people whose stories few know: Alice, Carmine, Cora, among others. Hulda did write her article about dredging and was a regular attendee of the community Bible study led by the Seventh-Day Adventists and faithfully attended the Presbyterian church. The characters of Nelia, Ruth, Shelly, Jasmine, Barney, and Cornelia are all fictitious but meant to invoke the distinctive range of people Hulda touched and whose generosity later helped restore the Klager garden. The Lowthorpe School was a real institution, and Wister did include a number of Klager lilac varieties in his famous book published in 1943. The descriptions of lilac varieties are taken in part from the article "The Hulda Klager Lilacs Reviewed" by Freek Vrugtman, registrar of the Royal Botanical Gardens, Hamilton, Canada, published in the summer 1999 issue of *Lilacs*. The review includes the most extensive listing of Hulda's lilacs on record.

Hulda was an ordinary woman with an extraordinary ability not only to see the details within individual plants so that she could breed for hardiness and resistance to disease in addition to color and size and scent, but also to imagine something more than the tiny pollen at the end of her turkey feather or smallest brush. Her dedication to detail and the specifics of science and her artful imagination are what drove her to develop more and more varieties. I like to think it was a gift she was given that she enhanced through study, determination, patience, and love. That she found comfort through flowers during the great many losses in her life is pure speculation on my part; but given her generous spirit and how the garden was rebuilt after the flood of 1948, I think it is speculation well founded.

Few records exist from Hulda's experimental work. Frank did make tags for her, and her grafting knife, hoe, and hat are ephemera that memorialize her life's work. Even in her lifetime, thousands came "to watch her burn."

The society still seeks plants that might have as their ancestors a Hulda Klager variety not yet returned to the garden.

If one misses Lilac Days, the gardens are still open for walking and viewing. The garden hosts Washington State's oldest ginkgo tree, five varieties of magnolia trees, and countless annuals and perennials. Guests are welcome to sit on benches and just breathe in beauty. The fragrance lingers long after Mother's Day, and the beauty of blooms of all kinds of flowers offer both a story worth remembering and a place of rest for the world where lilacs still bloom.

ACKNOWLEDGMENTS

Like a slow-moving river, this story came to me many years ago through Betty Carlson Mills. Once a Planter's Day Princess, Betty married Roland Mills, a grandson of Hulda Klager. Throughout her life in Woodland, Washington, Betty worked with family and volunteers to keep the Klager Lilac Gardens flourishing. One day several years ago, Betty sent me an invitation to come to Lilac Days, but I was busy and, not being a gardener, didn't appreciate what a treasure awaited me. A faithful reader of my other books, Betty expressed hope that this would be a story that would interest me, about a remarkable woman who taught herself horticulture and how her generosity came full circle to touch lives.

More years passed, and Betty occasionally sent me copies of newspaper articles about the garden, from *Sunset* magazine to the *Farm Journal* to the *American Magazine,* the latter a 1927 gem by Ruth Graham Case. Betty provided local histories, and every now and then reminded me of the dates for Lilac Days stretching nearly a month each spring.

Two years ago, with my friend Carol Tedder, I took Betty up on visiting the lilac gardens. There, in the midst of lilacs blooming, I was swept back to the early nineteen hundreds and my own lilac experiences: shrubs planted next to the one-room school gate just a quarter mile from our Wisconsin farm; lilac windbreaks, that heady scent in spring. There was so much more in Hulda's garden, and I knew that here was a story of resilience and pleasure that celebrated beauty and generosity, persistence and love. So I thanked Betty immensely for her persistence and belief in the gift of Hulda's story and for the privilege in being able to share it with others.

Judy Card, board member of the Hulda Klager Lilac Gardens, became an indelible part of whatever is good about my version of Hulda's story. A genealogist and historian, she located resources, drove me to the Cowlitz County Historical Museum, the Longview Public Library, the Kelso courthouse, up bluffs and along the river bottoms, and she and her husband, Stuart, offered hospitality to my husband and me (and our dogs) in their home. Her genealogy listings of descendants kept me straight on who belonged in what family, and her retyping of *Fields of Flowers and Forests of Firs: A History of the Woodland Community 1850–1958* helped me locate important dates and descriptions that I hope lend authenticity to the story about early Woodland life. Judy was always available for questions and shared speculations with me about events. She has become a friend, one of the gifts of sharing stories.

President Patti Audette gathered the board together to give me entrée into this remarkable story and provided important consents for access whenever I requested it. I am grateful. Ruth Wendt, Hulda Klager Lilac Gardens gardener and board member, answered questions and toured me through the site, sharing works she'd written about the garden and plants, and I'm grateful. Fran Northcut, horticulturist and board member, gave of her time and wisdom and provided me with the detailed accounting of individual Klager lilacs completed by the International Lilac Committee in 1999, a critical resource, and I thank Fran for sharing it. This list provided names of varieties attributed to Hulda's phenomenal efforts of hybridizing. The varieties listed included those identified in Cooley's catalog, from arboretums across the country, and more in Wister's *Lilacs for America,* published in 1943. Any horticultural errors noted by avid gardeners belong to me. Ruth and Fran and the Hulda Klager Lilac Gardens members and volunteers gave nothing but the best horticultural insights and Klager history.

Karen Eddy of the house committee of the board graciously answered questions, told stories, and reviewed items in the history room (on more than one occasion). Other board members met with me—Cicely Perry, Juanita Mac-Mahon—to share insights. Joyce Carlson, currently of the Woodland Historical Museum Society but former president of the Hulda Klager Lilac Gardens, shared her incredible scrapbook and retrieved other historical tidbits, such as Dr. Alice Chapman's accident that enhanced the history of early Woodland and the Klager family saga.

I also spoke with or exchanged e-mails with other descendants, such as great-nephew and Woodland City Mayor

Chuck Blum (who as a child lived next-door to Hulda's garden) and great-granddaughter Carolyn Wing, as well as Joyce Gilbert, Clara's daughter, who shared lively stories of visiting her grandma Hulda and the dogs, always named Bobby. There were others willing and offering, and so many descendants I didn't personally meet, but whose stories through the years have become a part of the lore of Hulda Klager's exceptional life. I'm grateful to them all.

Thanks as well go to my editor Shannon Marchese and all the WaterBrook team who I know prayed for me and my husband during his medical emergencies as this book was being finalized. I thank them and my prayer team, and my own family for their generosity and love.

Finally to Jerry, who researched with me and then began his own journey into healing, I thank you and see in you those Hulda Klager qualities of persistence, generosity, and love. I've taken to having fresh flowers on the table as often as possible for their healing presence.

When we moved from our remote ranch, I brought two Hulda Klager lilac plants with me. They bloomed this spring beside an older lilac bush on property recently purchased near Bend, Oregon, that is now our home. The previous owner said that bush had never bloomed. But as I finish this book in 2011, in a year when Jerry works to recover, there are buds ready to burst. It's a deep purple flower. I think Hulda would approve.

READERS GUIDE

Based on a true story, Hulda Klager's life reminds us of both strength and generosity as she endured hardships in the midst of unique achievements. It's my hope that her life will inspire our own lives as we experience challenges and disappointments on our way to present joys.

1. What was Hulda Klager's first love? Family? Flowers? Faith? The challenges of crossbreeding? Hulda's father urges her to be faithful to her gift. Did Hulda have a gift or a calling, or were her interests and abilities merely passions that she pursued?

2. What do you think about Hulda's father's comment: "Some would say that meddling with nature isn't wise. Frank might agree—especially if the one meddling is a mother who should be content with looking after her family"? Was her father right? Was Hulda "meddling" with creation? Should a mother be content with raising her family?

3. On page xii, poet David Whyte is quoted: "I am thinking of faith now... / and what we feel we are / worthy of in this world." Do you have a passion or gift or calling that you have yet to pursue? What barriers stand in your way? Do the voices suggesting

that you are not worthy of that dream speak more loudly than you'd like? Was Hulda lonely in her pursuit? Did she feel she was worthy of the joy of accomplishment?

4. Hulda comments on the consequences of progress: The electric lighting at the exposition that faded the stars; her objection to indoor plumbing; the impact of steamships docking and ruining the riverbanks. Yet she sent her children away to pursue their education, celebrated the work of Luther Burbank making changes in food production, worked to have a crisper, bigger apple and 254 individual varieties of lilacs. How do you account for these contradictions in Hulda's character? Did they make her more human or more difficult to understand?

5. Suffering, and its consequences and causes, was a theme in this book. How did Hulda come to terms with the losses her family endured? Do you think that suffering can be a consequence of pursuing a dream? What role did Hulda's garden play in helping her deal with life's trials?

6. Barney Reed challenges Hulda's work and points out the tragedies in her life. She says, "It did trouble me that so powerful a God would let bad things happen. And I often did learn something when a tragedy struck. But did I have to suffer to learn the lesson?"

How would you answer Hulda's questioning? Does she eventually answer her own question? What did you think of her conclusions?

7. Do you agree with Hulda when she tells her sister, "Beauty matters.... God gave us flowers for a reason. I think so we'd pay attention to the details of creation and remember to trust Him in all things big or little, no matter what the challenge. Flowers remind us to put away fear, to stop our rushing and running and worrying about this and that, and for a moment have a piece of paradise right here on earth."

8. What role did the characters of Jasmine, Nelia, Ruth, Shelly, and Cornelia play in this story? Could Hulda's story have been told without them?

9. Where did Hulda draw her strength from to keep going after the deaths of so many in her life? after the flood? Where do you draw your strength from? Are there ways Hulda (and you) enhanced those tools to better face an uncertain future?

10. Dr. Karl Menninger once wrote that the single most important indicator of a person's mental health was generosity. Who was generous in this story? How did generosity bring healing to people of Hulda's world?

11. Did Hulda pay a price for her obsession? Would she say that the price was worth it? Do you think it was? Why or why not?

Huldie, don't deny the dreams. They're a gift given
to make your life full. Accept them. Reach for them.
We are not here just to endure hard times until we
die. We are here to live, to serve, to trust, and to create
out of our longings.

Jane often participates in book groups through speakerphone
conversations. To have Jane "visit" your book group, contact
her at www.jkbooks.com/Pages/contact.html, indicating the
day and time, to see if Jane's schedule permits her joining
you. Please consider joining her *Story Sparks* newsletter for
inspiration and the latest news of her writing and speaking
events. Join at www.jkbooks.com.

A mother's tragedy, a daughter's desire, and *the walk* that changed their lives.

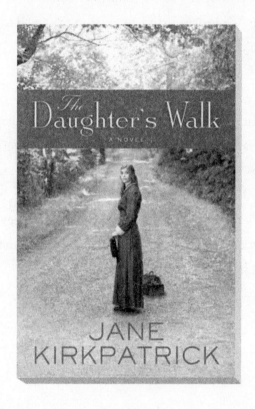

In 1896, in order to save the family farm, Clara Estby reluctantly accompanies her mother on a cross-country journey that redefines a mother's tragedy and a daughter's desire. Over two decades, friends and faith help Clara move through a family betrayal and into a future of her own design. But will the tentacles of the past keep her from finding the real joy in forgiveness?

Read a chapter excerpt at WaterBrookMultnomah.com!

APR 1 7 2012